X

THE
MOVEMENT
OF
MOUNTAINS

THE
MOVEMENT
OF
MOUNTAINS

MICHAEL BLUMLEIN

SIMON & SCHUSTER

LONDON • SYDNEY • NEW YORK • TOKYO • TORONTO

First published in Great Britain by
Simon & Schuster Ltd in 1988

Copyright © 1987 by Michael Blumlein

Simon & Schuster Ltd
West Garden Place
Kendal Street
London W2 2AQ

Simon & Schuster of Australia Pty Ltd
Sydney

British Library Cataloguing-in-Publication Data

Blumlein, Michael
The movement of mountains.
I. title
813′.54[F]   PS3552.L855
ISBN 0-671-65308-3

Printed and bound in Great Britain by
Biddles Ltd, Guildford & King's Lynn

To Betty and John

CONTENTS

Part Three EARTH

Part One

EARTH

Jessica once told me, before I knew all her thoughts, that if ever I lost the discipline or motivation of my profession I should become a gigolo. That was her way of encouraging me, and it served its purpose by bringing me back time and again. I remember that I laughed, but now, as I ponder the part I have played in this strange and labyrinthine drama, it seems no joke at all.

I was trained a physician and surgeon, and have practiced the art and moment of medicine for many years. The Oath, which was revived while we were students, has guided my judgment, and those of you who recognize my name will agree that the standards of my practice have always been of the highest caliber. Yet today the words of that ancient healer hold for me a different meaning. They sit like a chain about my neck, and one by one I find myself breaking the links. I have violated the spoken confidences of patients and engaged with them in the pleasures of sex. And far worse than failing to recognize the symptoms of a disease, I have chosen to be an agent of its dissemination. I am sure I have transgressed otherwise, and indeed, the words of the Oath become daily less and less distinct. Is it arrogance, then, that allows me to maintain that I am Doctor still, in truth, more a healer than ever?

If, at some time in the future I am no longer held in contempt by our society, this document may prove needless. If, on the other hand, we do not survive, it may represent the sole chronicle of the new age. If the latter comes to pass, I ask that you, Jerrold, brother and blood to me, likewise physician in the art, make public this record. Its facts are scientific; its truths, incontrovertible.

As is all truth, if we open our eyes.

1. Barea

I begin in the middle, for really there is no other place to begin. It was four years ago; I was forty-five. At Jessica's apartment in Pimplehill, propped on some pillows, staring at the single pane of glass above the boarded-up windows. The late afternoon sun sent a few rays slanting into the room.

Jessica lay beside me on the bed, flat (as I am unable to do), arms crossed behind her head. I inhaled her odor and touched a lock of her hair. She stared at the ceiling. I leaned over and kissed her on the neck, then licked down to her armpit. It was salty and wet. I drew my tongue farther, past the gentle mound to her belly. Her navel. An older flavor lay there, and I stopped and savored it. She made a sound, a sigh I think, and opened her legs.

"Eat me, fat man," she said, and I smiled. I shifted my weight so as not to crush her, then with my tongue found the taut skin of her thigh. She squirmed as I blew moist air upon her fur. I took a breath, then buried my lips between her legs.

By the time we had finished the room was dark. My forehead and face were wet; I was still panting long after Jessica had stopped. Shouts and cries from the crowds in the streets below penetrated the walls, and every now and then came the distant baying of hounds. Jessica stirred beside me.

"Come with me, Jules." She lay a hand on my thigh. "I want us to stay together."

"Then don't leave. Stay here."

"I'm sick of it. The noise. The decay. Do you hear the dogs? They've started to turn vicious. People are carrying plastic to protect themselves."

"Move to Ringhaven, Jessica. You could have the implantation . . ."

"Could I? I'm not so sure. I'm not so sure I want it."

"It's safer there. Quieter."

"It's different. But just as crazy. The whole city's crazy."

"You need to get away. A vacation . . ."

"Why won't you come, Jules? It's not forever. You have to leave the clinic anyway."

"I've already asked the NHD to keep me on Earth. In Barea, if possible. I like it here."

She dug her fingers into my leg and sat up. "You don't even know it here. You know your apartment, mine, the clinic . . . what else?"

"There are no hospitals on Eridis, no restaurants. Just domes and Domers."

"When was the last time you went somewhere new? Somewhere outside Barea? Or for that matter, in? When, Jules?"

"That's not the point."

"It is. You're afraid to try anything new."

"Why should I? I like the way things are."

"The way things are stinks. Try living in Sowall sometime. Or Westvale. Try living outside the wall . . ."

I was about to reply when there came a knock on the door.

"Who is it?" Jessica shouted.

"It's Mingo."

"What do you want?"

"I have a favor to ask. Could you open up?"

"Just a minute." She slid off the bed and flipped on a light. My clothes were lying neatly on a chair, and she picked them up and threw them to me.

"You better get dressed. It's my landlord."

While Jessica fished in her closet, I swung my legs to the floor to begin the labor of dressing. She brought out a cream-colored robe, which she tied loosely about her waist with a belt, then walked over and stood above me, tapping her foot.

"Skip the shoes, Jules. It's just Mingo."

"I will not meet the man partially clothed, thank you." I bent over and a small grunt escaped my chest. Hurriedly I drew on socks and shoes, then stood and tucked in the tails of my shirt. I nodded, and Jessica opened the door.

The man who stood there was dressed handsomely, his dark complexion set off by a light suit. He was tall and had long hair, well-greased and brushed neatly back from his forehead. He smiled when he saw Jessica, and clasped her hand in both of his.

"Hello, Mingo," she said.

"I'm sorry to bother you, Jessica. It's about my father . . ."

He stopped when he noticed me, and Jessica turned to introduce us. "Mingo Boyles, Jules Ebert."

He nodded diffidently. "I'm sorry if I'm interrupting . . ."

"Come in," Jessica told him. "Have a seat."

He accepted with an air of gratitude and took a small chair near the foot of the bed. Jessica sat on the mattress, facing him. I stood apart. She crossed her legs, and the edges of her robe slid open.

"You're a doctor?" he said, looking up at me.

"I am. Have I seen you before?"

He shook his head. "Jessica's mentioned your name."

"Has she?"

"It's something to be," he said. "A doctor's really something to be."

I inclined my head in acknowledgment. "And you? What is your profession?"

"I'm a sanitary controller." He cleared his throat. "I work in Ringhaven."

"I live there. The Pimella Arms. Do you know it?"

"I'm sure I've seen it. I go all over the place."

"He follows the dogs," Jessica said.

"Oh?"

He glanced at her, then looked at me and nodded.

"Yeah," she continued. "He collects their shit. Carts it to the Twins."

"I see."

"You don't have to be ashamed of it, Mingo. Someone's got to do it. It's as useful as anything else."

"I'm not ashamed. It's not what I came to talk about, anyway." He took a breath. "I was wondering if you could pay early this month, Jessica. My father's been getting kind of crazy . . . I'm afraid he's going to do something bad."

"I just paid a week ago, Mingo."

"I know. I'm asking a favor."

"Isn't there someone else?"

"He likes you the best."

"I'm flattered," she said. "When do you want it?"

"Tonight." He seemed ashamed and looked away. Jessica muttered something and turned to me.

"What do you say, Jules?"

"About what?"

"Is it all right?"

"Is what all right?"

She rolled her eyes. "Mingo's old man needs someone to quiet him down, and Mingo is paying me the compliment of coming here first."

"You're asking to leave here to service this man's father?"

"Don't be difficult, Jules. What I'm asking is for you to take care of yourself for a little while while I'm gone."

I stared at her. She glared back.

"Look, Mingo," she said, "maybe you better give us a few minutes together."

He nodded and got up. "I'm sorry if I caused some problem." His face was full of concern, and he kept glancing at me as he walked to the door.

"Shut it behind you," Jessica said, and when he was gone she turned on me angrily.

"What is the matter with you! You want to get me kicked out of here?"

"For refusing to service some man's father?"

"Not some man's. My landlord's."

"It's blackmail."

"Come off it, Jules. I owe it to him, just like he owes it to someone else. Maybe his boss, maybe the bank."

"I never expected you to do it while I was here."

"Who do you think I am? Some damsel in a golden tower? Maybe some duchess from Whitehill who's been spayed to keep sex from clouding her mind? I don't live behind a wall, Jules. I don't get to call the shots."

"It's how you want it, isn't it?"

"No, Jules." Her voice was like metal. "It's how it is."

"It could be different."

"It's not. I'm like everyone else."

"You're not. You're special. To me you're special."

She pinched her lip and pulled on it, then smiled. "You're sweet." She wrapped her arms around my neck.

"I've been doing this since I was a kid, Jules. Everyone has. Don't make it into something it isn't."

I felt the sleekness of her body under the gown. I swallowed. "I'm sorry. I didn't mean to cause trouble."

She kissed me. "Don't worry about it. Mingo's all right."

"Do you have to go?"

"I should. It'll put me ahead."

She embraced me, but after a moment I disengaged myself and moved away. "What's the matter with his father?"

"He's got some kind of nervous disease. Can't move his legs; gets agitated sometimes. Sex is the only thing that seems to calm him."

"How often do you have to . . . pay?"

"Once a month. Sometimes Mingo takes the payment himself, but usually he gives it to someone else. Most of the time it's his dad."

"A generous man," I said sarcastically.

"He is, Jules. There aren't many like him."

"You shouldn't keep him waiting."

"Oh, Jules," she said, coming and laying her hands on my chest. "Don't be like that. This has nothing to do with how I feel about you. It's just a kind of rent. Think of it as that."

"It's hard."

"Yeah." She kissed me on the forehead. "I'll be back before you know it."

She left, and I paced the room before settling back on the

bed. It was the only place in her apartment where I could be comfortable; the chairs were either too small for my physique or too weak. I turned idly through the pages of some journal, paying it no attention. Sleep was as distant as morning.

From the ceiling came a series of muffled sounds. Two voices, a man's and a woman's. Laughter. The squeaking of floorboards. I tried to put the noise from my mind, concentrating on the braised rack of lamb I had had for lunch. It was impossible. Each squeal of wood, each giggle stabbed me with jealousy. I rose from the bed and paced, trying in vain to calm myself. Suddenly, I could stay there no more.

I threw on my coat, not bothering to fasten the buttons, and rushed from the room. On the way downstairs I summoned Lark, which met me at the building's entrance. The night crowd of Pimplehill scattered as the vehicle approached. I climbed in and told it to take me home.

"Did you have a nice evening, Doctor?" it asked as we ascended.

"No." I reached in the seat compartment and uncapped a small bottle. I jiggled out a large blue soporific and threw it in my mouth.

"May I ask the reason?"

"I don't want to talk about it. Just take me home."

"Of course."

By the time we reached the edge of Ringhaven I was more composed, and when we finally docked at the Pimella Arms I could barely keep my eyes open. I weaved down the hall to my apartment and palmed open the door. No longer troubled by consciousness, I stumbled into bed.

Jessica called in the morning before I left for work. Her eyes were bloodshot and her face sagged.

"How come you left?" she asked, yawning.

"I didn't like hearing the two of you."

"I'm surprised you did. We were in the building next door."

"Next door?"

"It's just as well you went home; it took longer than I expected. The old man's gotten worse. It took him hours to get it up."

"Spare me the details."

She yawned again, then stretched. "I think I might go in late today. I only got a few hours' sleep."

"I'm on my way now."

"I'd like to see you tonight, Jules. No interruptions. Just you and me."

"I'd like that. Will you come here?"

"If I go in late, I'll have to stay late. Don't the Guards go on earlier now?"

"They activate at eight."

"Let's do it at my place then. I don't want to chance it."

"Next time here."

"Good. I'll talk to you later." She smiled sleepily. "I love you, Jules."

"I'll see you tonight."

I switched off the phone and the picture went dead. I had already eaten my breakfast, a well-rounded repast of toast, eggs, sausage, hotcakes, and sliced banana in cream, and had nothing further to attend to. Placing an after breakfast mint on my tongue, I straightened my coat and left the apartment.

Lark was docked in one of the balcony bays at the end of the floor, and I put my card in the slot and punched my name and number. The door slid open and the engine came on. I climbed in the backseat.

"Where to, Doctor?"

"Central Clinic."

"Directly?"

"Yes."

Lights flickered and the engine hummed. I sat back for liftoff, the worst aspect of a thoroughly unpleasant mode of transportation. The car disengaged from the balcony port, dropped slightly, then rapidly ascended. In a moment we were high above the Pimella Arms and most of the other buildings of Ringhaven. Lark banked hard to the left, and my stomach hung on a string.

"We're in no hurry," I chided. "Slow down."

"Of course."

The nausea subsided, and I managed to keep the vertigo to a minimum by keeping my eyes open and watching the city below. It has changed much, Jerrold, since we were children.

Whitehill is now full of tall buildings of every imaginable shape. A phallic theme predominates: missiles, spires, great cylinders with capped roofs vie with one another for the sky. There is a constant hum in the air, from the engines required to power these structures. Bridges connect one to the other so that it is possible, if one wishes, to avoid altogether contact with the ground. Indeed, the world within these edifices is filled with habitats of such multiplicity and variation that many therein find it unnecessary ever in their lives to step beyond.

Beside Whitehill lies Goldmont, but the one is hardly distinguishable now from the other. All but a few of the golden domes that used to cover the hill are gone. Those that remain are being converted into residences, their roofs cracked open to make way for the rising towers.

Surrounding these two districts (and Fidelity to the north) is the ringwall, a low barrier of hardened plastic. Embedded in it every hundred meters is a Guard, its sonic head facing inward. Beside each Guard is an opening for foot traffic.

In five minutes we were over the ringwall; to the south stretched the ancient tenements of Sowall. There were many barren areas, where buildings had been razed or had simply collapsed of old age. Pimplehill rose in the distance, and behind it towered the two great mounds of orange plastic, the Twins. The air was too murky to see beyond.

The clinic lay within a stone's throw of the wall, and I girded myself for descent. Lark landed smoothly on the roof.

"I'll be back at lunchtime," I said.

"Primum non nocere, Doctor."

"Thank you, Lark. I'll try to remember."

I left the craft and walked to the rooftop entrance, descending by way of the back stairs to the clinic proper. Ms. Imarra, our receptionist, greeted me with a smile half-hidden by the communication device that hung in her face. She handed me messages scrawled on paper and with a finger to her lips waved me through a side door next to the waiting room. Thus was I able to avoid the beseeching looks of my patients while I went to my office and prepared myself to become their doctor.

The clinic had changed little in the ten years that I had held my tenure. It retained the name Central, an anachronism of some past demographic: in none of our memories had it lay anywhere but on the uncomfortable border between Ringhaven and Sowall.

The ground entrance fronted a wide and dusty thoroughfare, across from which rose the ringwall. At one time the street had been a major avenue connecting the districts to the north with those to the south. After the wall was built, it had fallen into disrepair, eventually becoming more a buffer than a connector. Crowds still roamed it, especially in the morning when the Guards were silenced. Then the outsiders surged into Ringhaven to take up their jobs, to shop, or simply to marvel at the wealth and splendor.

Few from within the wall ever ventured beyond it on the ground, and Central's clientele, with rare exception, was drawn from the native and immigrant poor of Sowall. Even the most affluent among them were unable to afford such lavish treatments as gonadal selectics, pilitation, or appendage modification, all of which were fortunately beginning to fall from fashion. The care we provided was basic, and our patients fared just as well for it.

To some it seemed ironic that such poverty as we represented could stand so close to such largesse, but never to me. We were at the hem of wealth, the fringe, and to my mind it is always this part, like the moraine of a glacier, where the contrast is sharpest.

Once in my room I exchanged my suit jacket for the long white lab coat, emblematic of the purity and science of our profession. I straightened my desk, then opened the blinds of the window slit at the far corner of the room. I perused the ceiling to see if any piece had come loose during the night.

Central had been in existence for more than a hundred years, and it was at least thirty since it had received even token support from the government. The walls were peeling, the floors cracked, the ancient acoustical tiles stained and loose. I found one hanging precariously above my head, and tore it down. Many of my patients already faced one kind of danger or another in their lives; they needed not confront it in my office. Nor did I need further reminder of the poverty in which I worked. The lack of equipment, of laboratory materials and teaching devices bore on me sorely enough as it was.

Once assured that my office posed no bodily threat, I went to the door. Several charts lay in the tray and I took the one in front, calling the first patient of the day.

It was an uneventful morning—diabetics, asthmatics, alcoholics—until the last patient. The chart was thin, which gave me hope. The thicker a chart, the more recalcitrant the case, for the patient who regularly seeks out a physician's care is one who either suffers a disease for which we have not yet found the cure or has been offered the cure but for some reason is unwilling to take it. This chart was thin, which meant that the patient had either been healthy or had been elsewhere.

I went to the door of the waiting room and for the first time looked at the name. It startled me, and I quickly recovered my composure.

"Mr. Boyles," I called. "Mingo Boyles."

He was sitting with his hands folded in his lap, conversing with an elderly lady. He looked up when I called, then courteously excused himself from the woman and stood. He came to me and extended a hand.

"Dr. Ebert," he said.

"Mr. Boyles." We shook hands, and I motioned him through the door and toward my room.

I followed him inside, taking a seat at my desk. I noted that, as before, he was well-attired. His face was cleanly shaven and held no obvious signs of disease.

"How may I help you?" I asked.

"I want to apologize, Doctor, if I caused any problem last night."

"There was no problem. How may I help you?"

He fidgeted with his fingers and several times tried to initiate speech.

"Come now, Mr. Boyles. Unburden yourself. That is why you are here."

"I have a sore," he finally said. "On my penis."

"I see."

"It worries me."

That did not surprise me, for most men with a penile sore are worried. Those who are not are either very ignorant, very wise, or very busy with other, more important matters. I did not say this to him, inquiring instead as to the duration of the lesion.

"I'm not sure. A couple of weeks maybe. It only started bothering me the last few days."

"Do you know how you got it?"

He shook his head.

"Sexual partners? Have any of them had something like it?"

"Not that I know of. I haven't paid that much attention. The last few weeks have been kind of busy."

"I see. Do you have other symptoms?"

"Like what?"

"Burning when you urinate? A rash? Fever?"

"Uh-uh. None of those things. Just the sore."

"Have you ever had this before?"

"No. Never."

"Fine." I motioned him to the examining table. "Take off your pants and I'll have a look."

While he climbed up, I circled the desk; when his pants were down, I bent to examine the source of his complaint. What he had, in fact, was not one sore, but two. They lay next to one another on the penile shaft, about a centimeter below the prepuce. They were tiny vesicles, and sat on a reddish base. I touched them with a gloved finger, and he jumped.

"I'm sorry."

"They hurt, Doctor."

"I understand." I went to my desk for a magnifying glass, then bent down and studied the blisters more closely. I touched one gently with tip of a swab, and he drew his breath.

"What is it, Doctor?"

"I'm not sure."

I touched once more, as gently as I could, but it made no difference. He squirmed away.

"I'm sorry," I said. "I won't touch again."

A physician must be sensitive to his patients, but at times sensitivity can muddle judgment. This was one of those times, and whether it was because he was an acquaintance or simply a man in pain, I cannot say. I shied away from causing him further discomfort, choosing instead to wait. It was the wrong decision, and though I do not believe that a culture or biopsy at that time would have changed his ultimate course, it might have spared me the recriminations I subsequently inflicted upon myself.

I told him to get dressed, removed my gloves and washed my hands. Then I sat at my desk and turned my mind toward a diagnosis.

There was a time when Mr. Boyles's signs and symptoms were pathognomonic of the herpesvirus. All who are reading this document will be at least acquainted with its history. As a student I had the fortune of seeing an actual case, the last, I believe, in Barea. Shortly thereafter, the disease was eradicated. It was more than twenty years since it had been declared extinct.

I scribbled in the chart, unable to make a definitive diagnosis. I felt a vague pressure and realized that I was hunched uncomfortably forward. My belly was pressed against the edge of the desk, and I leaned back.

"Mr. Boyles," I asked. "You've sustained no trauma to your penis during any of your recent sexual encounters?"

"Trauma?"

"A pinch, a bite, perhaps some unusual device?"

"No, nothing like that."

"I see." I closed my eyes and drummed my fingers on the

desktop. I could not put a name to what he had. I told him this.

"But is it serious?" he asked anxiously.

"I cannot with certainty say."

"Please, Doctor . . ." He pulled on his fingers and began to blink rapidly. I watched this display, eventually feeling compelled to speak.

"The sores themselves do not worry me. They seem ready to burst. When they do, the pain should lessen." I paused, deliberating how best to present the rest.

"Are you familiar with Barea disease?" I asked.

He shook his head.

"It has only recently been described; the name isn't even agreed upon yet. It appears to be transmitted sexually, though the agent is not known. The few patients who have come to our attention complain of a variety of symptoms; a number of them, as I recall, describe various skin eruptions."

"Is it dangerous?"

"We know very little about it, but for the most part it seems benign. It appears to resolve of itself. I would be remiss, however, not to share the fact that a certain number of these patients suffer permanent morbidity."

"What does that mean?"

"Some are affected mentally. A small percentage die."

He stared at me, his fingers gripping one another until they turned white. "Am I going to die?"

"Of Barea disease?"

He nodded grimly.

"I doubt that you even have it. My guess is that within a few days you'll be the same man you were before this started. In the meantime I advise that you refrain from sexual activity, at least that involving your penis."

"What if it doesn't go away?"

"I want to see you again in a week. If you still have the sores, I'll take a specimen." I jotted a date on a slip of paper and handed it to him.

"You might try soaking the area in warm water . . . You do have warm water?"

"I can make it."

"Yes. Soak it several times a day. That should soothe the pain. It may hasten the healing."

"Am I going to be all right, Doctor?"

"I think you're going to be fine." I stood and offered my hand, which he clasped firmly. He seemed relieved to be holding someone else besides himself.

"Thank you," he muttered, and began to walk out. At the door he stopped and turned.

"I've always taken care of myself, Doctor. My health is important to me . . ."

"I understand."

"I keep myself clean."

"Of course. I am sure what you have is no reflection on your habits. If you'll bring that paper to Ms. Imarra, she'll give you your appointment."

"A week?"

"Yes. The date is on the slip."

"Thank you, Dr. Ebert. I won't forget. If it gets worse, I can call you?"

"Of course."

I ushered him out, then returned to my room. I closed the door and thought for a moment of Mr. Boyles. He seemed a pleasant and friendly fellow; it bothered me that I did not know what he had.

Of some things—certain aspects of the law, for example—I prefer to remain ignorant, for they offer to the mind little that is not either arbitrary or useless. Of things medical, however, I crave knowledge, and when it is not forthcoming, I oft become distempered and ill at ease.

Fortunately, it was time for lunch. As I changed coats, the images of disease and infection were replaced by those of food. It had been hours since I had had something in mouth, and the glands beneath my tongue were contracting painfully. As much as I was able I hurried up the stairs to the rooftop. Within minutes I was in the air, speeding northward to replenish my ebbing stores.

2. Falling, Rising, Falling

I went home that night after work, washed and tidied myself, then flew to the hovel that was Jessica's. It was after nine when I arrived, but she had not yet come home. Her door was secured with an old-fashioned lock, and I used a duplicate key to let myself in. After removing my coat, I lay on the bed, sucking in the faint scent that remained on the sheets and listening to the ambient noise outside. I must have fallen asleep, because the door, when it opened, startled me. It was Jessica.

She shut it and dropped her coat on the floor. Without moving, she peeled off the rest of her clothes. She stared at the bed, then leaned over and jostled me with her hand.

"Jules," she whispered.

"I'm awake."

"I'm exhausted." She climbed over me, kissing me below the ear on the way to the other side of the bed. Beneath the sheets she curled up into a ball.

"Come to bed," she muttered.

I pushed myself to a sitting position and began to undress, folding my clothes beside me in a pile. When I had disrobed completely and placed the garments neatly on the chair, I returned to the bed. I did not crawl in, for unlike Jessica, I was not ready for sleep.

"I saw your friend Mingo today in the clinic."

"Mmm."

"Are you interested?"

"He told me," she murmured.

"He has a sore on his penis. Did he tell you that?"

She sighed. "He said you said it wasn't serious. Can we sleep now?"

"Did he? I mentioned Barea disease to him."

She stirred. "He didn't tell me that."

"I'm not surprised."

"What makes you think he has it?" She yawned and opened her eyes.

"I don't. Not really. But there is an epidemic. It would have been irresponsible not to tell him."

"He's careful, Jules. As much as anyone can be."

"So he told me. But we may be seeing just the tip of the iceberg with this Barea thing."

"You're worried."

I nodded. "Each study keeps estimating a higher incidence than the last. A higher mortality too."

"There's a case at the hospital now," she said. "They're giving her Mutacillin. They say she's recovering."

"Coincidence. Mutacillin doesn't work. It's been shown. Whatever the agent is, it isn't bacteria."

She yawned and snuggled against me. "We're not going to find out tonight. Let's sleep, okay?"

"I want you to stop having sex with him, Jessica."

"Please, Jules. Not now."

"I mean it. His father too. Anyone. The risk is too great."

"I use an antiseptic."

"It may not kill it."

She sighed and sat up. "Look, I thought we already worked this out. Nothing's changed since last night."

"I have. I changed my mind."

"Well, I haven't."

"Be reasonable, Jessica."

"You be reasonable. And don't order me around. If you want to get away from the epidemic, then come with me to Eridis."

"That's ridiculous. It's blackmail."

"It's the same what you were doing. Trying to get your way by frightening me."

"I wasn't. And I won't engage in this petty bickering."

"Good. I've been wanting to sleep ever since you started talking." She rolled away from me and turned on her side.

"Jessica?"

"Be quiet. I want to sleep."

"I'm not finished."

"Talk to yourself then. I'm going to sleep."

She pulled the covers over her head; within minutes her breathing became regular and shallow. It angered me that sleep came so easily to her; to me it was uncomfortably far away. Many thoughts occurred to me in the darkness, most of them unpleasant, and I thrashed about for what seemed like hours before I finally fell into a fitful slumber.

In the morning I was wakened by the clatter of pots and pans. The window admitted a dull gray light, and I rubbed my eyes. I felt exhausted and wished I were alone.

Standing slowly, I shuffled to the dresser, where I had left my toiletry case the night before. I extracted the container of soap, then went to the sink on the other side of the room. Wherever I go, I carry my soap, an unscented and odorless variety. I eschew those brands that are perfumed, for not only are they medically unsound, but they obfuscate the vital organ of smell. For this same reason I allow no aerosols or other unnatural scents in my office, nor do I myself use them. When I perspire excessively, I change my clothing, and always carry an extra set of shirts and underwear in my briefcase.

I washed and dressed, then went to the kitchen alcove where Jessica was sitting on a chair. On the stove was a small pan with strips of bacon bubbling in deep fat. It is curious how a thing can be called food and yet disappear if it is cooked too long, and I turned off the burner before they shrank to nothingness. Jessica was sipping coffee and watching me. She had on a blue robe that matched her eyes.

"You look handsome," she said.

"I'm surprised you think so."

She began to reply, then stopped herself. "Sit down. I'll pour you some coffee."

"I'd rather stand."

"Suit yourself."

She poured a cup and handed it to me. "Before you tell me it's lousy, I'll say it. It's lousy. Half of it is burnt bread crumbs. And it's yesterday's."

"Why not spend the money, Jessica? Instead of skimping."

"Can't afford it."

"You shouldn't adulterate food."

"Coffee's not food."

"It's close enough. It has a taste, it goes in your mouth, you swallow it."

"I don't care that much, Jules. Food's food. It's not that important."

"I'll bring you a can."

"Fine." She stared into her cup, then looked up. "I've been thinking about Mannus's offer, Jules."

"Have you?"

"I'm young. Smart. This could be the break I need."

"What's wrong with the job you have?"

"What? Growing bacteria on agar plates? Working in a tiny lab in a tinier hospital? It's a dead end, Jules. I could grow old and die without ever using my brain."

"It's secure."

"It stinks. I'm sick of it."

"I don't want you to leave, Jessica."

"I know. And I don't want to stay."

"You want me to trade in my career for yours."

"You know that's not true. You already have a career, Jules. You have credentials. This is a chance to get some of my own."

"I don't want to go to Eridis, Jessica. I don't want to play doctor to a colony of slaves."

"They're people, Jules."

I took a last sip of the wretched drink and put the cup down. "They're not."

"They are. They have illnesses."

"The universe is full of illness. Why go someplace where it's inevitable?"

"Where isn't it? You know a place?"

"You know what I mean. They're made to die young. Or they do, which ends up the same. I can't think of a worse situation for a doctor to be in."

"I see."

"I want to stay with you, Jessica."

"So you've said."

"I mean it."

She looked at me coldly. "I'm sick of listening to you, Jules. Go away."

"Don't be like that . . ."

She stood up. "I mean it. Get out."

"Jessica . . ."

"Go!" She flung her coffee at the wall.

The outburst frightened me and I retreated, grabbing my coat on the way to the door. I left the apartment, slamming the door behind me. My hands were shaking as I summoned Lark from the hallway, but by the time I reached the ground my anger had turned inward. I thought of returning to apologize but judged that I needed to care for myself first.

I instructed Lark to fly to the bakery at Sixteenth and Alona. Its lights commenced to flash and its horn to beep, warning passersby that we were about to lift off.

After we were airborne for a short while, Lark interrupted my foul mood. "The bakery's below, Doctor. Are you strapped for descent?"

"Of course I'm strapped. Get on with it!"

We hovered, then abruptly the craft plummeted. I had paid extra for it to be able to handle such a maneuver, the few moments of weightlessness being the sole aspect of vehicular travel that I enjoyed. The padded straps dug into my shoulders, but still I seemed to float, and then we landed. We were on the flat top of a building, and in a moment, amid the flashing lights and beeped warning, had descended to the crowded street.

"Wait for me here."

"Yes, Doctor."

The door slid open, and I stepped out. Pushing people aside, I went in the store.

A rotund woman with a doughy face stood behind the counter. Her hair was piled on her head, held in place by a clasp shaped like a baguette. She had a faint moustache above her upper lip, upon which lay tiny beads of sweat. She smiled as I approached.

"Buenos días, Doctor."

"Buenos días, Señora." I looked through the glass beneath the counter at the trays full of cakes and cookies. "What is fresh?"

"All is fresh, Doctor."

"Yes. But today. What is fresh today?"

"Ah. Today . . . these"—she pointed—"and these. These are very good. Very sweet."

"They have jelly?"

"Yes. Look." She broke one open, and a cloud of steam rose up. "See, still hot."

"Good. I'll take a dozen. I'll take that one now."

She handed me the doughnut, then stooped to put the others in a bag. I blew off the steam and bit into it. I swallowed and took another bite. I began to feel better.

"Make that two. Another dozen."

"You have much hunger today, eh?"

"Yes." I finished the one and began another. "They are delicious."

She nodded and handed me two full bags. "I add it to the rest."

"Yes. Gracias."

"Hasta luego, Doctor."

"Hasta luego."

I turned and left, pushing through the crowd on the street. Several emaciated youths who were lounging against the car drifted off as I came up. I punched in the code and climbed in back.

"To the clinic, Lark. Slowly."

The lights and beeping commenced, and a halo of space opened quickly around us. We lifted off, and within moments the spot was filled again with people. From above, the swarming avenue reminded me of a blood vessel choked with corpuscles. I shook my head and turned away.

The doughnuts were superb, and it was a pity there was no one with whom to share. I stuffed another in my mouth. And another. Carefully, lest the jelly stain my clothing.

We took a leisurely flight, during which my spirits improved. By the time we landed on the clinic roof, I was feeling quite a bit better.

"Preserve the purity of life," Lark said as I stepped from the door. It was a phrase from the Oath.

"As always," I replied.

I walked into the clinic, stopping for a moment to exchange pleasantries with Ms. Imarra. The doughnuts had taken the edge off my anger, and in an act of spontaneity I offered her the remaining two. She accepted graciously, and I left to begin my morning.

It proved uneventful, as did the next several days at the clinic. There is a routine to the practice of medicine, to the procession of colds and warts, that is like the movement of the seasons. It is both reliable and reassuring, for the many small complaints that I treat are usually short-lived, and the patients recover their health. This pleases me; it makes me feel a part of something that is long.

On the other hand, there are times that I become terribly bored, seeing the same illnesses day in and out, treating them, watching them recur. I might as well be a man at a machine, punching a hole. At these times I feel I am not a physician (though perhaps it is when I am one most), but a kind of curator, preserving the ills of men and women so that we can have them for the next generation, and the one after. Perhaps it is not so much boredom as it is frustration, or disappointment that we are so helpless to change our lives.

It was in this unpromising state that my mood hovered for several days, until it was lifted in a surprising and unexpected way. A patient was responsible, a woman whom I had been seeing for many years. She was one of a handful I saw from Ringhaven. Her name was Ann Donovan, and she suffered from a constellation of symptoms—insomnia, fatigue, depression—without having any definite physical signs of illness. All laboratory data were normal, and several efforts with medication had been unsuccessful.

She was reclusive, though from time to time cast aside her solitude in desperate acts of outreach. These were often of a sexual nature, and always mismanaged. They never lasted more than a day or two, leaving her feeling hopeless and guilty. The forays were routinely followed by long periods of abstinence and withdrawal.

She held a minor government position, and lived alone in an apartment in Goldmont. Of her childhood she spoke rarely, though clearly it had been marked by little joy and less love. I had no great hopes that her adulthood would ever offer much more.

She came in one afternoon because of a rash. It seemed already to be fading; as I wrote a prescription for a mild cream, I remarked on her unusually good spirits. She sat straight up in the chair, which I had never before seen her do, and smiled at me.

"You notice too?"

I nodded. "It's a pleasure to see you so happy."

"To me too. I feel good, Doctor. I don't know why, but I do."

"Have you had any recent affairs, Ann? Any new friends?"

"As a matter of fact, yes. But three . . . no, nearly four weeks ago. By now I'm usually back in the dumps."

"Are you still seeing this person?"

She shook her head. "It only lasted a couple of days. I felt bad, as usual, for a week or two, but then all of a sudden I stopped putting myself down. Why bother, I said. It's not worth it."

"Indeed. This person seems to have had quite a salutary effect."

"Something has. I hope it lasts."

"As do I."

I reiterated my delight that she felt so well, concealing my suspicion that it was a transitory phenomenon. I was surprised that the mood had lasted nearly a month, for that had never been her pattern, and asked that she see me again in two weeks.

"Certainly," she replied pertly, and stood to leave. I was struck by her height, then realized that it was only that her carriage was more erect. Her clothes, too, were more complementary, greens and yellows rather than grays, and her face was alert. She smiled as she left, a genuine smile, not the pasted-on one of resignation I had so often seen.

Her cheerfulness was strangely contagious, staying with me the whole of that day. It might have lasted even longer had I not seen Jessica that night.

3. Commitment

Do you remember the time, Jerrold, that you challenged me to eat as many waffles at a sitting as I could? We were adolescents; you had invited some friends of yours over from school. It must have been the only time that you ever cooked anything, and I felt proud that you were doing it for me. I was to be the center of attention: except for jests, a fat boy has few opportunities to be the center of anything.

Eating the first few was wonderful, as though I were being filled with my success and your admiration. But you kept on cooking, forcing me to eat even after I was full. You were stuffing me, like a pig on a platter, and showing me off to your friends. I began to feel bad, which made me want to eat more, which made me feel worse. There is no end to the story, nor do I think there ever will be. It is the baggage I carry along with other such fragments, and if I am lucky enough to understand it someday in a different light, then perhaps it will serve as the beginning of a new tale. What made me think of it now was remembering the last few weeks Jessica and I spent together on Earth. They were as full of competition as they were of cooperation. Of love as they were of fury.

I picked her up after work one evening and we flew to an area of Goldmont known for its fine food shops. It was an older section, and many of the stores were on street level. At Jessica's suggestion we parked Lark and took to our feet.

Other shoppers were about, almost all of whom were from

Ringhaven. This I judged by their dress, which was generally lavish, and their faces, which were bejeweled. Also, we were in an area quite distant from the ringwall, and it was not long before the Guards would be activated. Few save those with an implant would be about.

We stopped in a cheese store, and then a meatery, where I purchased a marinade of beef. On the way out I suggested we make one more stop a block or two away, for there was a confectioner who sold the most delicious eclairs. Jessica looked at her watch and shook her head.

"The Guards go on in half an hour."

"We can make it," I promised.

"Forget it. If you want your sweets, take me to your apartment first."

"It's only a few minutes more."

"I've been with you in that store, Jules. I know how long a few minutes is." She started walking; after a moment's hesitation I caught up with her.

"I'm an outsider, Jules. It's not a game with the Guards."

"I know. Sometimes it's hard to remember."

"I can't afford to forget," she said flatly.

I began to walk faster, but she held onto my arm. "We're not in that much of a hurry." She laughed. "You don't have to run."

I laughed too, for I had never run in my life.

We reached Lark, and before entering, I removed the cheese from its plastic wrap. It needed time to breathe, and I crumpled the plastic into a ball and cast it to the far side of the street.

"It is a claim of our sanitary department," I said to Jessica, "that no scrap of refuse remains on the street for more than five minutes. Shall we test their boast?"

After consulting her watch she agreed, and we stood by Lark, waiting for one of the Fagos dogs. In minutes one appeared, walking briskly down the street with its nose to the ground. It had that odd Fagos air of single-minded intent. Like all creatures cloned to a purpose, it was oblivious to all else. Its stomach seemed already full, but when it came to the ball of plastic, it swallowed it in a single gulp. It sniffed around for other trash and, finding none, trotted down the block. At the corner was a fecal receptacle, set into the ground so that its top was level with the street. The hound stopped there and with its front paw pressed the receptacle's lever. A small hole opened, over which the dog squatted, depositing its load. When it had finished, it pressed the lever again, then disappeared around the corner.

"Remarkable," I said, turning to Jessica. She was no longer beside me. "Jessica?"

"In here." She was in the backseat. I joined her.

"The Fagos hounds . . . remarkable creations."

"Let's go, Jules."

"Of course. Home, Lark." I made myself comfortable. "Perfectly engineered and trained. Did you watch it perform?"

"They scare me."

"They're harmless. All they eat is plastic."

"They've attacked people in Sowall, Jules."

"That's hard to believe. Did you see how far the hound stayed from us? They're trained to avoid flesh."

"Maybe some of them don't learn so well."

"Perhaps there was provocation. At any rate, they keep the city clean."

"Ringhaven, you mean. In Sowall they shit wherever they want."

"They're trained to defecate in receptacles."

"So how come they don't? How come there're little piles of hard plastic all over the place?"

"Perhaps there are an insufficient number of receptacles."

She took a breath to reply, then exhaled. "Let's not argue, okay? I don't like them. You do. Let's leave it at that."

"With pleasure." I reached for the cheese, which sat in a small dish on the rear dash. "Would you care for a slice?"

She held out her hand without speaking, and I cut her a wedge. I was about to do the same for myself when Lark announced our arrival at the Pimella Arms. We docked in one of the balcony bays on my floor and debarked into the hallway. I looked at my watch: it was ten minutes to eight.

At the door to the apartment I handed Jessica the cheese and the marinade and palmed the plate in the wall. The door slid open, we entered, and I palmed it closed. Immediately, I set the deflectors.

Jessica deposited the food in the kitchen, then retired to a bath, a luxury of mine of which she always took advantage. I busied myself with the meal preparation, placing the marinade in the oven along with a half-dozen baking potatoes. In a pan I devised a light cream sauce, setting next to it a pot of diced zucchini. These I allowed to steam while I concocted a small salad, then sliced a loaf of wheat bread I had purchased that morning from the bakery.

Surveying what was to be our supper, I was acutely aware of the lack of a suitable dessert. I fleetingly blamed Jessica, then put the thought from my mind. Grabbing some crackers and a knife, I went into the living room to finish the cheese before dinner.

We supped pleasantly, in front of the one large window of my apartment. It faced west, and the warm light of the setting sun colored Jessica's skin. I was moved by her beauty, and when the sun set, and the lights of the apartment came on, I saw that her skin still glowed. I offered her more wine.

"It's beautiful," she said, gazing out the window.

"Live with me," I whispered.

She took my hand, cradling it in her own. Her eyes glistened. "I've always thought about living in Ringhaven. Ever since I was a kid."

"You could. You could have the implantation."

"I don't have the money, Jules."

"I'll give it to you. I'll get the references you need."

"I can get my own."

"Then do it. It doesn't hurt. It's over in a minute."

"It scares me, Jules."

"No." I shook my head. "You never even know it's there. And you can go anywhere. Anytime."

She nodded. I felt near to winning her.

"You could get a better job too. If you lived in Ringhaven, people would treat you differently."

"I know. I think that's what scares me."

"Freedom is frightening. So is success."

She sighed and let go of my hand. "It's tempting, Jules. So tempting."

"Live with me, Jessica."

"I'm so used to Pimplehill. To Sowall . . ."

"It's awful there."

She gave me a look.

"You yourself said it. The dogs, the noise . . ."

"I'm sick of it all. Outside the wall; inside, too."

"Then take a rest—"

"I need more than a rest. I need a change. I need to get out of this rut."

I felt the conversation slipping away. "You're still thinking about Eridis, aren't you?"

"I am. I'm thinking about it a lot."

My stomach growled. "It makes me uncomfortable to hear you say that."

"I bet it does."

"I'm not sure I could go with you."

"I thought you wanted to live with me, Jules. Weren't you the one who said that?"

"Here. I want you to live here."

Her manner turned cool. "What are *you* afraid of?"

I pursed my lips, then wiped them with the edge of my napkin. "I'm not afraid of anything." I began to clear the table.

She pushed her chair back and watched me.

"I'm concerned, Jessica." I put the plates in the kitchen and started to pace. "That I would be sacrificing my career for yours."

"That's absurd."

"That it would betray a weakness on my part . . ."

"It would be just the opposite, Jules. It would show that you're strong."

"I'm not so sure. I have a feeling that if we go to Eridis, your life will become more important than my own."

"I wouldn't worry too much about that," she said cruelly.

"You don't know me—"

"Don't I? Who knows you better? Who's been on the end of your selfishness more than me?"

"It's not so simple."

"What is? You say you're afraid of being weak, but when do you ever give in? When, Jules?"

"It's hard."

"Isn't it. And how do you suppose it is for me?"

"I'm not talking about you."

"So I've noticed. Try it sometime."

"You're as selfish as I am."

"I'm trying, Jules. It's hard, but I'm trying."

"You talk big, don't you? You say you love me, but all you care about is you. All you want from me is sex. A warm, fat body."

"There's plenty of others, Jules. Plenty."

"You're sick!" I shouted. "You don't love me—"

"More than you love yourself!"

"Get out!" I cried.

"I pity you, Jules."

"Go!"

She seemed about to make one last jibe, then shook her head and pushed the chair back. Her robe fanned behind her as she swept out of the room; with a vicious jab of my forearm I sent a table lamp shattering against the floor. I heard her slap the plate next to the front door and suddenly realized what was happening. I shouted for her to stop, but it was too late. She shrieked.

I rushed from the apartment and found her near the door, writhing on the floor. Her face was twisted and her fingers tore at her temples. Lines of blood welled up where she had dug her nails into her skin.

I lifted her, not bothering to straighten the robe, which had fallen open. Her exposed skin was pale and her muscles trembled. Beneath her breast her heart seemed ready to leap from her chest.

I carried her back to the apartment and laid her on the bed.

Once we entered, her screaming stopped and the muscles of her body began to relax. She had been exposed to the Guards for only a minute or two, but it took many more than that for the color to return to her face. I put my hand to her heart to be sure that it pulsed normally, and waited for her breathing to calm. When it did, and her pupils had begun to shrink, I went to the bathroom for a cloth to wipe the spittle from her lips.

"Jessica," I whispered.

She blinked.

"It's over. You're safe."

"I want to go home," she mumbled.

"You can't. Not until morning."

"I want to." She began to cry. "I want to go home."

"It's all right." I touched her cheek. "You're safe."

She blinked again, then bolted upright. "Don't touch me!" she hissed.

"Jessica . . ."

"I mean it! Leave me alone."

"It's over now. You're safe." I tried to hold her but she slapped me away.

"Don't touch me. Get out."

"Jessica, be reasonable."

"I said get out! I've had enough of you for an evening."

"I saved you!" I shouted.

"You brought me here. Now leave me alone."

"I'm sorry, Jessica. I'm sorry I got mad—"

"Go away." She turned on her side.

"Please . . ."

"Go!"

I backed out of the room, full of apprehension and guilt. She locked the door behind me, and I was forced to make my bed that night on the sofa. It was far from comfortable, though had I been given the most luxurious bedding I would not have slept. I feared that I had lost her, and all through the night I cursed having no eclairs to ease my pain.

In the morning she left with hardly a word. On the threshold of the door she paused, rubbing her temples, then strode resolutely into the hall. I called after her but she ignored me. I pleaded with her at the elevator, but the look of scorn she gave sent me staggering back. I returned to my apartment, glancing one last time over my shoulder. I felt a deep anguish, though by the end of the morning it had receded. Sometime in the afternoon my mind went blank. When next I remember, I had begun to binge.

I gave in to that desperate ritual, and in ten days had gained upwards of twenty pounds. I was no longer able to fit into my clothes, but it hardly mattered. My dress became slovenly; my manner, careless. I withdrew into myself, which was no pleasant place, refusing even to appear at the clinic. I told them I was ill, which was no fabrication. Had there been someone to purchase my food I would never have left the apartment.

What finally halted this destruction was the most insignificant of incidents. I was at home and had run out of food. I needed to go shopping, and to do that I needed to dress. I kept a number of loose-fitting garments for such situations (abrupt fluctuations in weight and size were not entirely unknown to me), and I put on underwear, baggy pants, and a shirt. I used my feet to kick a pair of shoes beside the bed, but when I sat and tried to put them on, I could not reach. I strained, bending as deep as I could, but each time my abdominal wall rose to halt me. It was as if a dozen fists were pushing against my chest, preventing me from reaching the floor. I tried once more, but the strain impeded my circulation, and I became flushed and dizzy. In frustration I tried to wriggle my feet in without using my hands, but the shoes slid on the floor, eluding the clumsy grasping of my toes. I went to the closet for a different pair, but none were any better. I stared at the floor, a fury building inside, and finally I began to weep. I sat on the bed and cried, catching my breath when I could. When it was over, when I had calmed, I picked up the phone and called Jessica. It was after work, but there was no answer. I tried again. And again. Finally, in an act of faith and desperation I flew to Pimplehill to wait for her.

It was early evening when I arrived, and still light. Lark managed to find an empty alley in which to land, and after I had stepped out, it ascended to a roof to wait. I pulled my coat tightly about me and walked into the street.

It was full of people, many of whom seemed as destitute as I. For this I was grateful, as I aroused little attention. I hurried toward Jessica's building, trying to avoid the numerous mounds of hardened Fagos droppings that littered the street. More than once I stubbed my toes, and was relieved when I finally reached her steps. I climbed up and passed through the front door, which was ajar.

Inside was darker, and malodorous. I went quickly to the stairs and began to go up, but at the first landing was forced to halt. Standing in the shadows was a man, and he appeared to be blocking the way.

"Excuse me," I said diffidently.

He made no reply, and as my eyes became accustomed to the dimness, I saw that I was speaking to his back. He was facing the wall.

"Excuse me," I repeated. "I'd like to pass."

Slowly he turned, and I recognized his face.

"Mr. Boyles," I said.

He looked at me blankly, then shuffled back until he was against the wall. He neither spoke nor gave other sign of recognition. I thought perhaps that I had offended him by my slovenly appearance, and I muttered some apology, then hurried up the remainder of the stairs. I glanced back once before letting myself into Jessica's apartment. He had not moved.

I entered and locked the door, then sat on the bed. In my mind I rehearsed what I would and would not say; as the minutes dragged on, I stood and began to pace. The sun had begun to set, and I stopped to gaze out the small window. It faced south and was set high in the wall, so that it was on a level with my eyes. I made out the shiny orange tips of the Twins, glinting like colored lava in the late sun. Every so often a vehicle flew overhead, adding a load of Fagos excrement to one or the other hill. The sun sank lower, and I turned from the window. I was beginning to fret.

I paced more, trying to maintain my resolve. With every

minute it was weakening: I felt both foolish and vulnerable. Several times I opened the door to leave, and each time I shut it. Finally I made up my mind and threw the door open. I took a step, then stopped when I heard the barking of dogs. It got louder, and then I heard human voices besides. They were raised. Yelling. I went to the window to look out.

I could see nothing below, until I pushed a chair up and stood on it. The balance was precarious, but curiosity overcame my uneasiness. With one hand on the wall and the other on the sill, I peered down to see wherein lay the commotion.

There was a crowd of people below, or there had been: it was in the process of scattering. In the middle of the street was a pack of Fagos hounds. One or two were growling, but the rest appeared to be munching contentedly on items at their feet. Two others trotted up from side streets, carrying large pieces of plastic in their teeth. Watching the dogs feed was not to me an unfamiliar sight, but seeing so many together was unsettling. I was about to turn from the window when I heard a scream.

A figure appeared, running madly up the street, a hound in pursuit. I thought the person a woman but could not be sure. The two of them passed the other dogs, one or two of which joined in the chase. The woman screamed again and threw a piece of crumpled plastic behind her. The lead dog caught it in midair and swallowed without losing a step. The woman tossed back her umbrella, her overcoat. This stopped some of the dogs, but not the lead. It bounded closer, baring its teeth within inches of her heels. The woman let out a shriek, and in a frantic motion tore the blouse from her chest. She flung it at the dog, which halted in midstride. Like a puppy receiving a tasty morsel, it began to wag its tail and yip with delight. The woman raced on, naked from the waist up, and disappeared around a corner. In a moment she reappeared, not far from the entrance to the building from which I watched. Suddenly I recognized her.

"Jessica!" I screamed. I clambered from my perch, with a haste that was my undoing. The chair tipped precariously, and while I strove desperately to recall an equilibrium, it toppled to the floor. I crashed upon it, then rolled away. Grimacing, I struggled to my feet. Jessica flew through the door.

She ran into me at a dreadful speed, nearly sending me down again. She was hysterical, weeping and moaning, and I cradled her in my arms.

"That does it!" she sobbed. "First the fuckin' Guards and now this!" Her body shook. "I can't take it anymore! I can't stand this fuckin' place! This goddamn fuckin' place!"

She went on, muttering expletives I had seen only in bathroom stalls. Over and over, when I thought that she had calmed, she burst again with invective and vilification. I had never seen her so full of rage.

Eventually her agitation dissipated. I relaxed my hold on her and she stepped back. Her face was flushed and stained with tears. Her hair was disheveled. She looked at me as if for the first time.

"Jules. What are you doing here?"

"I came to apologize."

She frowned. "You look awful."

"I've been on a binge."

She shook her head and sat on the bed. "I hate this city. I hate it."

"I've thought about Eridis, Jessica."

"I can't live here anymore. I can't stand it."

"All week. I've been asking myself if I'm right or just stubborn."

"I have to leave. I have to."

"I'm afraid if I don't look out for myself, no one will."

"I'm going to take the job, Jules." She looked at me. "I have to."

"If I come, Jessica, will you love me?"

She frowned again. "What?"

"I said will you love me?"

"I love you now."

"Say that you will."

"I will, Jules. Of course I will."

"And comfort me when I need it?"

"Yes."

I sighed. "I'll come then. I'll come with you to Eridis."

Her eyes, already swollen, swelled more. New tears began to stream down her face.

"Oh, Jules," she murmured, coming to me, melting into my soft belly and chest. "Jules, Jules . . ."

We made love. It was a tender moment when she reached her climax, for she called out my name. It was a rare thing for her to do. Whether she manufactured it for my benefit or whether it came from the heart I cannot say, but feeling as I did then, it filled me with warmth. I smelt the flow of her sex, and it caused mine to course. There is nothing like the relief of the troubled mind to open wide the gates: I believe it has something to do with the redistribution of blood from the brain.

Once I had recovered from myself, life took a turn for the better. I began to diet in order to reach my previous weight and reclaim my wardrobe. In the meantime I had myself fitted with several new suits and two pairs of specially constructed shoes which lacked the portion that wraps around the heel. They were not stylish, but they were shoes, and better than going barefoot.

Soon after I told Jessica of my decision, I made the formal announcement at work. Most already knew that I had been given relocation notice by the Government Health Agency but, as public employees themselves, they knew of the fickleness of paper orders. The actuality of my plans came as a surprise, and to many, a shock. After ten years they had come to think of me as a fixture, and some were apprehensive that my leaving might even threaten the existence of the clinic. Gratified as I was by it, their concern was ill-conceived, for I was neither indispensable nor irreplaceable. The clinic had survived for more than a century, through crises far more serious than my departure could possibly provoke.

On the other hand, it would have been irresponsible to minimize my position there. During the decade of my tenure I had accumulated the trust and following that that span of time permits from a group of patients. Disengagement would perforce be slow, for their sake as well as my own.

Jessica was leaving in a month, which seemed too short a time, but I nonetheless requested a berth with her aboard the Mannus vessel. My request was denied, and I approached the GHA to intercede on my behalf. I was told that it was the corporation's prerogative whom they carried. I responded that, as the appointed physician for the Eridian settlement, I should enjoy certain privileges. Surprisingly they agreed, offering a priority berth on the *Solis*, a government vessel scheduled to depart almost two months hence. With some venom I suggested that the GHA could surely do better, given the amount of money with which they subsidized Mannus. They replied that Mannus was a private corporation over which they had no control. This I knew to be false, but the knowledge was of little use. Others more powerful than myself have fared no better. Despite the fact that the government contributes enormous quantities of aid to Mannus in the form of contracts, technology and personnel (such as myself), despite the fact that it, in effect, holds the company's strings, the government, curiously, is always the one that seems the puppet. It would save a staggering sum were it to take Eridis for itself, for ourselves, but the sale will never occur. The situation for Mannus is too sweet, and the government too entrenched. At least for the present Mutacillin will continue to carry the Mannus trademark.

Mutacillin. It seems apt that the drug which has so irrevocably altered the face of medicine on Earth should play such a pivotal role in my own life. Had it not been discovered I would never have gone to Eridis, never been part of the world that unfolded there. As much as anything it has a place in this story: you must excuse me if I say some words about it.

4. Mutacillin

It has been said that the history of man is the tale of his quest for food; it is a claim I dare not dispute. As a physician, however, I would be remiss if I did not add another quest alongside that whose success sustains the myriad cells and streams of our bodily fluids. How we come to live, to die, and what forces make us rise and fall between: this is the riddle we have meditated on longest, and the one to which we give the name medicine.

The science began in our prehistory, and since it has been recorded has chronicled the struggles man has waged against those afflictions that would limit our lives. What we hear now, of viral infestations, cancerous tumors, diseases of the heart, is but the surface layer of a pit that is deeper by a thousand times than our furthest memories. The history of medicine, of death and suffering, is in the main the history of the bacterium. We forget it so easily because we live now without its scourge, but for three millennia the bacterium was master and we, its pitiful slaves.

Who has not read of the Plague of the Buboes, the Centuries of Leprosy and Tuberculosis, the Venom of Tetani? How many millions succumbed before we found measures to halt these microbes? We discovered the antibiotics, but as each new drug was developed so did new and resistant bacteria appear. For a while we kept pace, contriving agents potent enough to exterminate each new species. But the bacteria learned faster, mutating into forms we could no longer control. Our drugs became less and less useful, then barely better than placebo.

Perhaps it was the air, perhaps the water. Bacteria were once again slaying thousands, and costing billions in research and treatment. And then Mutacillin was discovered.

There are no panaceas in medicine, none except death, but in life Mutacillin comes as close as any. No case of therapeutic failure has ever been described, nor have there been serious untoward reactions. Since its introduction some forty years ago, the science of bacterial infection has not been the same.

As is so often the case with works that inspire great awe and wonderment, Mutacillin is the creation of nature, not man. To many this may seem an artificial distinction, since man itself is the creation of nature, but to me it has always been an important one. As a boy studying certain contrived mathematical sequences, I was amazed to find that nature had already described these in the spiral of the pine cone, the interlocking leaves of the artichoke, the swirl of the cochleate shell. Later, as my interest turned to the human body, I discovered again the sublime and intricate work of nature's art. Though as scientists we sometimes try to forge life of our own (indeed, on many occasions we have done so), we sit always between nature's palms. Always there, waiting for the hands to spread, or to clap together upon us.

Mutacillin is a living organism, or it derives from one, as have most of the antibiotics in the history of our medicine. It is a grayish black fungus and grows principally by vertical division. A mature plant approaches half a meter in height and resembles an inverted cone, but with a flatter and broader top. The grape-sized spores, by which it germinates, are clustered at the summit. At maturity the plant's base is no longer able to sustain its height, and the delicate walls crumble upon themselves. This motion releases the spores, which float or tumble to a new site of implantation.

Extremely low temperatures, below those compatible for long with human survival, are required for the plant's growth and successful germination. Its substrate is a slatelike rock that to this point has been found only on Eridis. It lies in great sheets, which can be cleaved to smaller sections of approximately four meters in length and several centimeters in thickness. These weigh on the order of one to three hundred kilos.

In its maturity, which is the only state useful to us, the fungus is exceedingly delicate. Its walls are thin and stretched to their limit; the least agitation will cause it to disintegrate. The spores, wherein lie the drug, are just as fragile, and if the plant crumbles, they are lost to us.

The mold clings tenaciously to its bed of rock, and any attempt to separate the one from the other, even with fingers far more agile than those of the Domers, is doomed to failure. This was amply demonstrated in the time before the Domers, when humans such as inhabit Earth worked the mines. These were the original settlers, the ones who came to dig the ores and metals that had fallen into such short supply elsewhere.

At first they worked the desolate Eridian surface, pocking the area around the settlement with shallow pits as they followed the veins into the ground. Later, they dug deeper, often finding that their tunnels ended in large underground caverns. It was in these caves that they first noticed the strangely shaped fungus, but it was nothing to them, who were after the rock. Deeper they went, chasing the deposits, working with hands and feet that became numb from the cold. They were nowhere near as deep as the tunnels go now (we have learned that the mold grows best where the temperature is least), but it was as deep as they could survive. The cold gripped them like granite, relentless, unyielding. It chilled beyond their bones, and they faltered.

Their minds became sluggish, and then their bodies turned clumsy. They cut themselves with their tools and dropped stones carelessly on their feet. They might work for hours before noticing such injuries, benumbed as they were by the cold. The incidence of broken and crushed bones, of abrasions and lacerations increased dramatically, but, surprisingly, there were no bacterial infections. Not one was ever recorded, not even the most localized cellulitis. Nor, for that matter, did the miners suffer from minor ones—acne, boils or abscesses.

In retrospect, we know that it was the floating mist of the spores that protected them, but it is the nature of serendipity to pass unnoticed until retrieved by exigency. In this case it did not occur until, threatened by the alarming rate of serious injury, the miners abruptly decided to abandon the planet. They left the machinery, the processing plants, the domes that had been constructed for their habitation. The mining company, an arm of what today is the Mannus Corporation, was faced with the loss of huge sums of capital. It was the goad serendipity needed.

Data were routinely analyzed, and some bright soul noticed the peculiar absence of infection. Studies were commenced, and in time the spores were identified as the prophylactic element. Efforts were made to grow them in vitro, on hundreds of different media, but not one was successful. The slaty Eridian rock seemed the necessary ingredient, and it had taken billions of years to be formed. It was untenable to transport it to Earth, not in the vast quantities that would be needed to make such an endeavor worthwhile. It was troublesome to Mannus but economically more feasible to retool the existing Eridian machinery and to harvest and process the spores on the planet itself.

Touching the fungus in anything but the most delicate manner is enough to send the spores flying into the air, disappearing into a dark tunnel or bursting against a piece of stone. Human hands are not deft enough, especially in such cold as the spores grow, to handle it with the requisite care. A machine is even clumsier. No way had been found to cultivate the plants off-planet, nor had they been able to be synthesized artificially. This was the adversity that confronted Mannus as they attempted to salvage their investment, and it was the fodder to which the Domers owe their lives.

It was decided to devise a race to harvest the plants, or rather the rock on which the plants grow. The race was designed to be big, to be able to lift the huge slabs of slate without disturbing the fragile spores, and fat, to be able to endure the interminable cold. The Domers are not as durable, perhaps, as a machine, but no machine has yet been constructed that rivals them in the care and efficiency with which they perform their task.

They hoist the slabs, then carry them to one of the hundreds of openings that worm into the tunnels. Within moves a conveyor system that lifts the rock upward to the processing plant. Here, under controlled, aseptic conditions, the spores are vacuumed from the fungi. Once this has been achieved, it simply becomes a matter of purifying, diluting and packaging the drug. Each step is interesting; I have seen them all. But none is more fascinating than watching the miraculous drug in action.

We call it an antibiotic, for it kills life. Yet it itself is alive, and for this reason we place it in a category apart from our other antibiotics. Mutacillin is both a deadly chemical and a living thing, a paradox which in nature is perhaps the rule rather than the exception.

Once injected into a host, the drug moves freely until it contacts a bacterium. Recognition occurs through a process we do not fully understand, though the multiple evaginations that appear on the drug's surface are thought to be a method of information transference. This is followed by a period of intense intranuclear activity that presages the extraordinary next phase. The drug alters radically its surface structure, transforming itself into the shape of a star. At the tip of each arm of the star is a membranous package, within which are clustered the chemical moieties manufactured specifically for the bacterium. These moieties have little or no effect on other species. When they come in contact with that particular one, they discharge, as though balloons pricked by a pin. I hardly have to say that the chemical is lethal: to watch an entire colony of virulent bacteria burst is a thrill few of us, at some time in our schooling, have not witnessed. There is no fear of resistance, because in each case the drug manufactures its toxin according to signals it receives from the bacterium: even a minimally different type invokes the production of a separate and distinct toxin.

Attempts at artificial synthesis of the Mutacillin entity have been fruitless. So, too, have efforts to collect its toxin. But we have the drug, and none of us needs stand in fear that a septicemica or some other fulminant bacterial infection will take the life of a patient. Perhaps somewhere in the cosmos is a medication that will likewise exterminate the viruses, and one to strengthen the vessels and make young again our aging sinews. In lore there is such a substance—a fountain, some say—but of its origin nothing of truth has ever been known.

Still, though, we are plagued by infection. Gonorrhea and syphilis continue to rage among us, and not for want of an agent to kill them. Mutacillin will easily do so, but it is only a drug. Except perhaps for the most rudimentary of consciousnesses, it has no mind of its own. We physicians wield it, and if a disease exists that might otherwise be eradicated, then we must brace ourselves to the challenge.

But the responsibility is not solely ours. Just as the gangrenous leg of a diabetic is not its own cause but the result of the diabetes, so are the epidemics of gonorrhea and the rest sustained, not by any one part, but by the body of society as a whole. A cure cannot exist apart from that which is to be cured. It is not, I am afraid, in the hands of medicine, but in those of government where the answer lies. If they are tremulous with old age, or diseased themselves, then what can any one of us expect?

5. Leaving the Clinic

Perhaps the sweetest moments in a physician's life are those in which a patient comes to grips with his problems. The silence that occurs is absolute, and often there is a new and fresh scent in the air. Though I was trained to minister to all who sought me out, I have never had cures for more than a handful. The majority must find their own. Those who are willing to try are the ones who make my work satisfying, for they ask for my knowledge and help, but not my domination.

Ann Donovan had never been one of these: up until the last weeks of my work at the clinic she had been a depressed and passive woman, one who carried an air of gloom into whichever room she entered. In no sense had she ever seemed to accept responsibility for the conditions of her life, and her visits frequently left me feeling that it was I who was somehow responsible for the troubles she suffered. Indeed, in the beginning I had tried to shoulder this burden, running tests, trying drugs, all for naught. The pall that cloaked her days and the frightening snakes that ringed the dreamy fires of her nights stayed with her month after month through the years.

And yet, for reasons obscure, I felt drawn to her. Perhaps it was that beneath her protestations of fatigue and sleeplessness lay a hint of humor. She seemed to have made a kind of gently mocking peace with her problems, accepting them as the crutch that she needed to confront a difficult world. Many of us who suffer aberrations learn to use them so, for life is hard, and oftentimes we must insulate ourselves from it. Though she entered each of our sessions with a downcast face and an air of despair, she would often leave with a twinkle in her eye. It was in those moments that I seemed to catch the drift of her purpose, and we would share a laugh.

Those times, to be honest, were rare, and though I counted her among my favorites, the thirty or forty minutes I was forced to endure each month listening to the repetition of her complaints were tiresome. Such people as she tend to duplicate their own symptoms in their listener, and I often found myself yawning and becoming strangely enervated. I had come to expect these reactions in myself, which made it all the more striking when, upon seeing her again, I experienced just the opposite.

It was perhaps three weeks since I had treated her for the rash, and as she entered the office, I found it hard to believe that this was the same woman I had been seeing for seven years. Her demean, of which I had been so skeptical the prior visit, seemed to have settled even deeper into her personality. She bore herself as confidently as before, and rather than shuffling along the ground as though she were carrying a burden, walked with a spring to her step. She had done something with her hair—I am not sure what—that made her face look younger and more exposed. I do not much follow fashion, but her clothes seemed more stylish, colorful, and cut to accent rather than obscure her body. She wore a scent that reminded me of lilac.

She sat opposite my desk and smiled. I smiled back, feeling uneasy with her sudden change. Suddenness in medicine, as in nature, augurs ill.

"I got your letter," she said. "I'm sorry that you're leaving."

"Yes. We need to arrange how to continue your care."

She looked at me thoughtfully. "The rash is gone. I feel pretty good, Doctor."

"You look good." I smiled. "Better than in a long time."

"It's amazing, isn't it?" She sounded in awe. "It's been nearly two months now. That's a long time for me."

"You sound puzzled."

"I am. It's strange. I look in the mirror and I see my face, but it's different. I mean, it's me, but it seems like I'm someone else."

"Oh?"

"Not really someone else." She made a small laugh. "Just not the me I'm used to."

"Are you using drugs, Ann?"

"No."

"Hallucinating?"

"You mean seeing things that aren't really there?"

"Or hearing voices . . ."

"No, not really. All the voices I hear are my own. They're just saying things I never said before."

"Like what?"

"Well, like I'm attractive, and smart. And interesting. I never told myself that before."

My uneasiness increased, and I waited for her to continue.

"I don't know what it is. I feel like I'm worth something. I feel . . ." She bit her lip and blushed. "I feel almost lovable."

"You've had phases like this before, Ann," I said gently. "When you've had more energy. More hope."

"I know. But those were out of desperation. This is . . . it's different. How can I explain it? It's more real, like before I was just acting different, but now I really am." She made a weak grin. "Do I sound crazy?"

"The suddenness concerns me. People change all the time, but rarely so quickly. Not without an explanation."

"Like what?"

"Drugs, toxins, some kinds of shock—"

"I told you I don't use drugs!" she snapped. I glanced at her.

"Is something the matter?"

She took a breath, then blew it out. "I'm sorry, Doctor. I'm a little nervous."

"Nervous?"

She chewed her lip and nodded. "I'm afraid it won't last."

"I understand your concern."

"I want to stay like this. I want to be happy, hopeful . . ."

"Of course." A diagnosis began to shape itself in my mind. It seemed unlikely, and yet I found myself pursuing it.

"Will you tell me about the affair you had, Ann?"

She looked up. "Why do you ask?"

"You mentioned it before. It seems noteworthy that it occurred shortly before you began to notice this change."

She shrugged. "It wasn't really any different than the ones before. I hardly knew the guy. He seemed friendly enough. Handsome, too. A little too full of himself for my tastes, but then I guess my tastes are changing . . ." She laughed. "Maybe he rubbed off on me."

"Sometimes," I replied, "in certain drugged states, for example, one person can be extremely susceptible to another. Take on their attributes—or what they suppose those are—and begin to act in entirely different ways."

"I wasn't drugged," she repeated.

"I understand. This man . . . he gave you nothing?"

She shook her head. "We had some wine. Sex. I was a little sore for a while afterwards . . ."

Suddenly the source of my discomfort crystallized. Barea disease. There was an epidemic, it was sexually transmitted, it was associated with mental symptoms. I told her this, as simply and directly as possible. I suggested she might have the illness. She frowned.

"Shouldn't I feel different if I did? On the news they say that people get depressed and start acting funny . . ."

"Most do. There are variations."

"I'm not sick, Doctor. I've never felt better in my life."

"It could be a prelude to something more serious."

"Is there some treatment?" she asked.

I shook my head. "We're not even sure of the agent."

"Well then," she said, "this is just talk. I'm not ill, and even if I were, there isn't anything to do about it." She smiled happily.

I thought to remonstrate, but in truth, there was very little to say. She was right.

"I have one request," I told her, and scribbled a name on a piece of paper. "This is the doctor who will be taking my place.

If for no reason other than my own peace of mind, I would ask that you make an appointment with her."

She nodded but did not take the paper. "I was thinking of trying it for a while on my own, Doctor."

"Please," I urged. "You may feel differently later. There is no obligation."

I held it out, and finally she accepted. "Just in case." She smiled, and I nodded, smiling in return. She stood, taking a last, slow turn about the room. Once again I was struck by her grace. She extended a hand, and I came from behind my desk. Her grip was strong, and warm, and I found myself cradling her hand in both of mine.

"Take good care of yourself, Ann."

"And you, Doctor."

For the briefest of seconds we held each other's eyes, and then she turned and left. I did not follow as I often did, but stood in the wake. The scent of lilac stayed on the air, and I closed my eyes to remember it. Not the smell, which was not truly hers, but the hint of a spring after so long a winter.

Days passed, some of them punctuated by moments such as I had shared with Ann Donovan, others by simpler and more formal disengagements. The few patients whom I was truly glad to be rid of did not balance the many whom I was not, and I finished my days exhausted and drained. Food constantly entered my mind, and had I not had Jessica's support and comfort I would certainly have succumbed to the wild excesses of my fantasies.

She was a bulwark in these days, despite being as occupied arranging her life as I was mine. My decision to accompany her had for the time erased whatever doubts existed between us, and we cleaved to one another like two teenagers in love. This, at any rate, is how she expressed it, and when I asked what she meant, she laughed, then sang me a verse from a song.

"Our love is bright,
And blind for any others;

Below the navel, above the knee,
It waits beneath the covers."

"You made it up," I replied.

"Uh-uh. It's an old song."

"I don't like it. It's coarse. What we have isn't."

"No." She smiled. "It isn't. But sometimes it's like that."

She huddled against me in the bed, and as my body involuntarily responded, I had to admit that she was right. To do so dismayed me, for it revealed ours to be what I felt then a lesser kind of love. I realize now that my attitude was, at best, priggish, but my experience up to then had been paltry. Prior to meeting Jessica romance had been unknown to me, and sex had been the sight of one rat mindlessly mounting another.

"You want it to be pure, don't you?" she whispered.

I nodded, and she touched me tenderly.

"It is, Jules. Like snow, and dirt."

"I don't understand."

For a moment she was quiet, and then she chuckled. "I'm going to appeal to the doctor in you. Think of a piece of fruit, a ripe one. Like a pear. A soft, ripe pear."

I hesitated. "A Bartlett," I ventured. "All right?"

"Good," she replied. "Imagine it on its tree, bathed in sunlight. Bright and sweet and golden. A perfect pear."

"Mmm." I tried to do my best. "I want to eat it."

"Good. Eat it. Think of how fine it is while you chew."

"It is fine, Jessica." I smiled. "But not as fine as if it were real."

"But you have it, don't you? You have it in your mind."

"Yes."

"Good. Now imagine that you've finished it, that it's in your stomach. And now in your small intestine, and now the colon. You no longer taste it, and your body's taken what nourishment it has, but it's still the pear. It's different now, it's in your rectum, and you push it out. Does this bother you?"

"No."

"Does it feel good?"

"It's not bad."

"All right. You push it out, and it's softer than before. And darker. Its smell is much stronger too."

"It's stool," I said.

"From the pear," she replied. "Is it baser?"

"What do you mean?"

"I mean, is it impure? Foul?"

"Stool is stool. It's not a question of being foul."

"That's how I feel about love, Jules. Sometimes it's dark, sometimes light. It's always changing for me."

"Stool and a pear hardly seem to capture how I feel."

"It's how I feel."

I sighed, shaking my head. "Sometimes it amazes me that we're together. We have such different ideas about things."

"Sex is all right, Jules."

"Is that why you love me?"

"It's part."

"It seems cheap. Like you're a victim."

"I like it, Jules. I choose it."

"I know. It bothers me."

"You'd rather not have it?"

"No. I like it too. Too much, I think."

"It's not food, Jules."

"Isn't it?" Suddenly my mouth began to water. I threw off the covers and went to the kitchen, hastily constructing a sandwich from the meats and cheeses in my larder. I returned to bed and readied myself to eat.

"Are you really hungry?" she asked.

"Ravenous."

"You have an erection, Jules."

I stopped and put the sandwich down. Looking over the edge of my belly, I could see the swollen tip of my penis. It hopped in time with my heart.

"Make love to me," Jessica whispered, draping her arms across my shoulders. "Eat later if you must."

I could not deny what I felt, and obeyed her like a child. The lovemaking was raw, provoking feelings I can put no name to. When I woke in the morning, the bread had already begun to stale.

Our last weeks together on Earth were like this, plunging into one another, struggling away, falling back. My greatest fear was that I would be consumed, and yet greater than fear was a sense of strength. I was parent to her, and child, and she was both to me. We were linked as we had never been, full of life and vitality. Such was my nourishment as I severed my ties with Earth.

6. Death and Life

There are moments in one's life when it becomes impossible to believe that we are not inhabited by other beings. You, Jerrold, dwell in me. Of course you do, for you are my brother, dark, and light. But there are others, not tangible, not even knowable. They live in secret, until the smallest of events, a cloud passing before the sun, a pungent odor, a memory provokes them. Suddenly we find ourselves overwhelmed by emotion. Often we weep. These hidden beings, it seems, love our tears.

It had been a long time since this had happened to me, and I scarcely knew that it was until I saw the ink smear. I was writing in a chart and the words began to blur, then run together in a stream. I felt a sudden wash of empathy for all things. I wept more.

As abruptly as it had begun the outburst stopped. Like a great wall my composure returned. I rewrote the note, then closed the chart and went to the door for the next. It was Mr. Boyles's. I wiped my eyes and called him to my office.

He was a different man than before. Not once did he meet my eyes, bowing his head so that his gaze struck me somewhere in the midsection. I have seen this before, from patients attempting to show deference, but the declivity of his attitude was something other than that. His hair was unkempt, his clothes in need of attention. An unclean odor rose from his vicinity.

He sat, shuffling in the chair, apparently unable to find a position of comfort. "I have an itch," he mumbled.

It did not surprise me, for he could not have bathed very recently. I asked if he still had the sores; from the look he gave I might have spoken an alien tongue.

"The sores," I repeated. "On your penis. You were going to return in a week."

"Sores?" He frowned, then suddenly seemed to remember. "Oh, them. They went away. Didn't come back. Now I have a rash. It itches."

"Is that why you are here?"

"I don't feel so good." A tic had developed in his right eye.

"What else besides the rash?"

"I don't know." He fidgeted. "I'm mixed up. Can't think straight. Can't sleep either."

"Do you use drugs, Mr. Boyles?"

"I think about it. Never did before." He made an odd little laugh, then began mumbling to himself.

"Take off your shirt, please."

He did not bother to unbutton it, pulling it over his head and dropping it to the floor. I bent to examine his chest and arms: there were no needle marks anywhere. The rash was on his back; it was a faint, serpiginous eruption, similar to what Ann Donovan had had. In view of his dissolute state I had expected something else, a verminous lesion, but it was not that. I prescribed a mild cream, and he prepared to leave.

"Please. Stay a moment."

He sat back in the chair and stared at his lap.

"I'm concerned, Mr. Boyles. About your health."

He mumbled to the floor.

"Before, I mentioned Barea disease. It seems more and more likely."

"Like me. Like you."

I frowned, and considered what to do. Ideally, he should have been hospitalized, but I was loath to become entangled in what could turn into a most difficult case. I was already overburdened trying to plan for my other patients, and this was a man I hardly knew. I decided to refer him to the physician taking my place.

"You may need to be hospitalized," I told him. "At the very least, you will have to be followed closely."

"Mostly," he said, "I swallow. When I'm hollow. Golly, dollies . . ." He chuckled to himself, and then abruptly his manner changed. He stopped squirming and sat straight.

"Doctor," he said. "I'm not well."

"I can see that."

"Look at me . . ." He picked at his shirt, his pants, as though they were someone else's dirty linen. "I'm not in control."

"You need help, Mr. Boyles. You may need to be hospitalized."

He stared at me, then looked down and nodded. I did not repeat what I thought he had.

"I am leaving the clinic soon and unfortunately will not be able to continue as your physician. I would like you to see a colleague of mine." I began to scribble the name, then crumpled the paper and threw it in the trash. Rising from my chair, I went to him.

"Come," I said, taking him by the arm, "I'll make the appointment for you."

I had become somewhat inured to his odor, but close at hand it was powerful. I found myself holding my breath as he stood. His face, which before had been nervous and distracted, now seemed merely tired. I steered him from the room to the receptionist's window.

Other patients waiting in line backed away as we approached; some nodded cordially to me. Ms. Imarra was gesticulating to the one in front, while talking to another on the phone. I caught her eye, then waited until she turned to me.

"It's crazy, Doctor. They all want to see you. Even the ones who haven't for years."

"They want to say goodbye."

She nodded. "They're sad. We're all going to miss you." The phone rang, and she asked the person to hold. It rang again, and she ignored it. "What can I do for you?"

"This is Mr. Boyles. He needs an appointment with Dr. Wilkins as soon as possible."

"Three weeks," she said, pulling out the book.

"That's too long. He needs it this week. Preferably tomorrow."

"You want to look?" She handed me the book and answered the phone.

"How about here?"

She put her hand over the receiver. "That's her lunchtime."

"Well, what's this?"

"Mrs. Ullyot wants a physical."

"I just gave her one."

"She wants another."

"She can wait."

"*You* want to tell her?"

"Lenore," I said, leaning forward and whispering. "This man is sick. He needs an appointment."

She glanced at me, then crossed out Mrs. Ullyot. "What's the name?"

"Boyles. Mingo." She penciled it in, and I turned to him.

"Ms. Imarra will give you your appointment. We'll call to remind you." I offered my hand, which he limply took. "If things get worse before then, call me. Or the clinic. Day or night."

He nodded. "I'm frightened, Doctor."

"I understand." I thought to say more but remembered that we were in public. "Just be sure to keep your appointment."

"I will."

I studied him one last time, then turned and walked back to my room.

Perhaps I should have taken more aggressive action with Mr. Boyles, but my mind was full of other things. Chief among these were the patients I had known far longer than him, and once I made the referral I put him out of my mind. In less than a week he reentered, when I received the call from the coroner.

I would have remembered the day even without the call, for it was my last at the clinic. A party had been planned, and the smells of various dishes hung thick in the air. The walls themselves seemed to exude the scents of turkey, ham, rice, vegetables, pies and cakes. Sundry decorative matter—bright paper, shards of metal, bits of glass—had been hung from the ceilings and walls, making the narrow hallways barely passable. I walked them carefully, full of excitement.

I had thought the day would be bittersweet, and I was not wrong. Friendship and felicity were laced with sadness, and tears as well as smiles fell upon me. All day there were hands upon my back, hugs, and kisses from those most familiar.

We had our party, ate, toasted, ate more. I was given a plaque to commemorate my years of service; on the back were the names of my fellow workers, stenciled on a plate of some thin metal. I received cards, flowers, small gifts such as people could afford. All touched me, and my mood was deep as I made my way to my office to begin the last afternoon.

I entered the room sucking a chocolate candy. The phone rang, and I sucked harder. I did not want to answer, but the ringing continued. I finally gave in, chewing the candy and swallowing it. I rinsed my mouth with water and picked up the receiver.

A gravelly voice identified itself as Dr. Toppas of the Barea Coroner's Office. He asked if I were Dr. Jules Ebert and then if I knew a Mingo Boyles.

"He's dead," he told me.

"Dead?"

"A friend found him this morning. We found a medicine jar with your name on it, so I thought I'd give you a call. You were his doctor?"

"I saw him twice. What did he die of?"

"Don't know for sure, but I have an idea. Did you know that he used drugs?"

"He didn't," I found myself saying.

"There was a needle and an empty syringe on the floor, and a puncture wound in the middle of his arm."

"I see."

"The guy was a mess, Doctor. Hadn't cleaned in who knows how long, clothes were filthy, apartment a sty. That surprise you?"

"I saw the man only twice, Doctor. The first time for a minor matter, a sore. He seemed at the time quite pleasant. Well-dressed, fastidious even."

"How long ago was that?"

"Five or six weeks. I saw him again less than a week ago. He was completely different. Slovenly. Distracted. Psychologically inconsistent . . ."

"Sounds like drugs."

"I entertained the notion too. It occurred to me, also, that he might have Barea disease."

The voice grunted. "We'll know when we do the autopsy. Why didn't you put him in the hospital?"

"I referred him to another physician. As of today I am retiring from my practice."

"Not a great note to end on, is it?"

I remained silent.

"Well, thanks for the help. The autopsy will be in a day or two. If we find out anything interesting, we'll let you know."

"I'd appreciate if you'd do so in any case."

"Will do," he said, and hung up.

I stood at my desk, staring at the receiver. I felt strangely incriminated and repeated the conversation in my mind to see if I had cause. I could not decide, though clearly the loudest voice of accusation was my own.

I could have put Mr. Boyles in the hospital. It is a risky place, but then so too is illness. At the least he could have been observed, prevented from harming himself if that, indeed, was his wont. Or supported, if his vital functions began to fail. There might even have been found some treatment for his condition, for there was a chance, however small, that he had had something other than Barea disease.

The coroner was right; the news did dampen the festivities of the day. But the mind is resilient, and my mood, though sobered, rebounded. I hardly knew Mingo Boyles, and a man's life, after all, is his own to live. Death, to me, is not cruel, merely the end to life. Jessica's homily of the feces and the pear came to mind, and I smiled, for it seemed apt. It made me all the more surprised when, that night at my apartment, she reacted so emotionally to the news of his death.

"I just don't believe it," she said over and over. Her eyes were swollen and red. "I can't believe that he's dead."

"Everyone dies," I said gently. "Sooner or later everyone does."

"He was young. My age. He was a sweet guy . . ."

"Even the sweetest die."

"He didn't deserve it, Jules. Not like that. Not any way."

She huddled in a chair, her knees drawn to her chest, and wept. "Shit," she sobbed. "Shit, shit, shit . . ."

I made no attempt to stop her; it is useless to try to hasten grief. I too was upset at his death, but for other reasons, and waited until she had calmed sufficiently to hear what I had to say.

"He had Barea disease, Jessica. I'm almost certain of it."

She lifted her forehead from her knees and looked at me.

"I'm worried about you."

She took a jerky breath and exhaled, then wiped her face with her hands. "I feel okay, Jules." She smiled feebly. "Can't you tell?"

"He might have given it to you."

"We only had sex a few times. Most of the time it was with his father. I told you that. And I used protection."

"We don't even know what causes it. How can we know what protects against it?"

She shrugged.

"You shouldn't have done it, Jessica."

"Is that why you're upset?"

"I'm worried."

"What do you want from me!" Her voice cracked. "You want me to say I'm sorry?"

"Jessica . . ."

"First you tell me my friend's dead, and then you say I might have the same thing he did." She trembled. "And now you want me to apologize?"

"I'm worried, Jessica. I love you."

"You sure have a lousy way of showing it."

"I don't want anything to happen to you. I don't know what I'd do . . ."

She looked at me and burst into tears.

I pulled her from the chair and hugged her to my chest. I became lachrymose myself, dampening the strands of her hair. After a while our sobbing quieted, and then it stopped. I coaxed her gently to dinner.

I had prepared a small repast that, when Jessica disclaimed hunger, I was forced to eat alone. It is no great joy to dine in solitude, and I was grateful for her company.

She was quiet, her mind obviously elsewhere, and between mouthfuls I carried the burden of conversation. It seemed best not to allow silence too firm a grip, and I recounted the small matters of the day, the party, the gifts, my farewells. I was careful not to mention Mr. Boyles again, though I confess that he seemed to be present, at least with Jessica, at the table.

By the time I finished, mopping the remaining sauce with the final bit of bread, her mood had lightened. Her friend's death was still in her eyes, but I think she understood that there would be time to grieve on her passage to Eridis. Together we had only a few days left.

We were at my apartment, where she had been staying since the Fagos incident. She took the plates and dishes from the table, placing them in the autoclave, and I deposited the capons' carcasses (it was fortunate that Jessica had had no appetite, for the birds were smaller than I had judged) into the shredder and compacter. I put a pot of water to boil and prepared two cups of coffee with new grounds. We took them into the living room, where I settled in my armchair. Jessica reclined on the sofa, her head resting on one of its arms while her bare feet brushed against the other. She stared at the ceiling, and I at her. We sipped.

"The ties are falling," she whispered. "Falling away."

"I'll miss you, Jessica. A month seems forever."

"It does, doesn't it? Look at the last one. How much has happened."

"It seems short to me, as though we're just beginning to know each other."

"Long and short." She sighed. "Death and life. In the same breath."

"I think of you as a slender tree, Jessica, and myself, something huge to wrap around it."

She smiled. "What will I do without you, my lover?"

"Take up with a Domer, I suppose."

"Maybe so. To remind me . . ."

"Jessica!"

She laughed. "I'll be working, Jules. Hard. They're not sending me all that way to have fun."

"I wish we could go together . . ."

"Me too. I'm excited, Jules. It feels like the beginning of an adventure."

"For both of us."

"Really? What's yours?"

"I'll tell you yours first."

"All right. What's mine?"

"Discovery. Achievement. Success."

"I think I can, Jules. I really do."

"So does Mannus. They wouldn't have hired you if they didn't."

"I guess so. It's funny, because there are plenty of other pharmacobiologists around, lots of them with more experience than I have."

"Don't sell yourself short. You do good work, you've published, you're young, you're . . ."

"What?"

"You're willing to go."

"Yeah. That's probably my most important qualification. Someone has to. That's where the plant grows. I wonder if Mannus really believes we can find some way to cultivate Mutacillin off Eridis, or if they're sending me for some other reason."

"Like what?"

"I don't know. Public relations. Maybe they have to satisfy some NHD regulation. Maybe I'm just a tax write-off."

"They would be elated to find a way to make the drug someplace closer than Eridis. Even if it's not on Earth."

"I'd love to be the one, Jules. If I discovered a way, then other companies could make it. It would be cheaper . . . anyone who needed it could get it."

"Mannus would still own the Mutacillin patent."

"Sooner or later it would leak out." She grinned craftily. "You wouldn't be able to keep something like that secret for long . . ."

"To benefit Mankind
She laid bare the vaults,
The pecuniary vaults of Mannus.

"It will be your epitaph."

"I wouldn't mind. It has a nice ring."

I smiled, and for a while we sat in silence.

"So what's yours, Jules?"

"My what?"

"Your adventure."

"To be with you, Jessica."

She sat up. "Really?"

"It is." I swallowed. "It's not easy to say. I've never been in love before. Never like this. My hunger has always been for something else . . . now it's for you."

She smiled. "I love you, Jules."

I started to get up, but she came to me first. She sat on my lap; a leg on either side, and pulled my head forward. At first I pushed her back, but then I grabbed her by the buttocks. I took a breath and buried my head against her chest. As light as a thought, as blazing, I stood and carried us to the bedroom.

How convergent our paths have become since then I could never have guessed. It fills me with awe, at times with sorrow. But that night I felt as buoyant and adventurous as she, and it was this that sustained me while we were apart.

7. The Party at the End of the World

Jessica left toward the end of June. I was with her as she boarded, then watched on the monitor while the Mannus vessel disappeared into space. In addition to its crew it carried supplies for the Eridian settlement. The special holds designed for the drug, which comprised the majority of cargo space, were empty. Transit time to Eridis from Earth was approximately a month's ship-time.

I was scheduled to depart three weeks later, July the eighteenth. I was to travel on the *Solis,* a government ship whose list of passengers was diverse, reflecting the various missions attached to the flight. My contract promised that, after a brief stopover at a planetary base on the outskirts of our system, the ship was to proceed directly to the transfer point for the Eridian region. I would trail Jessica by about a month.

After she left, I arranged my affairs. The majority of my attachments were material and easily settled. I sold my few luxury items, comforted to know that in a matter of years most would be obsolete. Lark was among these, and as I disposed of it I found myself secretly hoping that by the time I returned, other modes of transport would have been devised.

I purchased a small space for storage, which I reserved for those of my belongings that had been custom-made. These included my refrigerator, which was two meters in width and nearly three in height, my armchair, and the kitchen stools, whose seats had been built broad and sturdy enough to bear my mass.

Items of sentiment I singularly lacked—photographs, holographs, and the like. I have always preferred to preserve memories in my mind, which does not distort reality by attempting to freeze it. The few books that had meaning for me I packed and stored in the refrigerator; above them I hung the jackets, shirts, and slacks I chose to leave behind. Extra underwear fit handily in the cheese compartment, and dishes, utensils, bowls, and other kitchen items found their place in the freezer. The rest of my possessions I either gave away, sold, or kept for the trip. In the latter category were clothes, toiletries, two pots and a pan I was especially fond of, and the books and tapes I felt necessary for my practice. These were few, for Eridis was equipped with a medical library of sorts, and it was also possible to communicate when necessary with Earth.

I had assumed that this interim period, full as it was of the petty tasks of disengagement, would be rather unpleasant, but it was quite the contrary. I was busy enough to keep the havoc of gluttony at bay, and as I rid myself of each attachment, my mood became successively more sanguine. What astonished me most was that, after parting with Lark, I began to walk. Other than an occasional stroll in the gastronomic district of Goldmont, I had not done so since my youth, when childhood exuberance had managed to stave off the jeers of my companions. As an adult I had stayed for the most part indoors, eschewing the streets as, in one way or another, too dangerous.

The Pimella Arms lay in a valley, on three sides of which rose hills. Whitehill to the south (the Arms lay near its foot), Fidelity to the north, and Goldmont to the east. Over the years I had forgotten that this was so, accustomed as I was to flying with Lark above them. As I stood on the street in front of the Arms, staring at the gently ascending slopes surrounding me, I resolved to make no attempt to scale them. Conquering nature's terrain is the ambition of some, but it is not mine. My walks would be westward.

In the mornings I attended to matters of the trip and in the afternoons left the apartment and headed west. Within the wall most traffic was airborne, and the streets, though often

crowded, were not as choked as they were outside. Being
confined to one direction did not seem unduly limiting, for there
was a plethora of life to be smelt and seen. In the scant thirty-
odd years since I was a boy, Ringhaven had grown upon itself
enormously. Construction was in evidence everywhere, as were
a multitude of establishments and services that such a thriving
metropolis spawns. Some claimed that the city was out of control, making analogy to the carcinomatoses that ravage the
human body. I understood the intent of the observation, but it
did not seem apt. Cancer uniformly kills, and Ringhaven appeared to be flourishing.

One evening, emboldened by days of wandering without incident, I walked through an opening in the ringwall and ambled
into Westvale, a district remarkably similar to Sowall, to which
it is contiguous. The sun was low and orange, and the streets
were alive with people. Most were poorly dressed, many in
tatters. Hawking, milling, dancing, gambling, the atmosphere
was of a party or great festival. Beneath it, however, I could not
help but sense a current of desperation.

As I moved farther from the wall and more toward the
district's heart, I noticed that many in the throng wore masks.
I stopped and inquired of a woman if the day marked some
special occasion.

She was standing slightly apart and seemed to be watching
the others in much the same way as I. Her dress was tattered,
but her face seemed neat and friendly. In her arms she carried
a small child with sunken eyes and prominent cheekbones. Its
face was sickly, but when I looked closer I saw that it was a
mask.

"No occasion," she said, hardly moving her lips. "Don't
need no occasion."

A group of youths walked by, making music with desultory
instruments. One carried a flute; another, a spherical instrument that he beat on with a pale stick, producing a pleasant,
hollow sound. Others used similar sticks to add to the rhythm
and to syncopate. They neared and I smiled, nodding my head
to the beat. One of them saw me and handed me an extra pair

of the gray-white sticks. They were slightly curved, and as I took them, I realized that they were the dried rib bones of a human. The flute was a fibula, and the hard, hollow object a skull.

I could not bring myself to join in their music and returned the ribs quickly, before they fell to the ground. The woman, who had been watching dispassionately, grinned.

"Don't like music?"

I stared at her. "Some," I said.

"You be needing a mask. Got any paper?"

I had become suddenly self-conscious, and at her command fumbled in my pocket. I pulled out several crumpled bills and, without looking at them, held them out to her. She nodded, then bent and put the child on the ground. She straightened and brought her hands to her forehead. Carefully, she began to unpeel her skin.

When she finished, she asked if I wanted her breasts. I shook my head. In my hand I held her moist face.

She stuffed the bills somewhere in her dress, then picked up the child to go. Its pale and emaciated face seemed nothing but eyes, and the crone saw me watching it.

"Why such a mask?" I asked.

"You want its face?"

"Not the mask. I want to see its face."

She looked at me thoughtfully, then held out her hand. "Three bills."

I gave them to her, and she did as before. Placing the child down, she lifted its mask. Beneath it the face was the same. Its eyes stared at me, and suddenly the child grinned. Its gums were swollen and pocked with sores, and when I could look no more, I backed away. I was tossed about for what seemed like hours before finally losing myself in the swarm.

The pall that was cast upon me by the woman and her sickly child was lifted somewhat by the ambience of the crowd. I discarded the mask I had had the misfortune to purchase and resolved to delve no further into things that were beyond my ken. Such seemed the attitude of most others there, and once I had adopted it, my mood became decidedly more festive.

The swarm was greatest in the main avenue, spilling into side streets when the pressure reached too high. Most of these were dimly shadowed, cut from the sky by tall tenements. The people who were there invariably carried some article of plastic: a piece of car, an old phonograph disc, a tattered coat. I supposed these were, as Jessica had suggested, to fend off the more vigorous of the hounds.

On one occasion I was pushed into one of these side streets; when I became aware that I alone carried no piece of plastic, I turned quickly to depart. I was careless, stumbling over an object at my feet. When I regained my balance, I turned and saw that it was a Fagos hound, or what once had been one. Its limbs were stiff, its coat buzzing with maggots. A large rat scurried up and grabbed a piece of flesh from its hind leg. Hastily I retreated, using my weight to reenter the safety of the throng.

The flow was carrying me westward, where after several blocks the boulevard ended in what once had probably been a park. The skeletons of a few trees remained; the ground was dirt. Tables, stands and mats were scattered throughout the area, around which were clustered groups of people. Some were there to buy, others to sell, others merely to watch. At one of these a woman stood on a wooden crate, slowly turning in circles, assuming various attitudes and poses. Something about her struck me, as it seemed to have many others, for quite a crowd had gathered. Using my weight to advantage, I pushed my way forward, not stopping until I had reached the front. A cord of rope hung between several wooden posts encircling her, and another woman was within the cordon. With a basket she was collecting money from the crowd. I did not know her, but the other, her dancing partner, I did. It was Ann Donovan.

She was exquisite, and it took more than several moments to assure myself that it was she. It is always disorienting for a doctor to meet a client outside of the office, and I am sure that the reverse is true. In this case the momentary confusion was far greater than usual, for the woman was as changed from the last time I had seen her as she had been on that occasion from five years before. She was stunning, and I found my heart beating for her beauty.

She had somehow managed to find a practitioner adept at the art of pilitation. I have no great love for that surgery, nor for those others that, in the name of vanity, seek to alter the human body. Yet, as I gazed upon the gorgeous fur that grew from her flesh, I wished for a moment that all men and women were thusly garbed.

She wore no article of clothing, no vest or blouse, and yet there was nothing tawdry or egregious about her. A rich, tawny fur of short pile lay as a halter upon her breasts, curling beneath her arms to the upper part of her back. It reached to her neck, then swept down upon her shoulders, encircling the arms to the elbow. On her belly a narrow line trailed past her navel, then splayed out like a fan, becoming thicker and darker. It grew dense across the mounds of her thighs and buttocks, and between her legs was like a pelt. Below, it thinned, coiling in streaks around her calves and ending in a tuft on the dorsal arch of her feet.

Her scalp hair had been trimmed and dyed to match the rest, and on each malar eminence was a patch of sorrel down that feathered like a teardrop toward her temple. The orange light of dusk made what was bare on her body seem to blush, and the faint breeze that began to blow made her fur lay down and glisten the color of sunset.

She moved upon the crate in the most natural way, taking stances and poses that were as fluid as they were unlikely. Were it not for her face, which seemed content, and the language of her body, which was as relaxed as it had once been tense, I might have thought she were under the influence of some drug, or the compulsion of a hypnotic suggestion. As it was, I was not certain that neither was true, and when after a while she stopped to rest, I pushed my way through the cordon of rope and made it clear that I would have a word with her.

The other woman moved to bar my way, but fortunately Ann recognized me almost at once.

"Dr. Ebert!" she exclaimed, jumping from the crate on which she sat. "What a surprise."

I found that I wanted to touch her, but instead, I simply smiled. "The surprise is mine," I replied.

She laughed and turned on the balls of her feet, as though modeling a new outfit. Even among the strong scent of that crush of bodies on the field I could smell hers. It was musky, and I thought of the medical laboratories where animals were kept.

"What do you think?" she asked innocently. "Does it become me?"

My throat was drier than I thought, and I found it difficult to reply. A simple yes would have sufficed, but instead I found myself taking her hand and kissing it.

"You like it," she said. "I'm glad."

She stepped closer, and suddenly I felt without air. It frightened me, and I stepped back, panting and trying to gather my wits.

"Is something the matter?"

"I . . . I seem to be out of breath. I think I need to sit down."

"Sit here," she said quickly, taking me by the shoulders.

She sat me on the crate, which sagged but did not break, and waited while I calmed. It took no more than a few minutes, but when I started to stand, she kept me down with a finger.

"No. You rest. I'm fine."

I nodded, lacking the strength to be gallant. I was silent for several moments, until I recalled my intent.

"How do you happen to be here, Ann? I would not have imagined this your milieu."

"I've only been coming for a few days. Janice told me about it." She motioned to her comrade. "It's wild, isn't it?"

"Indeed. Is it always like this?"

"Since I've been here. Day, night . . . there's hardly any difference. They say it never stops. Never."

"It's like a great festival."

"That's what they call it. The party. The party at the end of the world."

"Ann, why are you here?"

"Who'd want to miss the final blowout?" She laughed and tossed her head.

"Ann!" I found myself commanding her. "Bend down so that I can see your face."

She did as I asked, and I examined her eyes. The pupils were normal, neither pinpointed nor widely dilated. Her breath was as I remembered it, slightly sweet; there was no trace of foreign chemical or toxin on it.

"Why are you here?" I repeated, gripping her shoulders with my hands.

"To make money, Doctor. I quit my job and spent my savings on the operation. Dr. Merkis provided me with a new source of income."

"Merkis? He is the one who performed the surgery?"

She nodded.

"And you do this for that old man? You advertise your body for him?"

"You misunderstand me. I do this for myself. I am proud of how I look. I am not ashamed to have others enjoy it, too."

I found nothing to reply, and stared.

"And you, Doctor. What brings you?"

"I am concerned for you, Ann. It is as though another person has invaded your life."

"Only a better one. There's no danger here, Dr. Ebert. It's only crazy to those who aren't."

She edged closer, and my eyes shut by reflex. The noise of the crowd became a roar, and I felt about to be flung to the floor of an animal's cave. Fur brushed against my arms, and a wild scent filled my nostrils. My chest ached, and inside I felt raw.

"Air," I choked. Her body lay within inches of my own. "Air."

As desperately as I wanted her at that moment, so did I push her away. I staggered to my feet and away from that spot, and when next I became aware of anything, found myself at the edge of the field and heading east.

I wonder now if I had been drugged. Perhaps something on the rib sticks, or the old lady's mask, some substance that could penetrate the skin. The events of that evening were too vivid, too strange and disconcerting to be merely real.

And yet the drugs of our own making are far stronger than any we might ingest. Perhaps what occupies me now had already begun. Perhaps what beheld the world that night was the first semblance.

I never returned to that part of the city, though I continued my daily walks. I sought to fill myself with the sights and sounds of humankind, for I imagined my future on Eridis to be nothing but dreariness. The thought of living in proximity to the Domers was particularly unsettling, and I attempted to saturate my mind with a more pleasant life, one that I could recall during my time away.

Days passed slowly and quickly, and eventually it came to the sixteenth of July. It was two days before our scheduled departure, and my apartment was ready for release. I had concluded all my arrangements, which was a mistake, for the forty-eight hours before such a journey can be harrowing indeed. Without some mundane preoccupation greater ones can develop, which is what happened with me. I began to doubt my decision, worry about the flight, even fear the commitment I had made to Jessica. The decision to play physician to the hopeless Domers seemed especially foolish.

One-half of the forty-eight passed, but it seemed tortuously slow. I thought of Zeno's paradox and for a moment convinced myself that I would never leave. The eighteenth finally arrived, and with two bags I made my way to the base. It lay in a desert south of Barea, inland from the sea by a hundred miles. We approached by air, which afforded a full view of the base. No vessel stood in sight, nor were any being prepared. In fact, there was little activity below us at all.

We landed, and I climbed out of the aircraft. My hand was shaking. A few of the people on the ground looked at me curiously. It was very hot there, and by the time I entered the main building and sat with the colonel, I was perspiring freely. I told him who I was and inquired of our vessel. He was cordial, but incredulous.

"The *Solis* is dysfunctional, Doctor. Were you not notified?"

I stared at him.

"There was a fire in its main chamber. Repairs have hardly begun."

"When?"

"A few days ago. You must have received notice."

"I received nothing."

"I'm sorry."

"What ship will take us, Colonel?"

"The *Solis* will. When it is repaired."

That, of course, was not good enough, but to recount the remainder of our conversation would merely be to subject you to outburst and invective. I circumvent the proceeding, and that of the next days and weeks, by telling you that the colonel was, at the expense of my everlasting animosity toward the government and all its minions, correct. It was the *Solis* that took us, and it did not do so until mid-October.

How I managed to occupy myself during those interminable days and nights might be the proper subject of a treatise on anger and impotence, but it has no place here. I retained my apartment, somehow managing to survive its austerity and emptiness. The most noteworthy event, the only one of interest, was a visit I made in late September to the coroner. It had occurred to me that I had never received the autopsy report on Mr. Boyles's death.

His office was in one of Goldmont's older buildings; it was set off from a large main room by an old-fashioned door. Part of it was glass, upon which I knocked. The man behind the desk looked up and motioned me in. I closed the door behind me and waited, but the man, whom I presumed to be Dr. Toppas, seemed momentarily to have forgotten me. He was absorbed with a screen on his desk, and I took the opportunity to look about.

The room was spacious, but drab. Three of the walls were in need of a coat of paint; the fourth contained a large window whose blinds were closed. Light was provided by a ghastly fluorescent fixture in the ceiling.

Decorating the walls were scanning electron micrographs of

various organelles. In one corner of the room was a holo of a tiny skeleton. I approached and saw that it had two heads. They were not skulls but actual heads, tiny ones, with faces. One was grinning, while the other frowned.

"A present when I graduated," the man behind the desk said, looking up. His voice was gruff. He sprang out of his chair, then walked over and extended a hand. "I'm Toppas."

"Jules Ebert."

He gestured toward the skeleton. "To remind me that there's a good side to every bad." He scratched his head. "Or is it the reverse?"

I looked at his face, his small chin and big ears, then back at the holo. "There seems to be a resemblance," I told him.

"There better be . . . I was the model." He motioned me to a chair, the only one besides his in the room. I jammed myself between the narrow arms, feeling pinned and mildly dyspneic. He did not seem to notice.

"You were the doctor for that man Boyles," he said.

"I saw him twice. You were going to send me a report."

"Was I? I've been swamped."

"I can refresh your memory. He was the man who died with a puncture mark . . ."

He waved me quiet with a hand. "I remember. Fascinating case."

He turned to his terminal and punched some keys. The green light of the screen shone on his face, and in a moment he nodded, then swiveled slowly until he faced me.

"Mingo Boyles. Cause of death: Barea disease."

"I was right."

"He had traces of narcotic in his blood, but not enough to kill him. We found something else. Just got it a couple of days ago. It may be a red herring, but it scares me. And not just me."

He pushed a button and part of one of the walls slid back to reveal a screen. He pushed another button, and a microscopic tissue section was projected on it from behind.

"You recognize the brain," he said matter-of-factly. "It was the only organ affected."

It looked vaguely familiar, and I grunted a response. He began to flash a series of slides.

"Medulla oblongata, pons, thalamic nuclei, neo-cortex: note that in none is there evidence of inflammation. No hemorrhage. No necrosis. Classic Barea . . . Now take a look at this."

I recognized an enlarged projection of a group of cortical neurons.

"Again," he continued, "note the typical absence of tissue damage or disruption of normal architecture. But take a look at the cells. Do you see the little particles?"

They were impossible not to see, once he called my attention to them. The cells were packed with them.

"I see them."

He turned off the projector and closed the wall, then turned on the room light. He scratched an ear and leaned forward in his chair. His desk was a mess, and he began shoving piles back and forth in search of something. Eventually he found it, a holo plate, blew some dust from its surface, then rubbed it with the back of his elbow.

"Like I said"—he clipped a light to one edge and pushed it across the desk to me—"it could be a red herring."

I picked it up and placed it in my lap. I turned on the light.

"We found this all over the brain," he said. "Worse in the cortex."

I studied the holo, slowly turning it in my hands. It was a model of a beautiful jewel, or so it appeared. The outermost part was a sphere, translucent and dotted with tiny rods. Within lay a lovely geometric shape, whose interlocking triangular sides numbered twenty.

"What is it?" I asked.

He made a snort. "I can tell you what it isn't."

"Indeed."

"It isn't zoster or simplex."

I looked up. "Herpes?"

"Blown up a million or so times. It was all over his brain."

"Is that what killed him?"

"Who knows what killed him? Barea disease did. This is the first time we've ever isolated anything like this."

"Herpesvirus hominis is extinct, Doctor."

"So we've been taught. What you're holding in your hands appears to contradict that notion."

"If it's not zoster and it's not simplex, then what is it?"

He shook his head and leaned back. "Don't know yet."

"*Are* there other kinds?"

"Not that infect people," he muttered. "Not until now."

I tried to take a deep breath but was impeded by the arms of the chair. I took several shallow ones and blew them out.

"The sore he had when he first saw me. It reminded me of herpes. I saw a case once."

He looked at me, his eyes moving from my face to the holo and back again. I squirmed a little in the chair.

"Couldn't he have had an encephalitis?" I asked. "As I recall, the herpesvirus lived in peripheral nerve cells and from time to time took it upon itself to ascend to the brain. He had all the symptoms . . ."

"He didn't have an encephalitis, Doctor. It was an infestation without apparent damage."

"Then what made him act so strangely?"

He shrugged. "Who knows. Maybe this did. Maybe Barea disease, whatever that is. Maybe they're the same. Or maybe it's neither one . . . Maybe he was just crazy to begin with."

I found myself shaking my head. "I don't think so."

"I hope he wasn't. I hope this isn't a red herring, or some kind of artifact. We need something hard. And soon. This Barea thing is getting out of hand."

"When will you know more?"

He shrugged. "When we do."

I withheld a nasty comment about laboratories run by the government. "I trust it will be soon."

He nodded, sighed and stood up. He seemed tired; it was clear that he wanted to end our chat. I was in no hurry, having nothing else planned for the immediate future, but propriety demanded that I stand and meet his hand.

"This Barea thing worries me, Ebert." He ushered me from the room. "We need to get a handle on it. And soon."

"I appreciate your time," I said. "If all goes well, I should be gone from this planet in a matter of weeks. If I have time before then, perhaps I'll stop by again."

"Sure," he replied, patting me on the back and turning away. "Or give me a call."

I left, and two weeks later returned, but he had no further information. After that I became busy with the anticipation of departure and did not call or visit him again.

The *Solis* finally departed Earth's atmosphere three months after the original date, four after Jessica had gone. The hyperdrive, which purportedly had been repaired, malfunctioned in the midst of flight. We did not abort the journey, but continued to and from the transfer point at but a fraction of our previous velocity. When finally I arrived on Eridis, more than a year had elapsed since Jessica and I had seen each other.

Part Two

ERIDIS

8. Arrival

Forgive me, Jerrold. I must gather my thoughts, for they whirl about like a flock of noisy birds. Science taught that explanations follow simple patterns, from A to B to C, but I have since discovered that the logic of events is otherwise. Time, I think, is not so much a thread as a lake, and chronology is simultaneous.

I arrived on Eridis and was met by a woman named Jeen. She gave me an amiable greeting, which I returned with a scowl. I had anticipated a different welcoming party.

"Where is Jessica?" I demanded.

"I don't know," she replied evenly.

"Why isn't she here?"

"She's probably in the mines working." She began to walk, and I tailed after her.

"Didn't she know I was coming?" My voice sounded shrill in the narrow corridor.

She shrugged and kept walking. "How was your trip?"

I stopped. "Where . . . is . . . she?"

She turned to face me. She looked exasperated, though not without sympathy. "Dr. Ebert, I was sent to escort you to your quarters. Ask me about the mines, or the layout of the settlement, or the recycling laboratories. I'm a biologist, not the administrator. I don't make out the schedules."

"Who does?"

"Guysin Hoke."

"I want to speak to him."

"You will. He would have welcomed you himself, but he was held up. He'll meet you in your room soon."

She turned and set off again, adopting a pace brisk enough that I could not catch her without running. This I chose not to do, and we did not speak again until we came to the juncture of the corridor we were in and a much wider one. She stepped into it, I followed, and then she stopped and pointed to the right. The light seemed to fail in that direction, though I imagined I saw the outline of a great door.

"That's Service," she said. "On the other side of it is the domeroom." Her finger moved until it pointed in the same direction but across the corridor. "That's the opening to the mines."

Impulsively, I started off in that direction, but she caught my arm. Her grip was strong.

"Don't be foolish, Doctor. It's dangerous there. And you'll never find her."

"Why isn't she here?"

"She'll be back soon. What's a little while longer to the time you've already waited?"

"Interminable! Do you know how long it's been?"

She nodded. "She told me."

"It's a travesty. The government has no shame."

"You'll find life here more reliable." She released my arm and began to walk down the corridor to the left. I did not follow, and she stopped.

"Doctor, please."

"When will she be back?"

"I don't know. Soon."

"Already I don't like it here."

She shrugged. "It's not so bad. Pay's good." She started off again.

"That's not why I'm here," I shouted, then cursed. I was helpless, and hurried to catch up with her. "I didn't come all this way for that."

"Everyone has his reason."

"Indeed. Yours is the pay."

"That, and a chance to do something different."

I scowled. "And is it?"

"It was. Now it's kind of boring."

"I expect it to be no less than that for me."

She laughed. "Don't be too quick, Doctor. You just got here. It took some time before I got tired of it."

"How long?"

"Longer than you'll be here."

I asked how she knew the tenure of my stay.

"No one stays here longer than a cycle. No one but me. And Guysin. He's been here since the beginning. This is my third."

We were approaching the end of the corridor, and the walls, which earlier had seemed a great distance apart, seemed now to be pressing closer upon us. All of us have been in tunnels whose parallel sides appear to converge in the distance only to spring apart when seen close at hand, but what I experienced then was the opposite. I felt the tunnel narrow as I progressed. I wondered if the long trip aboard the *Solis* had somehow damaged my sense of perspective, and I mentioned this to Jeen.

"It's no illusion," she said, pointing up. "The ceiling's lower, too. It's to keep the Domers out."

I looked to see if she were joking, but her face was turned away. For a dozen steps we were forced to walk in single file, and then suddenly the narrow tunnel burst out into a great circular pavilion. I breathed a sigh of relief, only then becoming aware of how short and tight my breaths had been.

We spilled into the center of the room, and I stopped for a moment to look about. The floor was opalescent and vast. Curling around it in an arc was a low wall full of doors. Above was a domed ceiling, suffused with a soft blue light. A few people were milling about the floor, but most of them were far away and paid us little attention. Jeen touched my arm and led me away from the center, toward a door at a right angle to the corridor where we had entered. Each door had a number, and we stopped at the one marked forty-nine. She pressed a plate and it slid open. I followed her in.

We stood in a narrow hallway, on either side of which was a door. She passed these and went into the room at the end, where she stood, waiting. I let her stand and palmed open each door to examine what lay behind. One was a bathroom and the other seemed to be a miniature kitchen. In it were a tiny stove, two sparsely stocked cupboards, a drawer and a counter. There was no running water and no refrigeration.

I closed the doors and took the few steps to the room at the end. It was by far the largest, and might have appeared more so were it not so cluttered with furniture. There was a table with two chairs, a desk with a chair, several empty shelves, a short couch, and scattered devices of leisure. Suspended from the ceiling and attached to two walls (the room was square) was a bed, from the side of which hung a metal ladder. I stared at it in disbelief.

"I presume you are about to tell me that these are my quarters."

Jeen, who had sat on the couch, nodded. Her arms were draped over its back and her legs were stretched out. "Jessica demanded that you have a kitchen."

"Has she seen it?"

"She designed it."

I took a deep breath and slowly blew it out. I pointed to the bed. "And that?"

She looked up. "Nice, huh?"

"I am not a bird," I told her, "who would perch above the ground, nor am I a simian who would swing and climb. I am a man, and one of cumbrous disposition. I prefer my bedding to be lodged against the bosom of the earth."

She gave me a wide-eyed look, then got up and climbed the ladder. For a woman her age (she was not by many years my junior) she was agile and strong. She reached the bed, stood on it (the ceiling above it was high), then jumped up and down several times. "Seems sturdy to me," she said. "Want to give it a try?"

"I do not," I replied. "Please come down."

She bounced a few more times, then shrugged and descended.

"I'm sorry," I told her politely, "but it's unacceptable. I am not prepared to hover while I sleep."

"Suit yourself."

"Are there other apartments?"

"One or two. This is the only one besides Guysin's that has the extra room. Believe me, it's luxurious."

"I would hardly call it that."

"The rest just have a bedroom and bathroom. That's it. We eat together, and there're common areas to play and relax."

"I am not accustomed to eating in large groups—"

"Then stay here. It's the best you're going to get."

I scowled, then surveyed once again the room in which we stood. It was larger than the other two but not commodious. I imagined the bed somewhere on the floor, but even with the table or desk removed the room would have been hopelessly cluttered. The choice, it seemed, came to dismantling the kitchen and putting the bed there, or leaving the bed where it was. It was a decision between food and sleep.

"If I am to tolerate the bed," I said, "I must have a refrigerator."

"What?"

"For the kitchen. There is no way to preserve food."

"We use one of the caves in the mines. Each day we bring up what we need."

"A small refrigerator would be preferable."

"Would it?" Her manner became formal. "Is there anything more you need? If not, I have work to do."

"I would like my luggage."

"When it's unloaded." She turned to leave, reached the door, then faced me. "We're on single name basis here, Doctor. What should I call you?"

The question disarmed me. I felt rebuked, and childish. I fumbled for a word.

"Jules," I finally said.

She nodded. "It's been a pleasure, Jules. Try not to be too upset. It's always hard at first."

Behind her the door slid open and a face appeared. Unaware of it, she turned to leave, and made a startled cry. She took a step back and put her hands to her chest. "You scared me," she said.

It was man of her height and, from what I could see, a slighter build. The hall was narrow, and Jeen backed into the living room as he came forward. She took a step to the side, and turned.

"Jules Ebert"—she motioned—"this is Guysin Hoke."

"Guysin," he said, smiling, and offered his hand. We looked at each other.

Names evoke mental images, whose basis, I would guess, lies in the obscure and pliant region of our subconscious. Before I met him, Guysin Hoke was a smell to me, a faintly sulphurous and eggy cloud. He had a large and hairless head and spindly limbs. His voice was shrill. To some degree the image persists, though it has been overlaid by the substance of him in space.

He was not as tall as I, nor as broad, and his hand was narrow and weak of grip. This was perhaps an affectation, for his torso and limbs seemed not devoid of strength. He held himself conspicuously erect, with his chin squared beneath rather small lips. His face was neither very young nor very old, and his eyes were dichromatic, one blue, the other gray. His scalp was bald, either naturally or shaved to be so; it glistened with some emollient. The scent of it emanated from him, and I stepped back, making some excuse so that I might breathe fresher air.

"I'm on my way out," Jeen said.

Guysin nodded without turning his head. "I'm very pleased to meet you."

Jeen shifted on her feet, then went to the door. "So long," she said and left.

"Did you have a pleasant voyage, Jules? May I call you that?"

"Where's Jessica? Why isn't she here?"

"There was a mix-up . . ." He glanced at me. "We weren't sure when you'd arrive."

"If Jeen could be there, why couldn't Jessica?"

"She's working, Jules. She's quite a fanatic about that—"

"You do not seem to understand," I said, trying to contain my fury. "I have just completed an interminably unpleasant journey to begin a job that I view at best with misgiving. At the very least, I expected Jessica to be here to greet me."

"She'll be here soon."

"Soon?" I exploded. "Soon isn't good enough!"

I was piqued by many things at that moment—the trip, Jessica's absence, the matter with the kitchen and the bed—and perhaps was too harsh with a man I had met but minutes before. But I felt abused, and had no other target. To my surprise he apologized.

"I'm sorry," he said. "The responsibility is fully mine."

"Words," I said with disgust.

"I know what it's like to wait."

"Do you?"

"Oh, yes. I know . . ."

His voice trailed off and I looked up. For an instant I thought I glimpsed a sadness in his face, and then it was gone. His manner became more circumspect, and he gestured toward the couch.

"Please, sit down. I know I am no substitute, but if you're willing to put aside your disappointment, we could use the time to get acquainted."

My anger had not disappeared, but there seemed little to do for it. He seemed genuinely contrite, and I sat as he suggested. He took a chair opposite me.

"I warn you not to ask about the trip . . ."

He smiled. "I was about to compliment you on Jessica."

"Oh?"

"She is a conscientious worker. Dedicated . . . intelligent . . ."

I nodded, trying with some difficulty to remember. "Her work . . . it's going well?"

"I believe it is. But to tell the truth, she rarely includes us."

"Perhaps she has little need as yet."

"Perhaps. But I'm sure I could help. I've been here for years . . ."

"Jeen mentioned that."

"I wonder if she's happy here. If it's the right place for her."

"Jessica? Why wouldn't it be?"

"We're a small community," he said. "Sometimes she seems unaware that there are others around . . ."

"She's always liked other people." Feeling the need to defend her put me ill at ease.

"Of course. Maybe I'm overreacting." He gave a little laugh. "I must not be used to people with such strong spirits. She has a real streak of that."

I nodded, picturing her during a quarrel. I smiled at her ferocity, and the image shifted to her in bed. She was naked, passionate, and I felt a quickening in my loins.

"Maybe too much of one . . ."

The daydream vanished. "What do you mean?"

He bridged his fingers on his chest and stared at them. He looked up. "I wonder if, perhaps, she is too independent."

"Say what you mean."

"The Domers . . ." He pushed his fingertips in and out. "She fraternizes with them quite freely."

"Is there something wrong in that?"

"There are rules, Jules. Perhaps you have read them . . ."

I nodded.

"The Domers were created to work. Any distraction is detrimental to that end. It is why we so strictly regulate the contact between them and staff."

"Of course."

"They are taught obedience, but nowhere friendship. Certainly not equality."

"Has Jessica violated some aspect of this?"

"Frankly, I do not know. She has been seen frequently in their company, both in the mines and the domeroom. She speaks with them openly, with a familiarity that is neither dignified nor politic." He paused and pursed his lips. "Forgive me if I am too blunt, but she seems in some peculiar way attracted to them . . ."

I began to reply but felt suddenly faint. I stood up, bracing myself with an arm on the couch.

"Are you all right?"

"Dizzy," I muttered. I fell back down. "Food . . . I need food."

He jumped up and disappeared from the room; in a moment he returned with a loaf of bread and a plastic jar. I watched weakly while he spread a smooth pink substance on a slice and handed it to me. The taste recalled salmon, and I devoured it. In a short time I had consumed both the loaf and the contents of the jar, and I sat back, feeling better.

"Thank you." I sighed, catching my breath. "I'd forgotten how long it had been."

"I should have offered you something sooner."

"No harm done." I wiped my forehead, which seemed to have beaded with sweat. "Where were we?"

He regarded me curiously. "Why don't you rest? We'll have plenty of time to talk later."

I nodded, suddenly feeling full of fatigue. "Jessica . . . when will she be here?"

"I'll send word immediately." He stood to leave. "In the meantime you get some rest."

He gave me a last glance. I thought he would speak, but he merely smiled, then left.

For the first time since my arrival I was alone. I realized that I had become accustomed to that state and had begun to prefer it to the company of others. I wondered what it would be like to consort again with Jessica, and I lay back on the couch, gazing at the platform above my head. How will I survive this place, I thought, and imagined the bed quaking beneath my weight and crashing to the floor. I cursed some epithet, then forced my imagination elsewhere. I closed my eyes and saw Jessica on the bed, covered with pelts of fur, dancing. She smelled of musk, and as the odor filled my nostrils, I became as light as smoke. I fell asleep drifting up the rungs of the ladder, gently insinuating myself among her supple and secret places.

·I dreamed of a bell signaling time for dinner, then woke to hear that it was ringing in the apartment. I was momentarily disoriented, then gathered myself and went to open the door.

It was Guysin Hoke, and there was a look of solicitude on his face.

"I sent word to Jessica. I wanted to tell you myself."

I muttered my thanks.

"She's deep in the mines, though. It will be a while yet. I thought I might show you around."

"Delay after delay. It's as bad here as Earth."

"Not so bad. But stay in your quarters if you'd like."

The word irritated me. There was nothing yet that I liked.

"I could use a walk," I said begrudgingly.

He smiled. "Good. I'll take you to the domeroom. You can see your prospective patients."

I had him wait while I went to the bathroom and relieved myself, then freshened my face with water. I straightened my clothes, and together we left the apartment. Behind, the door closed automatically.

We walked back the way I had come, and in a short while the corridor widened before us. The ceiling became much higher and then we passed the tunnel on the right that led to the landing field. I was in a taciturn frame, which seemed to suit Guysin fine. He was not.

"I love this place," he said, looking around. "I've been here all these years and still I love it. How many people can say that?"

I shrugged. He kept talking.

"There're not many surprises, it's true. Frankly, that's how I like it. I know what to expect: when I go to sleep at night, I sleep." He paused a moment.

"It does get lonely sometimes. Especially watching the young people come and go. Not many become friends . . ." He sighed wistfully. "I suppose I'm too old."

He stopped, waiting perhaps for me to gainsay him. When I said nothing, he went on.

"Still, I've never had a job I've liked better. And managing the colony is something I do well. It's not often that a man loves his work and does it well, too."

"I would think the one leads to the other," I said.

"I suppose it does. I'm a lucky man."

"I do not hold much stock in luck."

He laughed. "Neither do I. Good planning first. Then seeing things through."

As we had been walking, the light in the corridor had been growing steadily dimmer. Guysin pointed out the entrance to the mines on the left, an opening as broad and tall as the corridor we were in. In what seemed an unwavering dusk we approached the door Service.

I turned to him and asked what exigency necessitated such dimness. Sight has never for me been a keen sense and it serves even less in atmospheres ill-illumined.

"The Domers' eyes are made for the dark. The mines are even darker than this."

"Of course. The domeroom is dim, too?"

He nodded. "Bright light causes them pain."

The veil had begun to lift, and in front of us I made out Service. It was more than twice my height and many times my breadth, and I thought fleetingly of the creatures that lay beyond. I stood before it, waiting, and then Guysin touched me on the shoulder.

"We're not going in," he said. He pointed up. High in the wall that separated the corridor from the domeroom sat a window. "We're going up there," he said and turned to the right.

In the wall of the corridor was a doorless opening that I had not noticed before, and through it he walked. I followed, and in a few steps found myself in a small chamber. Guysin was waiting. He pushed a button and the chamber began to rise; perhaps thirty seconds later it stopped and we exited into a narrow hall. At the end was a room with several chairs and two large windows. They were set in adjacent walls, and I went first to the one nearest.

I looked out and saw from a great height the corridor down which we had come, its various branching passageways and the bright but narrow tunnel in the distance. I took a breath and turned.

Slowly I walked forward, trying to blanket my mind. I told

myself that I was a physician, that I must look but not judge, that I must be filled with dispassion and detachment. I recited the Oath and stepped to the window above the domeroom. I looked beyond.

9. The Domers

Memory is a fickle thing, but it is our only way of knowing. Sensation is its building block, and if it has a purpose, it is survival. Seen from one eye a close object is different than when seen from the other. How many eyes does it take to make a fact? How many memories?

Though I had read extensively of the Domers, I had avoided all images of them. I was not shocked when I first saw them, but something like a pit moved inside me. It expanded into my lungs and throat until I had barely air enough to breathe. I could not move, and my mind cast back to the first day of anatomy class, when we had viewed the faces and hands of the corpses we were to dissect. I was filled with aversion and awe.

I struggled to control myself, and became aware that Guysin was watching me. I turned from the window.

"I expect to be here a while," I told him. "There is no need for you to stay."

"I'm in no hurry," he said evenly.

"Please. I much prefer to be alone."

He eyed me. "Do you think you can find your way back?"

"I expect so," I said disdainfully.

He hesitated a moment, then smiled. "Enjoy yourself." He turned to leave. "By the way, the glass is one-way."

When I was alone, I returned to the window, relieved that I could watch without threat of being seen. I felt as though I were at some uncommon zoological park, enrapt by a strange and unsettling sight. It was not pleasant to look, but no force could have turned me away.

The domeroom was enormous, criss-crossed by rows upon rows of cubicles. Most of these I could see from the window; about half were occupied. Some Domers sat at the panels, but the great majority lay stretched upon the mats. The feeding tubes were in place, and though from my vantage I could not see the Domers' eyes, by the lack of movement I assumed that they were either sleeping or in a state indistinguishable from it. They were unclothed, and the mossy light from the dome gave their skin an algal tinge.

Even from a distance they seemed huge, and the extensive adiposity that at close range tends to iron out their features, from afar obliterated even further their resemblance to human beings. They sleep and rest with their arms at their sides and their legs together, and because my eyes had not fully adjusted to the light I fancied at first that they were limbless. Enveloped as they were in fat, I could make out little of their skeletal shapes, and since it is this that commonly allows us to distinguish at a distance one person's features from the next, the bodies below me seemed featureless as well. In a moment of casual fantasy I recalled the great banana slugs of our childhood. Do you remember, Jerrold, how we tormented them, forcing them to crawl over salt to get to food? It did not seem cruel then, nor did it now as I wondered of what use the Domers could be if they could move only as slugs. It was not a pleasant image, and was fortunately dispelled when I saw one go from a panel to a mat. It did not slither and I sighed. Its gait, though ponderous, was erect.

I stood in the room for some time, wondering what I could possibly offer these caricatures of human beings. By habitus they were destined to suffer; by design, to die young. This I knew before I accepted the position, though I had supposed that in some way I might be able to alleviate their pains. I had come to Eridis not simply as Jessica's lover but as a practicing physician, and this latter role was vital to my self-esteem. As I observed my future patients, I pondered what effect professional failure would have on that role, and on my life.

I decided to make a closer appraisal of the Domers and left the room. I took the elevator to ground level and stepped into the main corridor. I could see better, my eyes by that time having acclimatized to the light, and it made me feel smaller. Service loomed high above me and the arch of the corridor far above it. I could find no mechanism by which to open the door and was near to giving up when I spotted a smaller door to its right. I had missed it before; it was human-sized, and along its facing was a plate. I palmed it and the door slid open.

I hesitated, recalling briefly the restrictions on staff movement within the domeroom. As a physician I did not feel bound by them; in actuality, I felt a small need to make a point of my privilege. I did not, however, desire to be the cause of some offense, nor the provocateur of an unpleasant scene. I resolved to be professional, and with that left the verge upon which I paused and went forward.

From the floor the domeroom seemed even more vast than it had from the window. Directly in front of Service is an open space, the only one in the room. It is two, perhaps three dozen paces wide and seemed to swallow me as I crossed. In the middle of it I stopped to take my bearings.

Before me lay the Domer columns, fifty or more, and between each ran an aisle wide enough for two Domers to walk abreast. The columns stretched from one edge of the room to the other, then curved back, following the arc of the wall. I looked from side to side, barely able to make out the farthest columns, so distant were they from where I stood.

The walls of the room swoop up to become its dome, which is lit with a dull green light. I tilted my head and gazed up, sucking in my breath at the immensity of the hemisphere. Had it been darker, adorned, perhaps, with pinpoints of light, I might have imagined it a sky.

Where the ceiling intersects the floor are two other doors the size of Service. One is called Carefree; the other, Celeste. The three together mark the vertices of an equilateral triangle, but the vastness of the domeroom is such that from where I stood I could see neither of the other two. I turned once to make certain that Service and the small door beside it had not moved, then crossed the remainder of the open space.

At the head of the center aisle, not more than three steps away from my first contact with a Domer, I paused. Nightmarish images rose up, of turgid aliens with automatic brains and giants with inhuman antiseptic smells. I wiped the sheen of sweat from my forehead. I took a breath and crept forward.

On my right was the back side of a panel and slowly I looked left. The cubicle was empty. I sighed and walked to the next row. Again on my right was the back of a panel, beyond which I could not see. I realized that from this direction all the cubicles opened to the left, and I turned that way. There was a mat, a tube sticking out of the floor, the two sides of a panel with its bench, but no Domer. My nerve increased and I went quickly forward. At the fourth row I stopped, for lying face up on the mat, eyes closed and tube in place, was the massive creature I had come to examine.

Blood pounded in my ears; I tried to gather myself before going closer. The Domers are taught to disregard all occurrences outside their own cubicle, a lesson necessitated by the proximity in which they live, and I could not tell if this one was asleep or simply ignoring me. I watched it, and waited.

The creature was enormous, as they all are; to look at it made me sick. It lay flat, and at its tallest point—the peak of a great mound of epigastric fat—reached nearly to my waist. Below was the bulging adipose plain of its lower belly, and beyond, the swollen heaps of buttock and thigh. Its lower legs were like posts, and its feet nearly as broad at the heel as they were at the ball. I swallowed and stepped closer.

If you can imagine a huge barrel made of some soft and fleshy material, that was its chest. Another store of fat lay there, predominantly in the breasts, which hung to the sides like great, melting mounds of ice cream. The shoulder girdles were immense, the one part of the body where the outlines of muscle showed beneath fat. Its hand (I could only see one) was large and pudgy; of all the features save the face, it was most like our own.

I watched the chest rise and fall, and the waves of fat ripple across the breasts. It was breathing without effort, apparently unaffected by its extraordinary burden of adiposity. I am unable for long to tolerate the recumbent position, but this creature could, and was, before my eyes. My fascination turned to envy, and then through some bizarre metamorphosis I imagined myself in a similar posture. My breaths became shallow, as though I were starved for air. I sought to understand what was happening, but my thoughts would not cohere. I began to pant and my fingertips started to tingle. I was light-headed, becoming more so, and suddenly realized what I was doing to myself. In a panic I clamped my hand to my mouth. Though my lungs cried out, I did not let go for nearly a minute.

When I did, I thought I had aborted the episode, but in a moment I lost control again. This time my stomach convulsed and a sickness rose in my throat. I gagged and stumbled backward.

Waves of nausea swept through me, provoked by this foul and vile creature. My viscera churned, and I feared that I might lose control of some other bodily function. I should have left but could not, transfixed by a feeling alien and strange. The Domer was hideous to me, a mockery of the human form, and I was furious that I had allowed myself to come to Eridis. Violent thoughts overwhelmed me, and before I knew it I had stepped forward and jabbed the thing savagely in its belly. The action frightened me, but I felt that I had been provoked. I waited with bile in my throat.

It opened its eyes; its head was already facing me. It seemed to return from a distance.

"Your name," I demanded.

It looked confused and did not reply. It is rare that a Domer vocalizes in its cubicle, especially when it is feeding, but this I did not know at the time.

"Name!" I repeated sharply.

It blinked and creased its forehead. "Bulu," it finally said.

"I am a doctor. Ebert."

It stared.

"Do you know what 'doctor' means?"

It nodded.

"Good. It means you must obey me. I am going to examine you. Do what I say."

I had not really intended to do such a thing, had not even brought my tools, but for some reason I felt compelled to inspect the body at close range. The nausea had abated somewhat, and with trepidation I proceeded.

I began with the lower extremities, touching the flesh tentatively at first, then more vigorously as I became accustomed to it. The skin is smoother than ours (it is all but hairless) and soft, like a sponge. It is easy to have a finger, in certain parts a hand, disappear into its depth. The creature is warm, of course, and perspires; I felt the moisture of its sweat behind a knee. Some compulsion made me draw my wetted fingertips to my nostrils, and I sniffed, then gagged, for the smell was human.

I continued up the leg, poking, palpating, attempting to achieve some sort of command over the body. I touched the patella, whose width is greater than the outstretched distance between my thumb and small finger, and inched up the thigh. The mass of tissue dwarfed my hand; the buttock, though compressed by the supine weight above it, was tremendous. I stood at the haunch, at once spellbound and repelled.

I was looking toward the region of the genitalia but could see only the most external features. I leaned across the thigh to visualize more. The Domer's flesh gave before me, and I pitched suddenly forward. The smell between its legs slapped at me; I shoved myself frantically back. It was a vulgar and obscene moment.

I stood back, panting, violated. "Spread your legs," I commanded.

The Domer obeyed, and I went and stood between its feet. Forcing myself, I crept forward, stopping near its knees. I felt it incumbent to visualize the genitalia, and I crouched and looked.

I was sickened when I saw the penis and scrotal sac, for I had assumed this to be a female. It was appalling to me that a male could be so timorous, so passive, and I stepped back with disgust.

Lest you believe that I had lost all sense of objectivity, I must interject that the error I made is a common one. Domer males are frequently confused with females, for apart from the genitalia, which are hidden by the enormous folds of inguinal and femoral fat, there are no external clues to distinguish one from the other. Pubic hair is absent in both sexes, and the contour of the hips, waist, and shoulders, which usually demarcates human males from females, is obscured by the grossness of the Domers' obesity. Similarly, the breasts of the two sexes are equally pendulous, and since no Domer female has as yet given birth, the nipples and areola of the female are indistinguishable from those of the male. Apart from memorizing each face, the quickest way to know with certainty if a Domer is male or female is to look between the legs.

I had had enough of the examination yet felt impelled to continue. The bile had left my throat, but I had not yet gained the measure of control I sought. My viscera remained at a nauseous verge, and I felt far from a professional level of decorum. I wiped my forehead with the back of a hand and proceeded.

It was useless to palpate the abdomen, for it was far too thick. Also, I was reluctant to disturb the feeding tube, which had been functioning since my arrival. I was curious, however, as to the nature of its attachment to the abdominal wall and bent to inspect it closer. It was a mistake, for it provoked in the Domer a sudden, reflex response. His arm jerked from his side and propelled itself toward my head. It was as rapid a movement as I have witnessed from a Domer, but fortunately less rapid than mine. I jerked back, and his hand swept empty air. It gusted against my face.

"What do you think you're doing!" I cried out.

He shook his head, his eyes wide.

"Do you know what 'doctor' means?"

He quivered. "I'm sorry."

"Watch your step, Bulu."

"I'm sorry. I didn't mean to."

I wanted to slap him but restrained myself. I was fearful of his strength. "I'm here to examine you. I don't intend to hurt you. Don't try to hurt me."

"I wasn't trying." He was upset. "You tried to do something to my food."

"I was just looking. I'm a doctor."

"You scared me."

"I was examining you. I wasn't trying to take your food."

"You scared me. Don't touch it."

"Don't tell me what to do, Bulu."

"Please. I'm hungry. I need to feed."

"I have no intention of disturbing your meal."

"Please," he whined, distraught and frightened.

I was repulsed by his cringing attitude, and the bestial attachment he seemed to have toward his meal. I am no stranger to obsession, at times having craved food beyond endurance, but never have I begged for it, never shrunken before another in an act of debasement. His doing so was odious to me and the reason that I judged him so harshly. I did not know at the time how long it had been since he had eaten, though in my state I am not sure it would have mattered.

"Lie still," I commanded.

His arms were rigid at his sides and his flesh quivered with tension as I bent to examine the tube. I inspected it in a cursory fashion, finding myself no longer much interested. I had established a certain authority and felt calmer, less at the mercy of my emotions. As I returned to my quarters, I recalled that I had studied their method of feeding and already knew a great deal.

10. Seasons

Each Domer has a stoma, which on appearance is much the same as one an Earth surgeon might devise. On the Domer, however, it is not fashioned by craft. It is an inbred structure and serves a different purpose. Located in the upper gastric region, it marks the beginning of the alimentary tract. Having no need to transport food from the oral cavity, the Domers lack an esophagus, and the stoma functions for feeding purposes as their mouth. Whether it is capable of performing other acts we associate with that organ, such as whistling and vocalization, is a matter of speculation. I have witnessed neither, though I have been present when abdominal gas has been expelled with a sound remarkably similar to the primitive syllabications of our infants.

The stoma is ringed by a sphincter that prevents the inadvertent expulsion of material during off-feeding times. During feeding, it envelops the tube tightly, holding it in place and forming a barrier to hinder the entry of air. What little enters is quickly expelled from the stoma in the manner I have described. The Domers have no anus and are without the luxury of flatal discharge.

The alimentary tract ends in midcolon, by which point all nutrients, minerals and fluids have been absorbed. The nutritional engineers have achieved a food product—mush—of such efficiency that all is utilized. There is neither waste nor residue and, consequently, no need for elimination. An anus, or any other excretory orifice, is thus rendered superfluous.

There is a kind of beauty and logic to this design, wherein may lie a lesson for us. The most common illnesses of mankind—pharyngitis, rhinitis, vaginitis, urethritis—are the result of invasion of one or another of our body's sundry openings. Though I do not advise that we seal them off (nor, for that matter, can I envision a race without any), the idea of one or two less might be worth considering. At least in the case of the Domers it has proven both practical and harmless.

Elimination of urinary waste occurs in the same fashion as ours. Close to the feeding tube, which projects from the floor next to the mat, is a low, broad, funnel-shaped collector. The females squat upon it (when they are no longer able, they sit), and the males do as any males do. Beneath the floor the collectors converge, joining eventually into one large pipe that terminates in the recycling laboratory. Here the urinary solutes are separated and stored. Some sit until the end of the cycle, while others are utilized sooner, principally in the manufacture of mush. The solvent, of course, is water, and by the end of the process is pure enough to use again.

All that pertains to the Domers is recycled. The system for them is closed, and their survival depends upon its functioning smoothly and without waste. If the extraction of solute lags and affects the production of mush, they will go hungry. If one of the distillation machines breaks down, then they will go thirsty until it is repaired. If a process malfunctions to the degree that a sizable amount of recyclable material is actually destroyed, first they will go hungry, then thirsty, and finally, at the end of the cycle when the race is wiped out, only a portion will be seeded to return.

To my knowledge this occurred just once, at the end of the second cycle. A fire somehow started in the recycling laboratory, destroying kilograms of stored organic material. Before Mannus could replace it, the third cycle had begun, with the population of Domers drastically reduced. They toiled to its conclusion, but production suffered greatly. During the next cycle, after Manus had replaced what was lost, it rose to its normal level, where it has remained.

My arrival on Eridis came three years into the cycle. As I

looked at Bulu, I wondered if he had any sense at all of the passage of time. The Domers are dominated by it, by the cycle, in a way we can hardly imagine. For the first time something other than revulsion entered my heart. I felt pity for them, and then unexpectedly, for myself. We are all victims of some cycle. Mine is called hunger.

There are activities that can drive the thought of food from my mind—intense study, deduction, sexual excitement—but no day or half-day goes by that it does not reenter. Usually I fear that I am empty, starving, though at times my concern is the reverse. Constantly must I struggle to control myself, to contain the urge to have some item on my tongue, against my palate, traveling down my throat. Generally I am successful, for my will is strong and the memory is never far of the painful consequences of disinhibition.

I call this my season of temperance: though I consume large quantities of food, I do so regularly, snacking rarely. It is a calm period, and the longest of my three seasons. Yet it is the one I am apt to remember least. For the other two—engorgement and starvation—are violent, and lurk upon its borders ready at any moment to strike.

Engorgement, starvation: they make me sound like a beast, not a man. At times I believe it is so, that I am no more than a thinking cage for some primitive, feral creature. Without warning I am struck with an all-consuming hunger, a wind that sucks at my entrails with the horrid threat of famine. I become empty and fear that I will disappear if I do not eat. It matters little if I have recently gorged; I find that I must do so again. This is the beginning of a binge, and I will stuff myself with whatever is at hand until it stops. It can last for one night or many; when I was younger, there were periods when I glutted for months. Strangely, I am barely aware at these times that I have eaten at all, as though the glutton were someone other than myself.

I favor carbohydrates—confectionaries especially—but the type of food is not critical. In the fury of ingestion the taste of one substance is quickly overtaken by that of the next.

In any large binge there are multiple small ones. Gluttony

occasions remorse, which provokes an appetite to quaff it, which begins the circuit anew. These are the cycles within the cycle, and they will not end until the season itself does.

What signals its termination is as obscure to me as the trigger that starts it. It is precipitous, as no spring is, or winter, or any other thing of nature. The hunger does not vanish, but the craving to be filled with food becomes a compulsion to be depleted of it. The season of starvation begins.

It is the briefest of the three, and the most violent. It is colored by self-reproach and shame; to eat is to defile. I am as painfully aware of my body during this time as before I was not, and am plagued with fears of the damage I have done. I fear for my heart, my circulation, my joints, my pancreas. I avoid mirrors and have ugly dreams.

It is fortunate that this season is short, because it is the worst. Food, on which I rely for so much more than nutrition, is denied me. I am ashamed of my debauchery, my appearance, and believe myself to be permanently stigmatized. I am loath to enter the world.

It is said that those most victimized by their weaknesses are the ones most able in times of need to call upon their strengths. I believe that I am such a person, for time and again have I pulled myself from the abyss. Food, my demon, my weakness, ironically becomes the staff of my strength. My love of it is too great: I cannot starve myself for long. Eventually I begin to eat, resolving to do so in moderation, and once again temperance marks my life.

To remember my youth and adolescence is to recall the cycle of hunger. Where others think of a certain summer, a special fall, I recollect the times I was so obese as to fit into none of my clothes, or so voracious that I was ashamed to eat in public. Full of disgrace and embarrassment, all these memories are dark, all save one. I was ten maybe, or twelve. So fat that all I could wear was a bedsheet that had been fashioned for me, ridiculously large, billowing, with a hole in the middle for my head. Some friends came by; I had been absent for some time, and I think they suspected the cause. They asked to see me, but you would not let them in. Do you remember, Jerrold? They became more demanding, taunting with voices I could hear. You said I was ill and told them to go away. One of them laughed. There was a muffled sound and then a yelp. I assume you did something bodily to the boy. After that they were quiet, and then the door shut. You never talked about it to me, but I knew. I know now. You stood up for me. It is not something I will ever forget.

While I had been gone, my bags had been delivered. Jessica had yet to arrive, and the place was as dismal as ever. I paced the narrow hallway, cursing whomever and whatever entered my mind. I was frustrated, but more than that I was exhausted. I glowered at the bed; when I could no longer stand, I slumped onto the couch. Anger fought weariness and finally succumbed. I fell asleep.

11. In Whose Image

When I woke (or thought I did), the air was filled with huge balloons in the shape of humans. I was costumed and at the center of a throng. I tried to turn my head but could not. I opened my eyes and the colorful fragments died. I stared at a ceiling, for a moment thinking I was in Barea.

I pushed myself to a sitting position and rubbed my neck. I had slept with it turned obliquely against an arm of the couch, and it ached. The room smelled stale. I was alone. How many hours had passed since I had left the domeroom I did not know.

I stood and stretched, then put my bags on the couch to unpack. On the desk was a device that I assumed to be a communicator of some sort, and I toyed with the notion of placing a random call. It was an impulse to bridge the isolation with which I was suddenly possessed, and I lifted the transmitter and began to punch buttons. The screen remained blank, and the bell to my apartment rang. It startled me, and I wondered if I had inadvertently summoned someone. I went to the door and pressed it open. It was Jessica.

We stared, then rushed into each other's arms. I wrapped myself about her as I had imagined a thousand times, wanting to swallow her into my body. In a moment she squirmed away.

"You're crushing me," she said.

"I can't help it. I want you closer."

She smiled and hugged me, then squeezed past to the living room. I followed her, and we embraced again.

"It's been so long," I said, not yet believing that the wait was over.

"Too long." She clung to me hard. "How I've missed you . . ."

"And I you."

My gladness to see her veiled her in a glow, and yet it penetrated that she looked different. Thinner, perhaps; paler. Her hair not entirely kempt. The green suit she was wearing was soiled and wrinkled.

She saw my face and frowned. "What's wrong?"

I shook my head. "Nothing. You're beautiful, Jessica. So beautiful . . ." I kissed her until I had to stop for air.

"I wanted to be there to meet you, Jules."

"Yes. I was angry that you weren't."

"Guysin didn't tell me. I didn't know you were here until after you'd arrived."

"It's past. We're together now."

"I was working. I'm getting it, Jules."

"I heard. I'm glad."

"It's close," she murmured. "Close . . ."

I put a finger to her lips. "Not now, all right?"

She blinked, then looked at me and smiled. "I've missed you so."

"It's been a torture to me, Jessica. An endless, awful torture." Tears came to my eyes, and I hugged her. I felt as though she were the kernel, the life within me. After a while she drew back; with a sweep of her hands she took in the room.

"So how do you like it?"

I took a breath, then grinned. "Do you want honesty or tact?"

"Both." She smiled. "I arranged it."

"It's lovely. Perhaps a little cramped, but who would complain?"

"It's bigger than my place in Pimplehill was."

"Your place did not have *that.*"

She followed my finger and laughed. "The floating bed. I didn't think you'd like it."

"It's less a question of like than reach."

"There's no other way to fit everything else in."

"It serves no purpose," I pointed out, "if the bed remains above while I am below."

"You just need an incentive."

She went to the ladder and stepped on the first rung, then pivoted and arched her body out. "That's why I'm here."

She climbed swiftly to the top, then sat and draped her long legs over the edge of the bed. She swung them back and forth, humming innocently. With a seductive smile she began to lower the zipper at her throat.

Had my neck not been sore I might have reveled in her longer, for I felt uncommonly stirred by her position above me. As it was I could not, but her purpose had been achieved. I felt myself quicken, then lighten, and scurried up the ladder as though a squirrel running to its nest.

She had turned and propped herself on some pillows. I sat beside her. If the platform trembled or groaned beneath our weight, I did not notice. All my thoughts were on Jessica.

I leaned over and slid my finger through the metal circle attached to the zipper and slowly drew it down. Past her bosom, her belly, across the thigh and down to the ankle. I unpeeled the suit, brushing her skin with my fingers at every opportunity. She lay back, and I touched her ribs, outlining them beneath her breasts. She smiled.

"And now you, my lover."

It had been a year since I had been naked before another, a year since I had been touched and caressed. I was apprehensive, and beads of sweat began to pool under my breasts and in the humid area of my groin. I had not bathed since my arrival and sought to make some excuse if I smelled foul. Jessica quieted me with her tongue, tracing small spirals about my breasts. She touched my nipples with her lips and began to hum softly. I closed my eyes. My nipples hardened. Her lips seemed everywhere.

In a while I pushed her back, for my heart was racing too swiftly for my body to lie still. I needed to make some action of my own and rolled her onto the mattress. She fell upon it effortlessly, in a posture that was utterly her. Legs splayed, arms limp, she seemed to melt against the sheet as a shadow upon stones.

I loved her greatly and opened my mouth to lick her. The taste incited me. I began to grab at her flesh with my teeth.

"Eat me," she muttered. "Eat me, fat man."

I was there, eyes closed, giddy with the scent. I touched her lips with my own and kissed. She squirmed and let out a small cry. I kissed her again.

"Not there," she said. "It's sore. Other side."

Passion has no mind for questions, and I did as she asked. She began to rock, thrusting and holding herself against me. My mouth was full of liquid and my tongue felt as though it bore the weight of her pelvis. She cried again and I could not be sure if it was a sob of pain or pleasure. I was kissing her indiscriminately; she did not ask again that I halt. She rocked and groaned. Suddenly she strained against me, then arched above the bed. She gasped, then shuddered and collapsed.

I rolled away, flushed and panting and not yet satisfied. In a moment she was upon me, engaging me in ways I remembered so well. The river grew within me, surged, turned white. I groaned. It peaked, then exploded.

Minutes passed, or days. We lay side by side, panting, dozing.

"I love you," I murmured.

She snuggled closer. "I've been thinking up ways to please you."

"You're an artisan."

"I've missed you so. For a while I was afraid you'd changed your mind."

"Never."

"I didn't hear for months . . ."

"I sent a message, Jessica."

"Did you?"

"That we were delayed." I frowned. "It didn't arrive?"

"I'm not sure," she said vaguely. "Maybe it did. It seems like forever . . ."

"Jessica . . ."

"Does it for you, Jules? Does it seem like forever?"

"Longer. I didn't have work. Or you. All I had was a memory."

She murmured something I didn't hear.

"You had your research," I said. "At least you had that."

"Yes." She seemed to come alive. "It's going well, Jules."

"Guysin told me the same."

"Guysin? You met him?"

"Briefly. He seems to think highly of you."

She stiffened. "Are you serious?"

"That's what he said."

"He hates me, Jules. That's what he thinks."

"He said he was concerned about you. Worried . . ."

"I bet he is."

"Why? Why would he be?"

"I'm a threat to him. That's why."

"He said you aren't happy here."

"Only when he's around. The rest of the time I'm happy enough."

"Do you have friends, Jessica?"

"Why do you ask?"

"Do you?"

She pulled on her lip. "Sure. Jeen, Randy, a few others. Most of the time I'm too busy." She smiled. "And I was waiting."

I studied her, then found myself smiling back. "I'm glad."

"It's happening, Jules. I've almost got the mold growing on plates. Once I can do that, all I have to do is get it to germinate . . ."

"Can you?"

She looked at me and slowly nodded. "I think I can. I think . . ." She blinked and her face seemed to go blank. "Have you seen them?"

"What? Who?"

"Them. The Domers."

"Jessica. Are you all right?"

"Have you?"

"One. I saw one."

"They're beautiful."

"We were talking about your work."

"No."

"I'd prefer not to discuss them. Especially if you plan to make jokes."

"No jokes, Jules." She sat up.

"They're repulsive," I said flatly.

"Were you shocked?"

"Disgusted."

"I can see why."

I glanced at her sharply. "Do you have some point to make?"

"I just want to talk, Jules. That's all."

"Fine. Don't bait me."

"I didn't mean to. I'm sorry."

I scowled.

"What else besides disgusting?"

I took a breath, exhaling loudly. "Perhaps we can agree on some other subject. A more pleasant one."

"They're going to be your patients, Jules."

"I realize that. I pity myself for having to doctor the creatures."

"They're not creatures. They're human. They have thoughts and feelings."

"No." I shook my head. "Not human. Humanoid maybe, or humanesque. But not human."

"Whoever designed them did it without much thought to the distinction. They're not robots, Jules. They're flesh and blood. They have minds. Their bodies are the only thing that's different from us."

"It's a big difference. It's the chain around their necks."

"Slavery was outlawed a long time ago. Why does Mannus get to practice it?"

"Why does it bother you so much?"

She stood up and stalked to the edge of the bed, then back. "Live here for a while and see how it affects you. How it feels to be a doctor to slaves."

I recalled that I had said the same thing to her one night on

Earth, but I held my tongue. "I came here to be with you," I said. "Not to worry about the Domers."

"But they *know,* Jules. They know that they suffer."

"All of us suffer in our ways."

"No! It's not like that . . ." She was perturbed, and I did not understand why. I placed an arm about her shoulders.

"Listen to me," I said. "The Domers are our invention. We made them to supply the drug. Just as we made the Fagos hounds to clean the city. They could be robots, or insects. That they happen to be flesh and bone is incidental. And incidental, too, that they have feelings."

"No . . ."

."Yes. It's not worth getting upset about."

"I can't help it."

"You can. Please."

Suddenly her manner changed. She became very calm. "It's a battle, Jules."

"Don't be silly."

"I have to take sides."

I stared at her.

"Who is responsible? Aren't we them?"

"Jessica . . ."

"Who, Jules? In whose image are they made to suffer?"

"Stop it now!" I grabbed her arms. "Don't act crazy."

"I'm not crazy, my love. Look at them . . ." She wriggled free and came upon me, rubbing the upper part of her body against mine. "Look at you . . ."

Her breasts touched my own; against my will I became aroused. I beat the feeling down, for her words were a sickness upon me. I grabbed her shoulders and shook.

"You're mad!" I cried.

"Don't grab me."

"I am not them. Do you understand?"

"Let go."

She struggled but my grip was too strong. I dug my fingers into her harder, then stopped seeing her face. She screamed and bit my arm. I let go.

We were as close as could be without touching; I felt the heat of her breath. Her voice was cold.

"I had sex with a Domer, Jules. He fucked me and I fucked him. It was good. He reminded me of you."

A horrible vacuum sucked my chest. I tried to speak but couldn't. I couldn't move. A beast grabbed my arm and slapped Jessica across the face. She did not crumple and it slapped her again.

"I fucked him!" she cried. "Where were you? Where, Jules? Where?"

She was kneeling beside me, and the smell of her tears filled the air. I wanted her to return my blow but could not ask; then I was weeping too. I felt so hurt, so stripped and bare. Smaller than I had ever been. Beyond pride. I held out my arms and leaned against her.

"Hold me," I wept. "Don't leave me. Hold me."

12. An Assemblage of Reality

I wish I could say that after that everything was easy, but that would be a lie. It was not, at any rate, harder, at least not between Jessica and me. She discussed her affair without remorse, and I found that I could not maintain too harsh an attitude, remembering what had nearly transpired that day in the park with Ann Donovan.

In all truth, I was not so surprised that she had had a sexual encounter, for her appetite had always been great, and a year of abstinence would have seemed a decade or more to her. That she had coupled with a Domer was grotesque, but then I had never quite understood her tastes. Her attraction to the corpulent and surfeited was as much beyond my ken as was her belief that sex was an act purely of pleasure. Its romantic aspects to my knowledge had never occurred to her.

Understanding the need she must have felt and knowing that I (at least in thought) had experienced the same did not remove the hurt occasioned by her infidelity. Her demonstrations of affection, though, soothed me well, and I was surprised to find myself loving her more than before. It is said that a healed fracture is stronger than the original bone, and our rapprochement seemed to me an example. What doubt remained was cleared when she forswore further breach.

"I have no need," she told me, and I had no desire to disbelieve. We had already bathed and now were sharing the meager store that had been stocked in the cupboard. It was insubstantial, but for the moment I was content with our small privacy, unwilling yet to reenter the world outside. We made desultory talk, and for the final time I asked Jessica the name of the Domer. It was a halfhearted request, for in truth I did not want to know.

"Please, Jules. It's over."

"I have no grievance with him," I assured her. "I am merely curious."

"No. What if he comes to you later for care? Could you be objective? Would you?"

"I would treat him as I would any of them."

"You'd try, but what if you couldn't? What choice would he have? Where else could he go?"

Unexpectedly, Mingo Boyles came to mind, and with him a measure of guilt. I was glad Jessica made no mention of the man.

"It might be interesting," I said lamely.

"Can we drop it now? It's over. Let's talk about something else."

"You then."

She smiled. "You haven't had enough?"

"You need to eat more. You're getting too thin."

She had not fully dressed and looked down at her chest. She drew her thumb slowly over the stark cage of her ribs.

"You must eat, Jessica, or you will die."

She laughed. "I eat, Jules. I'll die whether I do or don't."

"It's not a joke."

"I'm sorry. I've been busy. Are you really worried?"

"I'm concerned. You look thinner. Paler."

"Everyone's pale here. All the light's artificial."

"The ones I've met so far had more color than you."

She shrugged. "They take treatments. I don't have time."

"Maybe you're working too hard."

"I am working hard. It's exciting . . ."

"Work isn't everything, Jessica."

She gave me a look. "What do you mean?"

"I mean, maybe you should slow down."

"I've heard that before, Jules. Guysin said the same thing."

"Maybe he was right."

Her eyes flashed. "I was hoping you'd be more supportive."

I had no ready reply and stared at the floor.

"Do you *want* me to succeed, Jules?"

"Of course I do."

"He doesn't. He wants me to fail."

"I find that hard to believe."

"Believe it. This is his operation. Do you know how long he's been here?"

"From the beginning." I stuffed a cracker in my mouth. She nodded.

"He's never left. Never. No one else has stayed more than a couple of cycles. Except for him. Doesn't that strike you as strange?"

"It's strange to me that anyone would want to stay for even one."

"Eridis is his life, Jules. His obsession. If I find a way to make Mutacillin off-planet, what reason will there be to continue the settlement?"

"He could find another job. He's high enough in the corporation."

"He doesn't want another job. He wants this one, Jules. *This* one." The tone of her voice made me glance up.

"Even if he does," I said, "it seems preposterous that he'd want the project to fail. He must realize Mutacillin's value—"

"He doesn't give a shit about Mutacillin."

"Is he interfering with you? With your work?"

"He undercuts me whenever he gets a chance."

"He said he's concerned for you. It seems appropriate, given his position."

"He's concerned for himself, Jules, not me. Himself." Her voice tightened. "Do you know why? Why he's so worried? Why he'll never leave?"

I stared at her, momentarily fearing another outburst. But her manner was different than before. Chilling. I found myself shaking my head.

"Shall I tell you?"

Like a puppet I nodded. My stomach growled.

"It begins before I came. Early in the cycle . . ."

"Jessica."

"The domeroom is dim, and no staff is there."

"Jessica."

"Listen. The door beside Service opens, and he steps through—"

"Jessica. Please. I'm hungry. I can't concentrate."

She glared at me.

"I'm sorry. I want to hear, but it's been too long. I need to eat."

"You need some manners," she said coldly.

"I'm sorry."

She took a deep breath and slowly let it out. "I need to talk, Jules. I've been waiting a long time."

"We'll have time. Neither of us is going anywhere."

She looked at me, then sighed. "I'd forgotten what it's like being with you."

"And how's that?"

"You know," she said.

"Everyone needs to eat, Jessica."

Her lips flattened in a smile. "That's what I mean."

Ten minutes later we walked through the wide entrance to the dining area. It lay in the center of the curved wall with the numbered doors. In anticipation of my first public appearance I had dressed formally, more so, perhaps, than was necessary. As we came to the threshold, I took a breath and assumed a dignified posture.

"Relax," Jessica whispered. "It's no big deal."

"I have my profession to uphold."

She raised her eyebrows and made a face.

"I'm only joking," I said, but she had already turned away, for we had entered the room.

It did not surprise me that it was domed, though the effect was quite different than in any of the rooms I had yet been. The ceiling was low, and recessed at regular intervals in the wall about six feet above the floor were a series of hidden lights. They shone upward, spilling across the milky dome, whose glossy surface reflected the light downward. The floor was azure and flecked with tiny silver specks. These did not glint —no light struck them directly—but as they captured the glow from above, they seemed to undulate, like waves. The entire floor was sunken several steps below the entryway in which we stood, and my first impression was that it was a deep sea grotto and that the tables, which were long and narrow, were ships floating upon water. All this occurred to me, and more, before I saw a single face. When finally I ventured to look, I was pleased to note that we had aroused but slight attention.

We descended the steps and weaved our way past tables toward the far side of the room. It was noisy, though not clamorous, and Jessica stopped frequently to chat and introduce me. She seemed to be enjoying herself, and if she lingered a bit too long on our way to the food I did not blame her. She was proud to have me there, and despite my own self-consciousness, I felt disposed to give her that small pleasure.

Eventually we arrived at the counter where the edibles were dispensed. Behind it were a man and a woman. Like most of the staff I had met they were young; they smiled as we approached.

"Hi," the man said to Jessica. He turned to me. "You must be the doctor." He reached across and shook my hand, and the woman did the same.

"I'm Randy."

"Oona."

"Jules," I said.

"We've been expecting you."

"Oh?"

"I warned them that they'd be seeing a lot of you." Jessica smiled.

"Someone's almost always here," said Oona. She was dark and tall, and wore an orange suit. "Either cleaning up the last meal or cooking the next one. If you want a snack, feel free to drop by."

"Thank you, but it is for just such exigencies, I believe, that I have been provided with my own small cooking facility."

"You have your own kitchen?"

"Kitchen is, perhaps, too generous a word. But yes, there is a stove and a cupboard. From time to time I might trouble you for provisions—"

"No trouble, Doc," Randy said.

"Jules," I remonstrated. "Or if you prefer, Doctor."

"Whichever. Come by even if you don't need anything. If you just want to hang out . . ."

"Thank you. I imagine that I will soon be quite busy. I'm surprised that you aren't."

"We are," said Oona, throwing up her hands. "Believe me. We should have four for the job the two of us do."

The orange of her suit seemed to blaze against her skin, and I found myself thinking of a mountain of sherbet on a bed of chocolate. I swallowed quickly before the saliva overflowed my mouth, then cut the conversation short.

"What is the bill of fare today?"

"Stew."

"I am not overly fond of stew," I said mildly. "What other choices have you?"

"Choices?"

"Jules. They have to cook for over a hundred. Everyone gets the same."

"I see."

"Don't grunt," Jessica whispered. "Be nice."

"The stew it is," I said as nicely as possible. "Is it permitted to have a double portion?"

"As much as you want." Randy piled a heap of the concoction on a plate and handed it to me. "There're biscuits in the warmer down there. Soup in a pot next to it. Dessert's pudding. Chocolate." He turned to Jessica.

"A small helping for me," she said, and when she thought I was out of earshot whispered, "Don't mind him. He'll get used to it."

"No problem. Everyone complains at first."

They smiled at each other, then Jessica hurried and caught

up with me. I had taken a course toward the periphery of the room, around which were lined a number of tables for two; she steered me away, toward a large table near the center. I argued briefly, then fell silent as heads began to turn.

We sat with three others who were just finishing their meals. One was named Rollin, a squat man with a wide face. Another was called Meril. The third was Jeen.

I nodded courteously to the first two, spoke a greeting to Jeen, then bent hastily to my plate. They must have understood my cue, for nothing was addressed to me until I had consumed a goodly portion of my meal.

"So," Jeen said. "I won't ask how you like our food."

I wiped my lips with a towelette. "Well enough. A hungry man won't complain."

"We do." The man Rollin grinned.

"They do the best they can," the other said. I was unable to decide if she were man or woman.

Jeen nodded. "It's better than mush."

"I wouldn't go near the stuff." Rollin grimaced. "They say it tastes like shit and sits in your stomach like a piece of granite."

I belched softly into the napkin and held up a hand. "Please," I implored. "I am still engaged with this . . . this stew."

"It's not as bad as you thought, is it?" Jessica had hardly touched her plate, and I was nearly finished.

"My objection to stew," I explained, "is not how it sits in the belly but how it lies on the plate. All foods eventually become mixed in our intestines; it seems redundant to have them mingled beforehand."

"Is that right?"

"I prefer the simplicity of a single flavor to the confusion of many. The problem with the latter arrangement is that each item struggles with the next, and none emerges the victor. A stew by its very nature defeats itself."

I took a final spoonful, which cleaned the plate. Beside me Jessica grinned, then said loud enough for all to hear: "And you, dear Jules, have defeated *it.*"

There were chuckles, and then Rollin raised his cup. "To the victor!"

The others joined, and I inclined my head. We all drank.

"To our new doctor," toasted Meril. The voice was husky.

"Principally," I said, taking the opportunity to clarify my position, "I'm here to minister to the Domers. Of course, if anything of urgency comes up . . ."

"Right now," said Jeen, "there are more staff than Domers who want to see you."

"Indeed."

"Cycle's been going over three years. That's long enough for almost everyone to have some kind of problem."

"Doesn't Mannus screen out the sick?"

"No one's sick. Not really. That doesn't stop them from wanting to see a doctor."

"Didn't you know," Meril whispered, "you have magic powers?"

I looked at her cheek, which was smooth, and decided she was a woman. She wore a deep blue suit that blended with the floor and obscured the contours of her body. Her fingers were long and delicate.

"I had an odd experience," I said to no one in particular. "I had the opportunity to examine one of the Domers . . ." Jeen glanced at me but said nothing. "Its name, as I recall, was Bulu."

"They're all the same to me," said Rollin.

"I assumed that they had been taught about doctors, examinations, treatment—that sort of thing—and indeed, the creature said that he had. And yet when I went to examine his feeding tube, he almost knocked me over. As though I had physically attacked him."

"You have to be careful. They're protective of their mush."

"Wouldn't you be," Jessica said sharply, "if you were only fed once a week?"

"Twice," Jeen corrected.

"Twice then. We get three meals a day and don't work anywhere near as hard."

"We're not designed to. They get as much as they need. More would be a waste of resources."

"Was he frightened, Jules?"

"Terrified."

"They live in fear that they won't get fed. First we fatten them up and then we starve them."

"They get what they need," Jeen repeated. "Enough so that their stores—and ours—aren't depleted."

"They don't even taste what they get. It goes in that hole in their stomach and they can't even taste it!"

"Jessica," I said quickly. "They can't. If it went in their mouths they'd choke. There's nowhere for it to go."

"Does that sound pleasant to you, Jules? Fair? They can't eat, taste, swallow . . ."

"Calm down. They're different from us. They're not meant to do those things."

She stared at me, then put her hands to her face. She bent her head.

"Jessica," I whispered. "What's wrong? What's the matter?"

"We're losing," she moaned. "They're tearing us apart."

"Stop it now. They're not worth it. Jessica . . . Jessica!"

She trembled, perhaps in response to my voice, then sat up and uncovered her face. It was flushed, but her eyes were clear. "I'm sorry," she said, forcing a weak smile. "I didn't mean to make a scene." She stood up. "I'll be back in a minute."

She turned, and I rose quickly to accompany her. She put a hand on my arm. "I'm all right, Jules. I'm just going to freshen up." She motioned to a door in the wall. "Really. I'm fine."

She started to walk away, and I watched anxiously. Jeen pushed her chair back.

"I'll go with her," she said. "We'll be back in a minute."

I started after her, then shook my head and sat down. "What's back there?"

"Toilets. Washroom. A couple of showers . . ."

I nodded, and the three of us sat in silence. Rollin shuffled his feet and Meril pushed a potato back and forth across her plate with a fork. I cleared my throat.

"What do the two of you do?" I asked.

"Maintenance," Meril answered quickly. "In the dome-room."

"Both of you?"

"I help when they need it," said Rollin. "Most of the time I handle communications."

"So you know them pretty well."

"The Domers?"

I nodded.

"Not much to know. They eat and sleep and listen to the teachers."

"Do they talk?"

"Not much."

"Not to us, anyway," Rollin said. "And vice versa."

"I see. I wonder if they think."

"Who knows?" He winked at Meril. "Me, I've got other things on my mind."

"You won't find out nothing by looking." She twirled a lock of her hair with a finger and grinned at him.

"Looking's not what I had in mind."

"Dream on, Rollin." She swung her legs around and stood. I expected her to be shorter, but her legs were long, tapering to narrow, mannish hips. The light from the ceiling fell upon her shoulders, which were broad, and lit the upper rise of her bosom.

"So long, you two. Nice to meet you, Jules." She strolled casually away, conscious, certainly, that we were watching.

"Nice piece, eh Doc?"

I nearly nodded.

"Been trying to get her for a year. It's all smiles and come-ons, until it gets to the nitty-gritty. Then she's as cool as cave fifty."

"Maybe she doesn't want a man."

"Flirts like she does . . ."

"Then maybe you're not the right one."

"Could be." His mouth widened in a kind of grin. "How 'bout you, Doc? She seemed to like you. . . . Didn't she say you were magic?"

"What?" I said absently, my mind elsewhere. He leered at me.

"I said, how 'bout you?"

I stared at him, slowly coming to my senses. "This is absurd! I am not here to engage in your lewd fantasies. And I am a doctor, my friend, not a 'doc.' "

He raised his eyebrows and held up his hands. "Hey, no offense, Doc . . . I mean, Doctor. I thought you were looking, too."

"My interest was clinical. She has an unusual habitus."

"Nice, huh?"

I opened my mouth to object but was interrupted by a man coming to the table. He acknowledged me with a nod, then bent to Rollin, who turned in his chair.

"I heard you're making book," the man said.

"Got it right here." Rollin patted his breast pocket.

"You laying odds?"

"It's a pool, Jack. The odds change."

The man considered for a moment. "Okay." He handed Rollin a scrap of paper and some money. "I'll lay a hundred. Ten on each."

"You're in," said Rollin. He counted the money, then tore off a piece of the paper and scribbled on it with a pen. "Your receipt."

The man took it and nodded. As he left, Rollin unzipped his breast pocket and took out a notebook. He opened it and started writing, looking every so often to the slip of paper on the table. When he finished, he recounted the money.

"So you're a bookie," I said.

"Nah. I'm not taking a cut. It's just a friendly pool." He looked up. "Maybe you'd like to join."

"I am not ordinarily a gambling man."

"It's nothing big time. Just about everybody's got something riding. And you being a doctor . . . I bet you'd be interested."

"I'll wager I'm not."

He grinned. "It's on the Domers. Who's the first to fall down a shaft."

"I don't think I understand."

"It's simple. They're all going to get sick, right? Well, sooner or later one of them's bound to trip, and some of those mine shafts down there are steep. So each of us picks ten Domers, and whoever picks the one who's the first to fall wins."

"Sir . . ." I said, my jaw starting to drop.

"It can't be just a fall to the ground, it has to be a long one, like to the bottom of a tunnel." He picked up the notebook and flipped the pages. "So how much are you good for?"

"Good for?" I stammered. "Good for?"

I kicked back my chair and stood, then leaned across the table. His face seemed to shrink as I bore down upon it. "I am a doctor." I quivered. "A physician. I do not wager on my patients. What kind of a man do you think I am!"

Drops of spittle flew from my mouth and I wheeled around, then strode from the room. From the corner of an eye I glimpsed Jessica but did not stop. I needed to be gone from that place, from that assemblage of masculine females, weeping lovers and ignorant fools. I had come millions of miles to escape loneliness, and now all I wanted was the solitude of my own thoughts. I went back to my quarters and locked the door, not opening it for Jessica, not even for her.

13. Some Unspeakable Joy

There are times when I feel that every decision I have made has been wrong. I used to think that about becoming a physician. Was I following your footsteps, Jerrold, or was I making my own? An imitation, or a man in my own right? I have admired you so, you see, that sometimes I have done things for your sake, only later realizing they were not for mine. The hours I spent after leaving the dining hall, staring at the floor, the walls, aroused similar feelings. I was frustrated, depressed, and I felt helpless. Deeper within I felt flawed for having allowed myself to become so. Had I been able to believe that I was the victim of some unkind fate the hours might have been less bleak, but I have never been such a person. I alone was responsible for coming to Eridis; the burden of unhappiness was mine.

For a long while I sat, motionless, like a hunk of stone. My thoughts were turned inward; they were deprecating and castigatory. I told Jessica, when she knocked, to leave me be. I sat and I stared.

For no obvious reason I began to think of the Domers. They who were so strong and yet so weak. Short-lived, yet ageless. In this there seemed to lie some lesson, though what it was eluded me. In the hope that I might somehow lift the pall that lay about, I turned my mind to them, to the lesson, if any, of their lives.

The Domers are our creation, and that they are both wondrously adapted and hopelessly flawed is testament to this fact. They were made in the human image, and what is human if not the sum of opposites? The left brain complements the right and one hand the other. Two legs are needed to walk. Dichotomy is the nature of thought, and what we hold to be our greatest virtue is at once our worst shortcoming. It is no wonder, then, that the Domers are governed by contradiction, for in truth they are but aspects of ourselves.

The idea of cloning is an old one, the production of complete beings dating back to Jacome's pioneering work with the Heads. Though his disastrous outcome was not occasioned by flaws in design or technique, it nonetheless resulted in strict regulation of total being clonification. Mannus was permitted (probably as a result of their intimate ties with government) to re-introduce the process, with the understanding that it would be limited in scope and confined to Eridis. Mores at the time dictated that artificial beings reflect the natural order: so it is that we have both male and female Domers. It was forty years ago that Mannus developed and patented the design, and Domers have been grown on a regular basis since.

Each cycle lasts five years. It ends (and begins) officially at the time of Festival, when the great doors Carefree and Celeste open to admit the Domers. The enormous rooms behind the doors are empty and brighter than the domeroom. The floors are metallic and slick. They slope gradually toward the center, where there is a large plugged hole. The ceiling in each room is domed; halfway between its peak and the floor is suspended a latticed scaffold. Mounted on its frame are the heads of numerous nozzles.

The Domers enter the rooms, and when all are inside, Carefree and Celeste close. From some of the nozzles issues a gas, a soporific, and within minutes the Domers are prostrate and senseless. Ducts hidden above the scaffold suck the gas from the room, and from a different set of nozzles begins a fine spray of liquid. I have not inquired as to its composition, though I suppose it to be a combination of organic acid and base, as well as solvents designed especially for human tissue.

It continues for some time, until a deep lake of liquid covers the floor. Slowly the bodies begin to disintegrate as skin and flesh dissolve in the liquid soup. Arms and legs, initially recog-

nizable, gradually become indistinct. The bodies come to resemble mounds, which bob about like corks. The shade of the
lake deepens; the texture becomes murky and thick. Last to
disappear are the organ tissues and bones; eventually no dis-
cernible structure remains. Days still must pass while the suspension is broken down further, until finally there exists a
solution of molecular and sub-molecular units.

This contains all the elements, the minerals and molecules
necessary to grow afresh the Domer body. It is, if you will, a
great sea of potential life, and when this stage is reached, the
hole at the center of the room opens. The solution flows into
a wide pipe that carries it to the recycling laboratory beneath
the domeroom. There it is joined in one enormous vat by the
same slurry from the other room. Over the next days and weeks
the soup is distilled, until eventually it is separated into its
component, elemental units. The processes that are used, such
as electrophoresis and ultracentrifugation, are not unique, but
the scale is tremendous and the degree of efficacy a matter of
record.

When all has been separated and purified, the molecules and
elements are joined again, including those that have been saved
from the urinary waste. The proportions are precise, and the
mass and volume of each aliquot identical. This stage is perhaps
the most demanding, for on the exactitude of the measure
depends the subsequent life of each Domer.

The substrate is transported by tube back to the rooms,
which have been cleaned and filled with rows upon rows of
large metal tubs. From the scaffold now hang a number of
retractable hoses that are the conduits through which the
Domer substrate is deposited into the tubs.

The rest is straightforward. A germ cell, which has been
cleaved from the undifferentiated neural tissue of each infant
Domer during the previous cycle, is placed in each tub, and
with it a variety of chemicals to stimulate embryonal mitosis.
The temperature in the rooms is increased to promote growth,
and in the ensuing weeks various hormones are added to accel-
erate it. In five weeks all structures are visible, and in seven the
bodies are near to exhausting the supply of substrate. They are

fully formed, but only in the sense that babies are, and will not achieve their adult size for several months. At this stage they must be moved from the vats to their permanent homes.

They are babies, but already weigh in excess of a hundred kilos. Ways could be contrived to transport them, devices to lift them from the tubs and ferry them into the domeroom, but these would be arduous and risky. At that age their bones are still weak, and a fall from any height could be lethal. Those who engineered the Domers foresaw this problem, and built into their genetics an ingenious solution.

There is an order of mammal—Marsupialia—in which the young are born immature and must crawl from the birth canal to a pouch, wherein are positioned the nipples. To an observer the journey is short, the span perhaps of two hands, but to the infantile being it must seem a great distance. How they know to set out, and in what direction, is a mystery we call instinct. In all likelihood it is founded in the genome, and for evidence I cite the Domers, who through genetic manipulation have been given a similar mechanism of survival.

At the time they are near to exhausting their substrate, they are seized by a powerful phototropic instinct. They orient to bright light, then seek by whatever means to follow it. They are unable yet to walk but can crawl, and to crawl is all that is necessary.

The rooms are dimmed, and staff approach each Domer with a bright light. I have not been present to watch, but they say it is a marvel, as though the light were a leash or some powerful hypnotic. One by one the Domers snake from their birth vats and are led to the mats and feeding tubes where they will grow to adulthood. The journey is slow, but it is safe, and at this stage of development it is the latter that is of paramount import.

Once on the mats the Domers are attached by staff to the feeding tubes, for though they are able to propel themselves along the floor with the muscles of the hip and shoulder girdles, they lack control of the finer movements of the arms and hands. Also at this time they are fitted with the first of a dozen teacher caps.

For the next week or two they lie in this state, learning the first lessons, feeding and growing at a phenomenal rate. The development of their central nervous system is accelerated, akin more to a lower level of primate than to the homo sapiens upon whom they are modeled. Within a few weeks they are able to roll over, sit, stand, and manipulate the feeding tube. They learn how to turn off its flow, detach it from the stoma, reinsert it. They have not left their cubicle, nor will they for a time, but at this point they are ready to leave the mat and sit at the panel. There, over the next two months they receive their lessons and refine their motor skills.

For practical purposes the beginning of a cycle is marked when the Domers worm their way into the domeroom. From this time to when they are ready to begin work is less than three months. The day they trod through Service on their way to the mines is the last day of their youth. It is the day they are fullest of health, of vigor and innocence.

The reason a cycle lasts but five years is that a Domer cannot function longer. Their bodies, which allow them to endure the cold, lift the great slabs of stone, suffer days without sustenance, succumb to the maladies that afflict the gigantic and the obese. Principally it is arthritis, which attacks their joints with a crippling savagery. Initially, as with all such diseases, the damage is microscopic, but by the latter part of the cycle it becomes clinically manifest. Arthritic burls begin to appear on their knees and ankles, and as time goes on, effusions limit the range of motion. The upper extremities, overburdened by the demands of work, are not spared, and bursitis of the shoulders and elbows is common. The finger joints become knobby and stiff, and the simplest motion, such as attaching the feeding tube, evokes a wincing pain.

Of course they continue to work, and their bodies continue to degenerate. The genes that are the source of their indispensability are the same that presage their demise. The great weight of the slabs of stone they hoist and carry accelerates the deterioration. Late in the cycle their hips begin to crumble, the sockets ground down and unstable. Their posture becomes crooked, as they try in vain to find a position of lesser pain. Their gait changes to a limp, and then a shuffle. They become barely able to lift their arms. Eventually joints begin to sublux, and the deformities become such that work is no longer possible. Pain, which has been present for years, is now accompanied by incapacity. This is the signal for Festival.

It coincides with the saturation of the recycling tanks and the depletion of mush stores. Enough Mutacillin has been harvested and refined to stock a number of ships over a period of months. The majority of Domers, their joints frozen, their bones splintering, lie crippled on their mats.

Surprisingly, it is not an unhappy time. There is great suffering, it is true, but on the day that Service no longer opens, the mood in the domeroom lightens. Pain turns to relief; resignation, to anticipation. Despite their agony, many of the Domers rise and begin to mill about Carefree and Celeste. A charge permeates the room, an expectation of something wondrous to come. "The greatest pleasure, the unspeakable joy": this is how Festival is taught.

A day passes. Two. Rumors circulate, and finally Guysin Hoke enters with the announcement. He appears high above them from a door concealed in the wall of the dome. He pushes a button and steps out on a balcony that opens before him. The effect is charismatic. The floor of the domeroom hushes and he speaks to the anxious throng below.

"Work has been completed," he says. "Service has been done. Toil brings reward, and hardship, pleasure. Congratulations. It is time for Festival."

He disappears, the balcony retracts, the door closes. Where there was an opening is now wall. It is as though he were a mirage: it catalyzes the excitement below. Those Domers who had remained on their mats somehow find the strength to leave them and hobble or crawl to the doors. All gather expectantly before Carefree and Celeste, awaiting the joyous moment.

The doors open and the two crowds surge forward. Blindly pushing and shoving, they enter, and then the doors close. The end of the cycle becomes its beginning, as Festival commences.

14. The Clinic

I accepted the position as staff physician with foreknowledge of the cycle's inevitability. I believed at the time, or made myself believe, that I would be able to temper some of the suffering with medication, to make the Domers' short lives, if not comfortable, then at least bearable. I foresaw it to be no pleasant task, but it was one I had faced often enough before. To succor the ill is an appointment all of us have chosen; it is a part of the Oath we promised to uphold.

Recalling this helped lift the gloom in which I faltered. I was a physician and bore the responsibilities of that office. None of them included self-pity or despair. If I could not be sanguine, I could at least try to be cooperative, and with this in mind I rose from the couch. I was determined to adapt to my new surroundings.

As a first step I turned to my personal belongings. I brought the two pots and the pan to the kitchenette and arranged my toiletries in the bathroom. In a drawer of the desk I placed my cassettes, and on its top the few medical texts I had carried with me. I flipped idly through one, then left it to draw a bath. When it was full, I removed my clothes and immersed the greater part of my body under the water. Silently I thanked Jessica for having supervised the rearrangement of my quarters: the tub, though not commodious enough to prevent some spillage over the side, had, by the signs of recent workmanship around its edges, been altered to fit the special needs of one such as I. I lay back and soaked, while I pondered what to do next.

It was not, after all, a difficult decision. I had come to Eridis as a physician. I should familiarize myself with the medical facilities and meet the ancillary personnel with whom I would be working. This I resolved to do and drained the tub, then dried myself. Hanging in a small closet was a white jumpsuit of the same type as the colored ones I had seen on other staff. I assumed that it had been cut to my proportions, but I shunned it. From what I had observed of others, the suit was designed to fit snugly against the body's contours, a style that would have been neither complimentary nor comfortable. I dressed instead in clothing I had brought, which was loose and familiar. Then I called Jessica.

"I'm sorry," I said as her image appeared on the screen. "I needed some time to myself."

"What happened in there?" Her face was full of worry. "Rollin looked like he'd been slapped."

"He didn't tell you?"

She shook her head.

"Some bet he wanted me to make. A pathetic man . . ."

"Are you all right, Jules?"

"I'm fine now. I had a nice bath."

She looked down. "I'm sorry about what happened."

"It was no one's fault. Let's forget about it."

"I didn't mean to fly off the handle like that. I don't know what's wrong with me."

"It was just one of those things, Jessica. It's over."

"I wish . . ."

"What?"

She looked up. "I wish you wouldn't shut me out."

"I needed to be alone, Jessica. I won't do it again."

"I need you."

"You have me."

The lines eased off her face. "Good." She smiled. "Are you ready to come out?"

I nodded. "I thought I'd take a tour of the medical facilities. Will you join me?"

"I'd like to, but I've got to get down to the lab. There's some stuff that can't wait."

"How long will you be gone?"

"A few hours. I can't stay much longer. It gets too cold."

"I'll warm you up when you get back."

"You make me warm now, fat man."

She puckered her lips, and I leaned over and kissed them. The screen was cool, and then the image faded. I drew back and adjusted my lab coat, then turned and left the apartment.

The medical clinic is housed in a large room that, like everything else, branches from the main corridor. The entrance, which I had failed to notice on my first excursion to the domeroom, lies in the short section of wall between Service and the entrance to the mines. It is a door as large as Service—it must be able to admit the bulk of a Domer—and can be opened by either of two palm plates. The one above my head I could barely reach, and I pressed the other.

The door slid open and I found myself in the vestibule of a short, high hall. I walked forward, passing a smaller hall to my left, and came into what appeared to be the main room. With a sense of familiarity I inhaled the antiseptic air, then paused to gaze about.

It was a vast space bracketed by numerous curtains hung from the ceiling, reminding me of the large public wards of our hospitals on Earth. I pushed one of them aside; behind it lay a pallet similar to the ones in the domeroom and a chair that, I supposed, was for an examiner. From above, strung also from the faraway ceiling, hung a retractable lamp. There was no table, or stand, or medical instrument. The space was rectangular and separated from identical ones on either side by only the thin curtain. There were two long rows of these booths, and between them an aisle to walk. Nowhere did I glimpse an implement that resembled one I might use, nor a machine, nor even a simple medication. This puzzled me, and as I retreated from the curtained columns my mind must have wandered, for the voice behind caught me by surprise.

"Doctor," it said, and my heart thumped as I wheeled around. It was a woman. "I didn't mean to startle you." She offered a hand. "I'm Martha."

"Jules Ebert." I recovered.

She nodded. "I saw you in the dining room. Randy pointed you out."

"Randy?"

"Stocky. Dark hair. He's the cook."

"Yes, I recall the stew. And again, you are . . ."

"Martha Higgins. I'm a technologist, nurse, general assistant. I work here."

"I see. I have a number of questions."

She smiled, but only one side of her mouth lifted. "I'm sure you do. You've only been here, what, a few days?"

"Something like that."

"I bet it seems a lifetime."

"In a sense."

"It helps to be working." She turned and motioned for me to join her. "C'mon, I'll show you around."

She pushed aside one of the curtains and pointed inside. "This is a Domer examining room."

"I'd assumed that. Why are there no instruments?"

"For what?"

"To examine them, of course."

Her left eyebrow came down and the half of her forehead above it furrowed. "There's no need, Doctor. The problems they have are quite predictable."

"You treat without examination?"

"Most of the time. It's rare that we use more than our hands and eyes to diagnose."

"On Earth," I said, "that would be felonious."

"We are not on Earth, Doctor. The situation is quite different."

"Standards of medical practice should not depend on situations, Ms. Higgins."

"Everything depends on situations," she replied.

"You seem quite sure of yourself."

She shrugged. "Would you treat a narcotic addict with terminal cancer the same as an addict who is otherwise healthy?"

"Are you asking if I would prescribe narcotics to each?"

She nodded.

"Within the realm of the law, yes, I would." I smiled. "I have
an unorthodox view of addiction. If you knew me better, you
would not have chosen that particular example."

"Then use another. There're thousands . . . How about an
eighty-year-old hypertensive and a thirty-year-old one? Would
you treat them the same?"

"It depends . . . But no, I probably wouldn't. But the standard for one is different than the other. The example does not
negate my point."

"Nor mine. You base your standard on the patient, not the
disease. That's all I was saying."

"But without an examination how can you know your patient?"

"If you were in the midst of an epidemic of encephalitis, and
you'd seen a hundred patients, all comatose, all with a characteristic rash, wouldn't it be safe to assume that the hundred and
first who presented that way had the same illness?"

"It might be."

"It would be foolish not to."

"I have never accounted myself a fool, Ms. Higgins."

She looked at me and smiled, unconsciously rubbing the
right side of her face. "The discussion is philosophic, Doctor."

"Of course."

We strolled down the aisle between the curtained booths,
from time to time glancing furtively at one another. When our
eyes met, we smiled self-consciously and looked away. She had
a plain face, which was striking only when she made some
gesture with it. Then the muscles on the left side contracted,
while those on the right remained flaccid. It seemed at first that
it was the left side that was ill, leaping in periodic contortions,
but this was an illusion. She had a classic case of palsy, with
virtually complete paralysis of all the muscles of the right side
of her face. From her manner, which was not particularly self-
conscious, I guessed that it was of long-standing duration.

She looked older than most of the other staff I had met, her dark and wavy hair streaked with gray. Her eyebrows were dark also, and thick; her eyes, a venous blue. She wore a white jumpsuit, similar to the one I had spurned, but with a higher collar. It was unzipped to the base of her throat.

"So," I said. "No examination. How about treatment?"

"Over here." She steered me to a wall that ran parallel to one of the rows of curtains. Just as I recognized that it was not a wall at all, she pushed a button and it slid into the floor. Behind it was a vast array of trays, instruments and bottles.

"There's an identical compartment on the other side. If you need anything, just push a curtain aside and grab it. You don't have to walk all the way around."

I looked at several of the instruments and many of the bottles. Some were filled with pills, others with fluid.

"Most of these are analgesics and anti-inflammatories. The injectable stuff is mostly steroids. You can see that we go through a lot."

"Have you been using it already?"

"Not yet. Pretty soon though."

"You speak as though you've done this before."

"I have," she said.

"Indeed. Jeen told me that other than she and Guysin, no one has been here for more than a cycle."

"I guess she forgot about me. This is my second."

I picked up a forceps; it was old, with bits of debris lodged in its teeth. Many of the instruments were like this, or worse.

"We could use some new equipment."

"Don't hold your breath."

"At least they could be cleaned. Sterilized."

"What for? No one gets infected."

"Of course. I'd forgotten. A better scar then, in case we have to suture."

"Doctor, why would we care about a scar?"

"Well, what if we have to operate on a staff member? That must happen. *We're* not recyclable."

"There's a separate area for staff. Over here."

She led me back to the hall where I had entered, then turned right. We entered the smaller hall I had passed; it ran straight for a dozen steps, curved right, and ended in a doorway without a door. A Domer, had he been strongly motivated, might have reached to that point, but never beyond. We walked through the opening into a room with a couch and several chairs; she did not have to tell me what it was. There are a million arrangements for a waiting room, and they all look the same. She palmed open a door and we walked through.

"Two examination and treatment rooms." She pointed to either side of the short hall we were in, then to a door at the end. "On the other side of that is the surgical suite. Do you do surgery?"

"In a pinch. There was a time when I fancied that I might devote myself to it."

"And?"

"I chose to be a sleuth rather than a craftsman. Neither of which, it appears, is needed on this planet."

"Why did you come?"

"To succor the sick and heal the lame . . ."

One side of her mouth curled up. "You should have gone somewhere else."

"That's what I told Jessica."

"You came here for her?"

Rarely am I inclined to discuss with others my personal affairs but something about the woman—her face, perhaps—loosened my tongue.

"Yes," I told her. "And for the government. I owe them time."

"Do you?" she said curiously.

"My academics were not of a quality deemed proper for medical school. High scholarship, as you must know, is considered requisite for such training. The dogma deserves scrutiny, but it is, however, entrenched. In my case, strings were pulled, and doors miraculously opened. About a year ago—out of the blue—the government snatched me up and said it was time to repay. Soon after, Jessica was offered a job here. I chose to accompany her."

"You came a bit behind."

"The fools bandied me about for a year before finally depositing me here."

"I'm not surprised."

"They're blithering and incompetent."

"Immoral," she added. "Contemptible."

I glanced at her. "You have some grievance with them."

She nodded sullenly.

"Is it because you must stay a second cycle?"

"Who said that I must?"

I shrugged. "Who would voluntarily stay more than one?"

"With all due respect, Doctor, you are beyond your reach. I have no great affection for our government. If I thought that by staying three cycles, or five, there would be time for it to improve, I would do so."

"It has not changed in fifty years . . ."

"It has worsened."

"It's stagnant, that is all."

She shook her head. "There's no such thing. It's diseased." Her blue eyes were cold. "It's dying."

I coughed nervously. "Aren't we all?"

"We are not it."

"There's an analogy . . ."

"The government—society—has a life of its own. We comprise it, but it is more."

"It reflects us. Its flaws are no more than ours."

"Do you really believe that? I would hate to think that my friends are as full of malice and injustice as it is. Or that you are."

"Perhaps not us. But others."

"We are the enlightened?"

"The conscious."

She smiled. "Everyone is conscious, Doctor, in one way or another. Isn't that the challenge of medicine?"

"Of psychiatry, perhaps."

"Of all medicine. To help people become more aware. Help them see how they contribute to their own sickness and health."

"To the degree that they do."

"Of course."

"It's an ideal. I have found that few patients are interested. Perhaps because they have such little control . . ."

"Yes," she said. "I've seen that. Too often." She started back toward the waiting room. "If you think it's bad on Earth, wait until the Domers start getting sick. They have no control at all."

I followed her out. "Jeen said there's already quite a few staff who want to be seen."

She nodded. "The ones that couldn't wait I saw myself. Nothing very serious."

"Rarely is it."

"Most of them just want someone who will listen. At least it's something to do. Keeps things from getting boring."

"If I'd wanted to chat, I would have entered a different line of work."

She laughed. "If you didn't want to, you should have."

She was right, of course, and I agreed to begin seeing patients that very day.

"I'll try to contact some," she said, then went into the office that had a communicator. After a while she came out.

"I couldn't get Bardis or Connor. Trish, Pook, and Seff are on their way."

"Fine," I said. "I think I can handle three."

"Break you in slowly."

"I could do it in my sleep."

She smiled. "If you need me, I'll be back in the surgical suite. There's an intercom in each room, or just open the door and call."

I nodded and she left. I took the time before the patients arrived to explore in more detail the examining rooms. Each had two chairs, one behind a desk, the other in front, a glass-enclosed cabinet, a sink, and an examining table. Next to the table was a metal instrument stand on wheels. The rooms were square and painted white; they were unimaginative, remarkably similar to their counterparts on Earth. Illumination, as I had feared, was fluorescent, and I instinctively turned the lights off.

The rooms became totally dark, and though I waited for more than a minute for my eyes to adjust, the blackness did not recede. I had no choice but to use what light Mannus had provided.

It was not true that there were no examining instruments in the clinic; only that there were none for the Domers. The staff rooms were equipped with the latest and most sophisticated diagnostic tools. Due to the years I had spent in the impoverished milieu of Central, some of them were unfamiliar to me, but that did not last long. Treatment is the forte of some, but mine is diagnosis. With the eagerness of a young surgeon attempting to master the complex ligations of his craft, I strove to attain mastery of the tools of medical progress.

There was a binocular-shaped instrument, one end of which fit onto the orbit of each eye. The other was a small box with a screen. Inside were two laser tubes that could be positioned into an axis parallel to the optic nerves. Impulses were transmitted down the nerves and continued along the neurovisual pathways. A sensing device recorded the speed and integrity of the impulses and translated the information onto the screen in analog form as an anatomic picture. With practice it was possible to discern the optic chiasm, the geniculate bodies, and the occipital lobes. Defects in the pathway showed up as gaps in the picture, and by varying the frequency of the impulse, it was possible to differentiate one disease process from another. The instrument's value lay in its versatility: it was capable of diagnosing diseases not only of the visual system but also, by implication, of the cerebrum as a whole.

Another instrument, which I had read of but never seen, was the neural tail. This was a long and flexible tube of narrow diameter, composed of millions of tiny filaments twined around one another. The filaments, which were synthetic, were modeled after the long axons of the central nervous system and were able to conduct electrical current. At each tip was a microscopic sensor of such sensitivity that it was able to detect the most minute of electrical potentials, such as that generated by the flux of ions across a cell's membrane.

The tube is passed through the mouth and fed down the

trachea into the mainstem bronchus, where the sensing operation begins. A mechanism on the operator's end of the tube is
pushed, releasing the force that binds the filaments together.
Slowly they begin to separate and, as the tube is advanced, they
snake their way into the various pulmonary passages, touching
and sensing the cells along the way. Abnormal potentials—
those, for example, that exist across the disordered membrane
of a cancer cell—are easily differentiated from normal ones.
Because of the multiplicity of filaments the area of abnormality
can be localized exactly. A negative test is confirmative of a
pulmonary tree free of disease.

There were other instruments—the transcutaneous grid, a
biogenic pipette, a resonance suit—that no doubt are as commonplace to you as the binopticon and the tail. To me, however,
they were fascinating, and the experience of mastering them,
sublime.

Modern diagnosis may be considered the art of entering—
without disrupting—the body in as many ways as possible. Into
every orifice there are dozens of instruments designed to fit, and
likewise across the pupil of the eye, the skin, and the skull. Were
a diagnostician able to disassemble, without harm, cell by cell
the human body, I believe he would do so. Or better yet, shrink
down and enter himself into each cell. That would be a brilliant
clinician, though a tiny one. Try as I might I could not imagine
myself to be he. I had no choice but be content with what tools
I had been given, and those I found in the clinic on Eridis.

After poking about for a while, I wandered into the waiting
room. Two of the three staff had arrived, and after introducing
myself, I showed each into an examining room. Trish, a young,
attractive woman, was worried about her hair falling out. It
seemed unwarranted—her hair was thick and full of luster—
but when she parted the dense strands at the peak of her scalp,
I understood her concern.

There was a large and circular hairless patch that she had
managed to cover with her coif. The skin of the exposed scalp
was pallid; to the touch it was spongy. It was a classic case of
alopecia areata, and I apprised her of it and its benign nature.

"It will resolve of itself," I promised. "Probably within a matter of months."

Her face, which was covered with bright rouges and strong penciled lines of color, remained tense, and I realized that I would have to offer more than reassurance.

"It's already been there for months," she said tightly.

"It will go away. Be patient."

"There must be something . . . Can't you give me some medicine?"

I shook my head.

"Doctor! Please. Anything."

I sighed. "I'll give you an injection. It might help."

She nodded, and I found a syringe with a long needle. Solemnly I drew the medicine from a vial, meaning for her to watch, which she did with a look of nervous satisfaction. I had no illusions that the drug would hasten her cure, but I felt that at least I could provide the healing powers of a good performance. As I injected the suspension into the bald area, she winced. It did not take but a few moments, and when I had done, she restyled her hair to conceal the offensive spot.

"Thank you," she said with relief, batting her eyes.

"My pleasure."

We shook hands, smiled, and she left. I disposed of the needle and syringe, washed my hands, then crossed to the other room. Seff was waiting, and when I offered my hand to him, he refused to take it.

"I'm not sure you want to touch me," he said.

"Indeed. And why not?"

"Look." He lifted his palms and held them in front of my face. The skin was flaky and dry; in several spots it was scaling off in sheets.

"How long have you had this?"

"A couple of weeks. I'm afraid to touch anybody."

"I understand, but your fear may be unwarranted. Have a seat; I'll scrape off a bit of that skin to look at under the microscope."

He did as I asked, and while I searched for a scalpel and

slide, I took a brief history. He worked in engineering and was responsible for maintenance of the conveyor system in the mines. His job involved the use of multiple different solvents and degreasing agents, and I asked if he wore gloves.

"Nah. Don't need 'em. I got tough skin."

"I can see that. Would they interfere with your work?"

He shrugged. "Might. I'd rather not use 'em."

"You could cut out the fingers . . ."

"You think I gotta wear 'em?"

"We'll see," I said and punched the intercom. "Ms. Higgins? Where is there a microscope?"

In a few seconds she answered. "Back here. You need to use it?"

"Yes. And potassium hydroxide."

"What?"

"Potassium hydroxide."

There was a pause. "I'll try to dig some up."

"Please. I'm on my way."

I carried the slide and scrapings carefully through the swinging doors to the surgical suite. It was similar to ones on Earth—central table, large and adjustable lamps, cabinets, instrument benches—except that along one wall was a bank of machines. Ms. Higgins was bent over one of them.

"Microscope's over there." She pointed without looking up. "Potassium hydroxide's next to it."

I went over and put a drop of the solution on the slide. "I need a flame."

She patted the counter next to her. "In here."

I heated the bottom of the slide, withdrawing it from the flame just before the liquid boiled.

"What are you doing?" she asked, raising her head.

"Looking for fungus."

"Why not use the analyzer?" She pointed down the wall to a machine under a hood.

"I didn't know we had any of this."

"I didn't get a chance to show you. It's our laboratory." She straightened and stretched her neck. "What's potassium hydroxide for?"

"It digests the skin cell membranes. Leaves the fungus intact. Whatever you see under the microscope that isn't debris is fungus."

"I've never used the stuff."

"I hadn't either, until I started to work at Central."

"Central?"

"The clinic where I was before the government drafted me. Impoverished but resourceful. A vestige from our more liberal past."

"The old ways . . ."

I nodded. "And the cheap ones. I learned a lot of things there that I'd never been taught in school."

"Who's the patient?"

"Seff."

"Is that what he has?"

"I don't think so, but it's easy to find out." I walked over and put the slide under the microscope. After a minute or two I drew back.

"No fungus. Irritant dermatitis, as I thought."

I discarded the slide into a receptacle, then turned to go.

"Come back when you're finished," she said. "I'll show you what we have. There's some nice equipment here."

I returned to the room, and Seff met me with an anxious glance. "Contagious, huh?"

I shook my head. "Not in the slightest. It's an irritation, from all the solvents you use. They dissolve the natural oils of your skin, and then there's nothing to protect it."

"I wash my hands."

"That makes it worse. Soap and water do the same thing. You need to protect your hands with gloves."

"I don't need medicine?"

"Use a hand cream after you wash. And wear gloves."

"I really gotta wear 'em?"

"You really gotta." I ushered him to the door. "Come see me in a couple of weeks. If you do as I suggest, I guarantee you'll be better." I made a point of shaking his hand and not washing my own until he had left.

I went to the waiting room to see if the one named Pook had

arrived. She had, and rose when I entered. The top of her head reached barely to my chest. Though I am not given to the bias that those of short stature are childlike, I could not help but think that she was quite young. Her face lacked any of the characteristic furrows of aging, and she held herself with that shy, yet haughty posture of adolescence. I introduced myself and showed her to a room. After she had sat in one of the chairs and I in the other, I asked what had brought her to me.

"I can't taste anything."

I raised my eyebrows. "Nothing?"

She shook her head.

"How long have you had this problem?"

"A few days. Maybe a week."

"I see." I attempted to lean back in the chair, but it was not the type that allowed such movement. I was not comfortable.

"Have you had any illnesses . . . stuffy nose, sores in the mouth, anything like that?"

She shook her head.

"No burning of the tongue or the nostrils?"

"Uh-uh."

"Contusions to the head? Perhaps a mild concussion?"

"Huh?"

"Like a fall, a sharp blow."

"No, nothing like that . . ." Her voice trailed off.

"I see. Please have a seat on the table; I'd like to examine you."

She sat without speaking, her legs slightly spread, a hand on each thigh. I looked at her tongue and oral cavity, which were unremarkable, and then her nose. The mucosa overlying the septum was pale.

"Do you have allergies?" I asked.

"Not that I know of. Is something wrong?"

I told her what I had seen. She said nothing.

"That's all," I said. "You can have a seat."

While she returned to her chair, I stood with my hands in the pockets of my lab coat. I leaned against a wall and closed my eyes.

Ageusia. The absence of taste. Little is known of the malady, for it is considered minor, a mere inconvenience when compared to disorders of sight or hearing. But it is more than minor, more than a nuisance. I have had patients who, deprived of the sensation, have become emotionally labile, depressed, even suicidal. Such conduct is not surprising when one considers that the olfactory bulb (damage to which can produce the ageustic state) is intimately associated with that part of the cortex involved in emotional behavior. It may explain why I myself am so sensitive to certain odors, and why particular flavors provoke in me such profound effects.

I walked to my desk and looked at Pook. Her head was downcast; her manner, retiring. I have seen my share of depressive states, and it was not that.

"Pook," I asked. "How old are you?"

"Twenty-two."

"Eighteen." I sat down.

She shook her head.

"Nineteen?"

She was silent. Ever so slightly she nodded.

"Does anyone know?"

She shook her head. "Will you tell them?"

"You're supposed to be twenty-one, aren't you?"

"Are you going to tell?"

I shrugged. "Did you really come to me because you can't taste?"

"I'm not lying. I can't."

"Is there any reason . . . any that you can think of?"

She was silent for many moments, biting her lower lip with her teeth. Then she muttered something.

"I didn't hear you."

"I said gel. I put it in my nose. Only for a minute."

"What's gel?"

For the first time she looked at me. "You don't know?"

I shook my head.

"Everyone uses it. I don't know what it is . . . it's pink."

"It's a drug?"

"I guess. It takes you to other places, makes you think funny things."

"I see. And you used it recently?"

She nodded. "In my nose. You're supposed to put it on your skin."

"Why your nose?"

"I don't know. I thought I'd get a better rush."

"Did you?"

"It made me laugh. I couldn't stop. When it finally ended, and I got around to eating, I couldn't taste anything."

"You can smell?"

"Uh-uh. I can't smell either."

I arranged myself as best I could in the chair and considered her case. Every society has its drugs, and the vast majority of users never come to medical attention. This I take to mean that the majority are in control of their situation. Some, however, are not, and these I feel obliged to counsel. What this gel was—probably some psychosomimetic, possibly a short-acting alkaloid of the ergot class—did not much concern me. What did was the girl.

"I know nothing about this gel," I told her, "which makes it difficult to prognosticate. It does, however, take quite an insult to destroy the olfactory receptors. Hopefully more of one than you produced in your attempt to experience nirvana . . ."

I saw by the line of concentration across her eyes and the exasperation rising on her face that she was failing to understand me. I tried again.

"The cells that smell are resilient. When they are damaged, they usually grow back. But it takes a minimum of thirty days."

"You mean I'm going to be this way for a month?"

I nodded. "Possibly longer."

"I can't stand it."

"I sympathize, but I'm afraid you have little choice."

"You're a doctor. You're supposed to help."

"If I could, Pook, I would. Believe me."

"I might as well eat mush."

The thought made me nauseous. "You're young. You'll heal quickly."

She bit her lip and stood up. "So that's it? You can't help?"

"Only with advice." She hung there as though expecting punishment. "Stay away from the gel. It doesn't seem to do you any good."

"That's what I expected you to say." She turned and walked to the door. "So are you going to tell?"

"About your age?"

"Yeah."

"Everybody has a secret," I said. "Yours isn't so bad."

She hesitated, her back to me. "Thanks," she muttered, then opened the door and left.

There were no more patients that day, and I took leave of the clinic and returned to my quarters. I lay on the sofa with a book, expecting to read until Jessica got back, but in a matter of minutes had fallen asleep. I roused when she arrived, but only long enough to ascend the ladder. I was exhausted, and once I attained the bed said perhaps three sentences to her before I lapsed again into a deep slumber. I woke once and she was beside me, and then again and she was gone. A clock in the room said that it was morning; I had slept sixteen hours.

I rose, washed, dressed, then found my way to the refectory. It was busy, too much so for the morning meal, which I prefer to take in a muted environment. When I could not find Jessica among the crowd, I decided to carry my tray of edibles to the apartment. There I ate in peace, augmenting the fare with a cup of bitter, though welcome, coffee and a buttered roll. When I had done, I cleaned the utensils, cup and plate, relieved myself in the privy, straightened my clothes, then set off for the clinic at a brisk pace. It had been months since I had been able to take such exercise, and though my legs had weakened, the walk was exhilarating.

I arrived at the clinic, where I was met by Ms. Higgins and a waiting room half full of staff. So began my second day as physician to the people of Eridis.

I do not intend to recount each and every day of my tenure

there. The first few weeks were busy, as I saw and attempted to treat a good portion of the Eridian staff. Most of the problems were commonplace, not much different than what I had been accustomed to handling on Earth. There were, of course, fewer bacterial infections, but such illnesses had never comprised a particularly large percentage of my practice. Since the majority of the clientele were young, there were little of the chronic illnesses and more of those associated with that age group: skin disorders, viral infections, problems of adjustment. Many came to me because of symptoms resulting from the strain of living in such a small community, or for feelings of separation and isolation. Most responded well to reassurance, though for some I instituted short-term, directive psychotherapy.

While the practice was generally not demanding, it managed to keep me occupied. Every evening (and during the day when I could coax her) I spent with Jessica. She was proud of herself and her work, and this made her happy. At times she was genuinely loving.

In her presence I had similar feelings: I remember the first months on Eridis with more than passing fondness. Our time together was sweet; our moments of conflict, evanescent. Halcyon was our cleavage. Fervent, and rare.

In retrospect, it seems strange that discord kept its distance, for the canker, I am sure, had already entered Jessica's life. But such was the case, and I am as grateful now for those days as I was then.

As often as our energies allowed we made love. It was a recreation for which we were well-matched. After one such interlude, as we were lying on the bed, Jessica began to chatter.

She seemed to be speaking random phrases, whose meanings eluded me, but I was drowsy and in a state on the edge of dream. With an effort I forced myself awake; the movement seemed to startle her. She blinked several times before sighing and nestling against me.

"Jules," she whispered. "How nice to have you. I was afraid you'd gone."

"I'm here. You were dreaming."

"I love you. Don't leave me."

"How could I?"

She smiled dreamily and hugged me. After a while she drew back.

"Can we talk, Jules?"

"About what?"

"I never got to finish what I started to tell you. About Guysin."

"Is it long?" I yawned.

"I don't want you to fall asleep."

"I'm exhausted. Can it wait?"

"It's already waited a month . . ."

"I want to hear, Jessica." My eyelids drooped. "Just not now . . ."

She sighed. "All right. But soon. It can't wait forever."

I mumbled some reply and heard no more words after that. I fell asleep dreaming that we were a cloud, billowing darkly across the sky.

15. Jessica's Story

Soon turned out to be several weeks and might have been longer had I not taken the initiative. In the past I had always relied on Jessica to do so, and when she did not, I assumed that important matters regarding her work had intervened. I let the matter lie, but after several weeks became curious. At first I wondered if she were hiding something, then later, if she felt merely that I was uninterested. I decided to act and made arrangements with Ms. Higgins to close the clinic for half a day. I went to the main kitchen, where Oona was kind enough to provide me with a provision of goods, and I carried these to my quarters. Then I called Jessica.

"We're having a picnic," I told her.

"We are?"

"In my apartment. You're the guest of honor."

"I'm flattered. Who else will be there?"

"No one. Just me."

"That's sweet, Jules. But I have work to do. Don't you?"

"I canceled clinic. You can take some time, too. You could use a break."

She smiled. "You don't have to twist my arm. What's the occasion?"

"We could use some time together. And I want to hear your story."

"Story?"

"The one that you've been trying to tell me for months. About Guysin."

"Oh, that. I'd forgotten." She rubbed her forehead. "My mind seems so full of other things these days."

"You need to relax."

"Noisy birds, Jules. Do you ever hear them?"

"Come over. I'm just about to start cooking."

"I'm on my way."

The screen went blank, and I went to prepare the food. After a while Jessica came. She wore a light green jumpsuit, and I could not take my eyes off her.

"You're ravishing," I said, embracing her swiftly.

"Am I?"

"But still too thin. You must eat."

"Food is the farthest thing from my mind."

"No," I said. "It mustn't be."

She laughed and allowed me to lead her to the table. I began to feed her, but after several spoonfuls she pushed my hand away.

"Enough," she sputtered.

"You must eat the rest."

"I will, Jules. Give me time."

I gave her a stern look, then turned to my plate. I guided a buttered broccoli stem to my mouth, and while I sucked on it found myself musing on the past.

"Do you know that this is the first peaceful meal we've shared, just the two of us, since Earth?"

"It's been a long time, hasn't it?"

"It has. I remember the last one before you left. It was after your friend died."

"Mingo," she said softly.

"You liked him, didn't you?"

"Yeah. He was all right."

"I wonder if they ever found out what killed him."

She looked up. "You told me it was Barea disease."

"It was. But they found some virus too. The doctor with whom I spoke thought that perhaps the two were connected."

She shrugged. "It doesn't matter much, does it? Not to Mingo."

"No. I didn't mean to upset you."

"What's gone is gone." She sighed.

I reached across the table and took her hand. "I love you, Jessica."

She squeezed me and smiled.

"Now eat your food, will you? Before I have to eat it all myself."

We finished the meal, then retired to the couch with cups of coffee.

"Weak," I muttered.

"Like old times."

"So, tell me your story."

"Why all of a sudden do you want to know?"

"It seemed important to you. Isn't it?"

She looked at me and took a last swallow of her coffee. She put the cup on a table. "It is."

"Then tell me."

"You should get comfortable. It's kind of long."

I arranged myself on the sofa. "Go ahead."

"It began before I came. Early in the cycle. The Domers were feeding and learning; hardly any staff were in the room. The door next to Service opened and Guysin stepped through. He crossed the space in front, toward the rows of Domers. Every so often he glanced back to make sure he was alone—"

"Jessica?"

"Hush. He went to a stall near the back and stopped. There was a Domer there, a female, and she was sitting in front of her panel with her eyes closed. A teacher was on her scalp, and he gazed at her for a long time before going forward. He reached up and touched her on the waist; his fingers sank into the soft flesh—"

"How do you know this?"

"Listen, Jules."

"But how do you know?"

Her face got hard, and I feared she would reprimand me. "Guysin told me most of it. The rest I just know."

"He told you? I don't understand."

"If you wouldn't interrupt—"

"Why did he tell you?"

"Will you listen, Jules? Please."

"I'm sorry. Go ahead."

She shot me a look of warning, and I clapped my hand over my mouth. She continued.

"He reached up and touched her. 'Sandra-hoop,' he said. 'Sandra-hoop.'

"Her eyes moved lethargically toward the sound, as though she were in a trance. They blinked open.

" 'Sandra-hoop,' he repeated. 'Remove the teacher. I am Guysin Hoke. The Manager. Remove it.'

"In a daze she looked at him, piecing the words together. Finally she understood and raised her hands. She was young, her movements clumsy, and it was a little while before she was able to peel the membrane from her head. She turned and peered at the small man beside her.

" 'I am Guysin Hoke,' he repeated. 'The Manager. Guysin Hoke.'

" 'I'm learning about you.' Her voice was like a child's, the words halting and not exactly clear.

" 'Yes. I've come so we can meet.'

"She waited, unaccustomed to speech. Guysin shifted on his feet. Despite having done this many times before he was nervous.

" 'I want you to remember me,' he said. 'Look at my face.'

"He smiled while she did; after a while she smiled back.

" 'Are you learning?' he asked.

" 'Yes. It is my duty.' She held up the delicate cap. 'I have the teacher.'

" 'Have you been taught about me?'

"She nodded, a look of eagerness on her face. 'Yes. And I am learning more today.'

" 'Good. I want you to learn, Sandra-hoop. I want you to remember what you are taught, and I want you to remember me.' He placed a hand on her bare chest. 'Will you do that?'

" 'Yes,' she replied, looking at the hand and feeling its strange and bony hardness.

"Guysin did not end the touch for a long time. When he did, his fingertips tingled, and he fought down an urge to return them to her chest. He told her simply that he would be back, then left her to continue her studies. She obeyed, barely understanding that something out of the ordinary had happened. Soon, she had all but forgotten.

"He returned often in the first few weeks, familiarizing her with his face, his manner, his touch. He told her that she was special, chosen by him for special attention and duties. He appealed to the pride in performance she had been taught and the strict dogma of obedience. He was the Manager: she must listen to him. She must learn, and she must not talk.

" 'I am counting on you,' he told her, 'because you're special. You're beautiful, Sandra-hoop, and you're my choice.'

"Her eyes sparkled and she felt even bigger than she was. Special was not a concept the teachers taught, and yet the Manager had singled her out. Her initial bewilderment turned to curiosity, and then to a rising sense of importance. She anticipated his visits, was excited when he came and disappointed when he didn't.

"He began to come irregularly, varying the intervals so that she would learn to welcome him at any hour, whether she was sleeping, feeding, or learning. Slowly, meticulously, he taught her how to use her body, how to think of it in ways not taught in the lessons. He explored it with her, naming and touching the parts, and did the same on himself. Gradually, and without knowing, she began to waken to a new possibility.

"Each time they met Guysin craved her more, and the restraint he had to exercise got harder and harder. But he had no choice: even though she was fully formed, during the early visits she lacked completely the kinesthetic skills necessary for the acts he envisioned. Developmentally she was an infant, barely able to stand. To take her, even in the passive mode, would have been a dangerous act; in a clumsy and awkward moment she might easily have crushed him.

"This preparatory phase lasted no more than two or three months, but to Guysin it was an eternity. He bolstered his spirits with memories of past cycles, and then one day he decided it was time.

"He chose an hour when he knew no other staff would be there and entered the domeroom. He paused, his ears and eyes alive, then crept forward. When he reached the first row, he stopped being so cautious. He hurried down the aisle, every so often glancing to the side, at the Domers in their cubicles. Some were sitting at the panels, teachers wrapped on their skulls; others were on the mats, feeding or sleeping. All had learned well the early lessons of privacy, of creating walls where there are none. He passed unnoticed, and this gave him courage. He hurried on.

"When he neared Sandra-hoop's cubicle, he coughed, then whistled, intentionally trying to arouse attention. The mechanical looks he received relieved him. Even so, by the time he reached his destination, his throat was tight and his head was spinning.

"Sandra-hoop was on her bench, being taught. When he saw her, his heart began to pound. His breaths got shallow and fast. Lifting a trembling hand, he touched her massive buttock; ripples of fat spread from his fingertips. She opened her eyes.

" 'Guysin.' She peeled back the teacher, gracefully hanging it on a peg. 'Hello.'

"He did not speak, for he was unable. Instead, he moved his hand slowly along her thigh.

" 'That's nice,' she said, and waited to be told what to do. Finally he spoke.

" 'Sandra-hoop,' he whispered hoarsely, 'I want you. Tonight.'

"She understood the words, but something in the meaning confused her. He was talking in a different tone from the one he used when he was her tutor. She squirmed on the bench. 'Here I am,' she said.

" 'Yes,' he whispered. 'Yes.'

"He touched her waist, pushing his hand into the rolls of her fat. He moved closer, until his chest brushed against the side of her thigh. Her excess flesh spilled over the edge of the bench, and against this he began to rub his nipples.

" 'Guysin, what is this?'

"He continued, apparently not hearing.

" 'Guysin?' She stood, and his hands fell away.

" 'Sandra-hoop,' he stammered. 'Sandra-hoop, I love you.' He was panting and had a look on his face that frightened her. She drew back.

" 'No!' he said hotly. 'Please!' He reached for her, and her eyes widened. His jaw was quivering, and then suddenly he froze. He pressed his hands to his face, then shook his head violently. 'No, no, no,' he muttered angrily to himself. 'Not like this. Patience. Just a little more.'

"Sandra-hoop watched, puzzled, alarmed. She waited, while Guysin fought to regain his composure.

" 'Sandra-hoop,' he said finally, his voice strained but under control. 'Tonight I have a special lesson. Something new, and wonderful.'

"Immediately she relaxed, for he was speaking in a manner she recognized. He motioned her to the mat, and with a developing grace she sat beside him.

" 'I have taught you the unknown parts of the body,' he began. 'Mine, yours, and some of their purposes. Tonight we will continue the lesson, and if you are ready, I will teach you the principle of pleasure.'

" 'I know about pleasure, Guysin.'

" 'Tell me.'

" 'It lies in service . . .'

"He nodded, waiting for her to recite the litany. His patience had returned, for his goal was in sight.

" '. . . in duty to Mannus and obedience to staff. These are the three pleasures of our material and productive life. The greatest, the finest, waits at the end of cycle. It lies behind Carefree and Celeste and is so wondrous that it cannot be told.'

" 'That is right, Sandra-hoop. You have learned your lessons well.' He paused, running a hand down her enormous spine. 'You know you are my special and in this way are different from the others. Tonight I will add to that difference, for tonight I will teach you the fifth pleasure.'

"He told her to lie down, and with his fingers began to teach. Starting at her head, which cropped now with tiny hairs, he touched her, caressing her face, her ears, her lips. He fondled her breasts, where his hands were dwarfed, and her huge belly. Kneeling at her side, he stroked her thigh, then whispered for her to spread her legs. He stepped inside, touching the soft skin with his fingers, caressing it. He moved forward. If Sandra-hoop had not yet understood the fifth pleasure, it began now to dawn.

"Guysin took his time, working hard until finally he could do no more. He fell back, exhausted. His face was hot and wet; his skin was flushed. In front of him Sandra-hoop heaved like a mountain. He smiled at her.

" 'Now I will teach you the rest.'

"He had her move and lay on the mat himself, then began to coach her. He had judged the time right, for her motor skills were good enough to please him without doing harm. He showed her different positions that were pleasant and safe, and warned her against ever mounting him. He allowed her to touch his penis, but little more than touch, for she was still several weeks away from being adept with the small muscles of her hand. Being toothless, she was quickly able to learn other ways to please.

"Eventually the lesson was finished, and Guysin crept back to his quarters. Sandra-hoop did not return to the teacher; instead, she lay on the mat wondering how it was that she among all the Domers had been chosen to know this thing. She wished she would know it again, and as her fingers played absently in the dark vee of her legs, she hoped it would be soon.

"In his apartment Guysin hoped the same. It had gone well, this final and hardest lesson, and he was both exhausted and relieved. From now on, at least for some years to come, his appetite would be satisfied. He fell asleep in the imagined folds of his lover's obedient flesh.

"From that time on he visited her often, becoming more and

more bold as the months wore on. He had become an addict; each time he saw her he wanted her more. Before long he believed that he couldn't live without her . . ."

Jessica paused, then stood and stretched. "All this talking makes my throat dry." She left and I heard sounds in the kitchen. She returned with a cup filled with liquid and took a swallow.

"Want some?"

She handed me the cup and I took a sip. I should have smelled it first. Gagging, I tried desperately to spit it out.

"Strong, isn't it?" Jessica said. "Jeen makes it in the lab."

"What does she use?" I sputtered. "Urine?"

She grinned. "Not bad, Jules. I can ask her to explain it herself."

"No, don't. Just bring me some water. Plain water."

She brought another cup, which I sniffed before drinking. Cautiously I sipped it. "What is that foul drink?"

"It's some sort of liquor. She calls it brew."

"She could call it ambrosia . . . it won't touch my lips again."

"I said the same thing." She laughed. "Wait and see. Being here changes a lot of things."

I grumbled to myself, then chanced to look up. Jessica seemed to have frozen. Her eyes were fixed on the wall, and I glanced there to see what had caught her attention. There was nothing, and I looked back. I stared at her.

"Jessica?" She did not blink, and I grabbed her by the shoulders. "Jessica?"

Several seconds passed and then suddenly her body relaxed. Her head slumped to her chest; in a moment she raised it.

"Jules?"

"Jessica? Are you all right?"

"I . . . I . . ." She frowned. "For a moment it just seemed to go blank."

"What happened? You looked like you were in a trance."

She shook her head, as though to clear it, and I guided her to the couch. "What happened?"

She gave me a dull look. I shook her.

"Answer me!"

"Don't hurt me, Jules. I don't know. I'm not sure."

"I don't like it, Jessica."

"I'm all right now."

"It's not like you . . ."

"Maybe it's Jeen's brew." She smiled weakly.

In my mind a light went on, then off. I stared at her. "Why don't you try water for a while?"

"I was only joking."

"I wasn't. There are some grisly stories about native concoctions."

"Jeen's a biologist."

"Yes. Not a brewer."

"I'll think about it." She settled on the couch. "So, do you want to hear the rest?"

"Yes. But don't do that again. Don't frighten me."

"I promise." She motioned me to the other end of the couch. "The rest happened after I got here. Guysin had been seeing Sandra-hoop regularly, which of course I didn't know, and then something came up, some problem in recycling. He had to deal with it, and a week went by, and then two, when he didn't get a chance to see her. He began to get tense and started snapping at people for no reason. The pressure kept building, and then it got too much. He just had to see her. He had to.

"He checked the staff schedules to make sure no one else would be in the domeroom, but once he got inside he got reckless. He didn't listen or look carefully, or else he might have known that I was there too. Instead, he rushed to Sandra-hoop's cubicle. She barely had time to open her eyes before he was on her.

"She had not forgotten the fifth pleasure, but the unexpectedness of his visit—he had never been absent for more than two or three days—and the frenzy of his advance caught her by surprise. She uttered a cry, which I heard. I went to look.

"Neither of them seemed to notice me, and when I figured out what they were doing, I got a little embarrassed and turned to leave. My feet got tangled and I tripped; when I got back up,

I became aware of the silence. I glanced over my shoulder. Guysin was struggling to his feet. He was naked, and suddenly I felt that I had done something foolish. I left as fast as I could, not stopping until I reached my apartment."

"You were there . . . with your Domer?"

She nodded. "After that our relationship changed. Guysin had never been that warm to me, but now each time we met he seemed even cooler. I thought to tell him that it was not that big a deal, and I even considered confiding in him that I was having my own affair. But he never allowed it and kept his distance.

"I did not stop my own visits to the domeroom, but I was careful to come and go by other routes. I never saw him there again, and as time passed, his attitude seemed to change. I sensed that he was putting out feelers to me, and I thought that he had finally forgotten the episode. He sat with me sometimes to eat, initiated conversation, asked about my life and my work. He became more and more friendly, and then one day he invited me to his quarters for a visit.

"I was flattered and hoped to improve our friendship. I even thought that he might offer to help me in my work. I arrived, and he met me with a smile. His breath smelled of liquor.

" 'Jessica,' he said. 'Come in. Can I offer you a drink?'

" 'I'm not crazy about the stuff,' I told him.

" 'It's a developed taste.' He laughed and poured me a cup. He sat in a chair opposite me and proposed a toast. 'To your work . . . and our friendship.' He downed the drink and poured himself another.

"We talked, mostly about small matters, and Guysin kept on drinking. Later on, he made another toast.

" 'To Eridis.'

" 'Eridis,' I replied.

" 'To the Domers!'

" 'The Domers.'

" 'The Domers,' he repeated, watching me.

"I lifted my cup in response and took a sip. I had had more than I was used to and was feeling pretty good. He took another swallow, then put his cup on a table. His eyes were red and seemed to dance, but when he spoke again his voice was as sober as mine is now.

" 'You like them, don't you?'

" 'Who?' I asked.

" 'The Domers.'

" 'They seem nice,' I said cautiously.

" 'Nice?' He chuckled. 'Yes. Nice. That they are. But you like them, don't you? I mean, you're really . . . fond of them.'

" 'What do you mean?'

"He smiled. 'I mean, you want them. You have a lust . . .'

" 'Guysin.'

"He quieted me with a hand. 'I've seen you, Jessica. I've watched from the window. I've seen what you do.'

" 'So what?' I said angrily. 'You do the same.'

" 'Yes,' he said, his eyes gleaming.

" 'Say what you mean.'

" 'You just said it, Jessica. We're the same. Except that I train her. I teach her how to act.'

" 'You're crazy! We're not. And they don't need to be trained. They're people, Guysin, not slaves.'

" 'Don't be naive. You have more sense than that. They are exactly slaves. Our tools, made to do our bidding. In all things, Jessica. All things.'

" 'I don't believe that.'

" 'No? Then what were you doing with him? Giving him the choice?' He laughed, as though he had made some preposterous joke. 'You were taking him just as I do her. And with less foresight and preparation. I watched. I watched you mount him.'

"He leaned forward, and his voice, which was already thick, got thicker. Maybe it was the alcohol, or maybe the years of pent-up emotion.

" 'Jessica,' he said, 'open up your heart. Don't you see we're the same? The obsession, the lust for them. It's strong in you, isn't it? Stay here for a few cycles. You'll see. It will build. They are here for us, for the ones who want them. They were made for us, for our pleasure, our use—'

" 'Stop it!' I said, but he kept on as if he hadn't heard.

" 'But be careful. You must teach them to obey, and it is not so easy. The other teachers are strong, and it takes patience. And later on, they won't want to obey, because they're hungry, or tired, or they hurt. You must teach your Domer, Jessica, teach him well, so that he obeys even later on.'

"He bent closer. 'I'll tell you, Jessica. I'll tell you how. Listen now. Listen.' And he told me the story that I just told you.

"By the time he finished, his face was flushed and his eyes even redder than before. He poured himself another drink, then sat back and watched me.

" 'They're not playthings,' I muttered. 'You and I . . . we're not the same.'

" 'But we are, Jessica. We are. Think of their flesh, how soft and warm it is. Don't you want to lose yourself there? Feel yourself sink in it, deeper and deeper . . .'

"He seemed to have gained some power over me, and I couldn't reply. It was a horrible moment, Jules, because in a way what he was saying was right. I did want those things, but he made it sound so sick. Up to then I hadn't felt that I had done anything wrong, except to break some silly rule, but when he talked like that, I started to feel ashamed. And he knew that I did, and he used it.

" 'Don't feel guilty,' he told me. 'They're here for us. How you treat them, within reason, is entirely up to you.'

"I couldn't stand it anymore and struggled to my feet. My head was light and I grabbed the edge of a chair to steady myself. He used the moment to move in front of me, barring my way to the door.

" 'One more thing you should consider,' he said, and his voice made me cringe. 'Your research. What happens if you succeed? What happens to the colony here, to the Domers? What happens to us? Think about it, Jessica . . . think about what success means.'

"He stepped aside and I lurched forward, stumbling to the door as if I had been drugged."

"You'd had too much to drink. He was used to it."

"No." She shook her head. "It wasn't that. It was what he said, Jules. It frightened me."

"It sounds as though that is what he had in mind."

"He treats them like they're his toys, like he has the right to control their lives."

"Doesn't he? Isn't that the purpose of this place?"

"Making Mutacillin is the purpose. What he does with Sandra-hoop is something different."

"Different than what you do with yours?"

"Did, Jules. Yes. One's sex, the other's more like rape."

"I'm not sure he'd agree."

"Stop it! You don't even know him. We're not the same. He's crazy, Jules. Twisted. He does what he does for power. To dominate."

"Calm down."

"I see him now." Her voice trembled. "I see what he is."

"Jessica. Please."

"He's a plunderer, Jules." Her eyes flashed. "A plunderer, and a rapist!"

16. The Mines

I held up my arms as if to deflect blows, for the charge seemed venomous and not entirely singular. I was disturbed by it, and by her behavior. Always she had been opinionated, but rarely as abusive as she now appeared. It was unlike her or so I chose to believe.

Additionally, I felt the discomfort of being called upon to judge a man I hardly knew. I was not about to gainsay Jessica, but neither in fairness could I support her wholeheartedly. Even if the facts were as she had stated, and I did not doubt that they were, their significance seemed open to interpretation. For once I had the forbearance to stay my tongue, until I found a comment of temperance with which to respond.

"If that is so," I told her, "then we must find some way to bring it to light. Such a man is not fit to be Manager."

"I need your help, Jules."

"And you shall have it. But I need time. I've been here a scant two months."

"Sometimes I feel like I'm going to burst."

"Is it me?" I asked, suddenly worried. "Have I done something wrong?"

"No." She shook her head. "It's this place. Sometimes it just gets too tight." She put her palms against her temples and squeezed. "Do you know what I mean?"

"Give me time. I'm sure I will."

"I wish it weren't so hard, Jules."

"It's the price of adventure." I smiled, sliding toward her. "It's what you wanted."

"Is it?"

I laid a hand on her thigh and began to stroke it. She sighed. "I suppose so. It seemed more exciting from a distance."

"Most things do," I whispered, letting my hand wander between her legs. She sighed again, then smiled and turned to me. In a moment we had embarked on the exception.

Over the course of the next months I acquainted myself further with the colony and its inhabitants. I continued to treat staff members, even going so far as to mingle with them from time to time in their various social activities. If I was generally detached, I tried never to be aloof and was by and large successful.

My relationship with the Domers was more problematic. Initially, my feeling toward them hovered between distaste and pity (closer to the former than the latter), but over time it began to change. I was all but unaware of the shift and would probably have remained so had it not been for a dream. It was a vivid one, so much so that for a while I did not believe that the events had not actually occurred.

It began in the midst of a great parade or festival of some kind. This became a circus, in the center of which lay an enormous ring. Inside of it, milling and prancing, was a throng of live performers, cacogens and freaks. From the center I emerged, spangled, glittering beneath a single red spotlight. With various gesticulations I took command. The crowd, which had been desultory, began to take shape. In a few moments it became a circle several bodies deep with me at its hub. I made a gesture with my hand and was copied by a hundred others; a sound, and my voice was echoed back a thousand times. This filled me with pride and a feeling of importance. When I woke the dream died, but the feeling it begat stayed with me a long while after.

I seldom interpret my dreams, but this one seemed to require no great acumen. I was at the center (on Eridis) of a unique and fascinating experiment in medicine. Rather than shun the Domers, I should immerse myself in them, study their health and disease, observe their behavior. There existed an opportunity to edify our art and make a contribution of scientific merit to our profession.

The prospect excited me, for it offered an alternative to the apathy with which I had been approaching my job. Further, it allowed me to substitute curiosity for aversion, and science for emotion.

As I thought upon it, I realized that I had already begun my study that first day when I had entered the domeroom and examined the surprised Domer. I would have ample opportunity to examine more of them soon, for the time was drawing nigh for their bodies to begin to fail. I decided, therefore, to focus for a while my attention on their work in the mines. It was there that I saw for the first time the wisdom of their design, and felt for them something other than disdain.

The mines. How can I describe them to you? From my meager knowledge I recall that there still exist some on Earth, though I cannot say where. Have you ever been to one, Jerrold? Ever crawled beneath the ground into a dim tunnel, drawn upon air that is dank and filled with particles? All light is artificial and all sound, be it shrill or muffled, seems unnatural. Dirt and detritus are ubiquitous, and there is no way to remain unsullied. Those who work the mine have it ground into the very pores of their skin, so that after a while they darken, as wood does with age. And the air there is chill; the stone, cold. On Eridis the stone is as cold as ice.

The entrance to the mines is near Service; it gapes in the wall of the corridor like the opening of a gigantic burrow. An enlargement of one of the original excavations, within about twenty feet of the surface it makes the first of perhaps two dozen branches. In order to get as deep under the surface—and into the cold—as possible, the shafts are all quite steep. Descent, though hazardous, is relatively effortless, while return is arduous, especially if moisture has slickened the stony floors. In the steepest shafts there are conveyances for staff, but Domers must exit under their own strength. The floors have been scored with foot- and hand-holds for this purpose.

Springing from every shaft, like grapes from a stem, are Domer-made caves of varying size where the actual growth and harvest of the fungus occur. Some of these are large enough to accommodate a great many workers, while others have space for just one or two. The former are more desirable to Domers, for there is less need to bend and stoop.

Throughout the tunnels, but in none of the caves, are paired elliptical openings in the walls, called mouths. In each pair the mouth on the left is the entry point and the one on the right the exit for the vast system that conveys the rock and its adherent fungus from the mines to the processing laboratories above. Each orifice is huge, two meters, perhaps, in the long axis by one in the short, and must be so to accommodate the enormous slabs of stone on which lie the delicate fungal pyramids. There are a great number of these mouths, though not as many as there might be: to walk any distance with the slabs, even for the Domers who are designed to do so, can be treacherous. Remarkably, accidents are rare, except in the latter part of the cycle when the bodies begin to fail.

The first day I ventured into the mines I stayed but a short time, for the environment was too alien to tolerate longer. I returned the next day, doubling my length of stay. The third day I remained longer, and so on. By the end of a week I had become sufficiently acclimated that my tolerance approached that of other staff who worked there. Without a suit it was perhaps twenty minutes; with one, three to four hours.

The suits are cumbersome, but for any save the most perfunctory exploration an absolute necessity. In the lower reaches of the mines the temperature hovers near freezing, and the small drafts that come and go from the mouths make it colder still. The Domers, whose extensive adiposity acts as both insulator and heat generator, are able to tolerate such an extreme, but were a normal human forced to be there without protection he would never survive. Even with suits, which cover all but the face, staying in the lower portions of the mine more than the appointed time carries the certainty of frostbite and the risk of much worse.

For this reason, among others, most staff tend to congregate in the upper reaches of the mine. Periodically they round to the deeper sections but the trips are brief. Initially, I followed their example, remaining for the most part near the surface. I found myself often in their company, and they seemed pleased to have me. I represented for them a diversion, I suppose, from a tedious task.

On one such occasion I came upon a group of three staff huddled about a brazier notched into the wall of rock. A blue flame lit the otherwise dim passage and cast out a small measure of warmth. Even though we were in one of the upper tunnels where the air was less than frigid, the heat was welcome, and instinctively I stepped forward to join them. One looked up, her face ruddy and played upon by blue shadow.

"Hello," she said. "I'm not sure that we've met."

"You must be one of the few then." I extended a gloved hand. "Jules Ebert. I'm the village doctor."

"Sidia. Welcome to the mines."

She rubbed her hands together and stepped closer to the fire. One of her companions, a man with a crooked nose, muttered something. The third one, whose collar was pulled tightly about his face, nodded and lifted a narrow-necked bottle to his lips. Tilting his head, he took a long swallow. He finished, then thrust the bottle in my direction.

"Want some, Doctor?"

The voice was familiar, but without more of the face I couldn't place it. "I'm sorry. I seem to have forgotten your name."

"Bardis. I saw you once in the clinic."

"Of course. I didn't know that you worked here."

"If you call it that. Most of the time we just stand around."

"It's work enough just keeping warm," said the one with the bent nose. He hugged himself and shivered. "It's so damn cold."

"How long do you have to stay?" I asked.

"Too long."

"Four hours," Sidia said. "If you keep moving you stay warm enough. The suits are pretty good."

"And the brew. The suits keep you from getting cold, but the brew makes you warm. Have a slug, Doc."

Reluctantly I took the bottle. I would have preferred to pass it on, but the moment dictated otherwise. I wiped its lip with my glove, then took a small sip. I handed it to Sidia, who had a gulp.

"Rudy?"

He smiled, his mouth curling in the opposite direction from his nose. "Have I ever said no?"

He took a long swallow, and for a time we all watched the soft flames. I was aware of our shadows, magnified on the wall behind us; fleetingly, I imagined that they were cast by someone else, by Domers crouched nearby or poised behind the rock itself. I sucked in my breath and asked for the bottle. All of a sudden the brew seemed less foul.

I took another swallow and the shadows receded. Bardis reached for the bottle.

"It passes the time," he said, drinking. "Warms up the insides . . ."

"Why aren't there other sources of heat in the mines? Other spots like this?"

"There are," said Sidia. "One in shaft five and another in twelve."

"There should be more."

"Talk to the Chief. He says there's not enough fuel."

"Yeah, talk to Guysin Hoke." Rudy chuckled. "Tell him to shit more. Tell him to issue an order for all of us to shit more."

"Maybe you've got a medicine, Doc. The more you can make to come out, the more we've got to burn . . ."

"I see," I said. "I hadn't realized."

"No problem, Doc. While you're at it, why don't you get him to do something about the smell? Maybe he could plant some flowers." He took a gulp from the bottle. "Roses would be nice."

"Does no one like it in the mines?"

"The Domers don't mind. They like it just fine."

"It's so boring here," said Sidia. "We just stand around. We're supposed to supervise, but there's no need to. The Domers know what to do."

"They're like robots."

"Yeah. We just watch them . . . and let them know that we are."

"I suppose there's value in that," I observed. "Establishing your authority now, so that later, if it's needed, you have it."

"I suppose," Sidia said, unconvinced. "I'm just glad our shift's only four hours. I think I'd go crazy if I had to stay longer."

"How long do the Domers stay?"

"Twenty-four. Half of them work while the other half feed and rest. Then they switch."

"I see." I cleared my throat. "I had thought, perhaps, of speaking to one or two."

Sidia glanced at me. "Why?"

"Scientific curiosity. Medical research. They are, after all, my patients."

"You could talk to them in the domeroom. When they're not working."

"I have, and will do so again. But they are not so receptive there. They would rather sleep than talk. And when they are feeding, their minds seem enfeebled . . ."

"They're the same here."

"Certainly to work they must be more alert."

"Have you talked to Guysin?"

I paused for a moment, debating how to proceed. "Sidia," I said gently, as though I were instructing a student in some particular of the art, "would you have me treat a patient without knowledge of her condition? If you came to me with a problem, wouldn't you want me to know as much about you as possible?"

"I suppose, but—"

"The same holds for any patient, be she human or Domer."

"They have their job to do."

"And I mine. I have no intention of disrupting them. Given their intellects, I doubt I could converse with any for more than a few moments."

"They haven't said more than a dozen words to me since I've been here," said Bardis. "Yes, no, bows, nods . . . that's about it."

"Let him go." Rudy belched. "He can tell us if they have anything interesting to say." He laughed and Sidia shrugged.

"I guess it's no big deal. Just don't talk too long. Everything's figured so close here, they probably can tell the difference between a thousand slabs and a thousand and one."

"The responsibility is entirely mine," I said. "Entirely." I turned to go. "Thank you for the brew. And the warmth."

"Anytime. Thanks for breaking the monotony."

I nodded and walked away. Their conversation continued, but after a few steps I could no longer make out the words. A bit farther along the arc of the shaft I was in, the sounds ceased altogether. I stopped momentarily, waiting for my eyes to adjust to the dimmer light below. The tunnel was illuminated, as all of them are, by widely spaced bowls attached to the ceiling. They are of a translucent material and their source of light, I presume, biologic. When my pupils had dilated maximally, I continued my descent. I had a particular destination in mind, and as I wound my way downward, I thought for a moment about boredom.

It was a complaint I heard frequently from staff who worked in the mines, but one that had never occurred to me. I found them fascinating, and far from oppressive. True, others had been there longer, but that was not, I believe, the basis of our difference. Nor was it the smell, which was as distasteful to me as it was to them. It was something else. The space, I think, and the feeling it engendered in me.

I am no agoraphobe, but neither have I ever been especially fond of wide-open spaces. In the same way that the extremely thin often become threatened within the confines of a small room, menaced, perhaps, by a reflection of their own emaciation in the closed space, so are the unnaturally large disenchanted by the outdoors. It is as if we, by standing in comparison to some great plain, or the sky overhead, become ourselves diminished. It is why I have always preferred the city to the country, and a modest office to a spacious one. And why, I believe, I was attracted to the mines.

I felt enclosed by them, comforted by the immeasurable thickness of stone and earth around me. Bounded. Embraced.

I continued my descent, feeling rather fine. On either side I passed numerous caves, all of them full of Domers. Several times I had to halt while one, with a deferential bow, crossed in front of me with a slab of stone. When it was full of fungi, the Domers bore it on their back, stooped so that the slab was nearly parallel to the ground. With a kind of grace they maneuvered the front end into a left-sided mouth, sliding it gently forward until the conveyor took hold. Then they moved to the right-sided mouth, where they waited for an empty slab to appear. This they grabbed, either hoisting it above their heads or else carrying it under their massive arms back to the caves. The latter method was more common, for the openings of most of the caves barely exceeded a Domer's height.

None of the Domers initiated conversation with me, and their responses to the various salutations I offered were never more than a few clipped words. I assumed that they talked among themselves, as most who are engaged in prolonged and intimate work will, but I never heard more than indistinct murmurs. Once, I thought I detected the faint melody of some song but was never able to locate the source.

For the most part, they seemed too busy to engage in idle chatter. Those who were not carrying the slabs to and from the mouths were occupied with other strenuous work. New slabs were constantly being cut, hoisted, and positioned. The caves were continually being enlarged and had to be buttressed lest they collapse and destroy valuable material. The bigger they became, the farther they grew from the mouths, and the longer the trek with the sheets of stone. Those with fungi had to be carried with great care, which made the task that much more difficult. In the larger caves scores of slab-bearing Domers were in motion, manuevering about one another in a complex and arduous dance. I marveled at their agility and stamina.

At one point I came upon a line of Domers who were busy digging at a section of wall. At their feet lay a number of the small, powerful explosives used to break through the rock. Either they were rendering another branch to the tunnel or else creating a new cave, and I decided to pass without disturbing them. Their faces were intent on the wall in front of them, and I squeezed behind, flattening myself as best I could against the opposite wall. The peak of my stomach, which I had attempted to suck in, accidentally brushed the rear of one of them. He froze (it may have been a female), and then the ones on either side did the same. Slowly they turned.

Not for the first time was I struck by the similarity of their faces: all the Domers seem cut of a single mold. Their expressions were troubled, and they bowed their heads.

"We are sorry," one of them muttered.

"For what?" I found myself saying.

They stood silently, motionless save for the faint ripples of fat as they breathed.

"*I* touched *you*," I explained.

Still they replied nothing.

"This is absurd! Will you not talk?"

One of them nodded.

"Well?"

"We are sorry."

"I told you I am to blame."

"Yes."

"Well?"

"We must work."

"Go ahead."

He scraped his feet and stared at the ground. "We cannot while you are standing there."

I moved down the tunnel until I stood free of them. "There."

He turned to face the wall, and the others followed. None, however, began to work, and I had the impression that they were waiting for me to leave. It was an impasse, and I felt obliged to break it. I backed down the tunnel, and when I was out of sight, the sound of their tools commenced against the stone. I shook my head, displeased, vowing that my next interaction would be different. It was to come soon.

Several days before, I had decided to approach a Domer who seemed different than the rest. I had discovered him fortuitously: on one of my earlier sojourns I had chanced to be a dozen or so paces behind a staff person who was rounding a lower tunnel. She had passed the opening to a cave (fifty-four), said a few words, then moved on. I stopped momentarily to catch my breath—I was not accustomed to the sharpness of the incline—before proceeding. By that time she was out of sight. As I neared the cave's opening, I heard the sound of a single voice. It held a fervent tone and seemed to be berating the others. I sneaked forward and peered around the edge of the stone wall. The cave held, perhaps, twenty Domers; about half were working, half listening to the one who was talking. I could not hear the words—I was too far away—but the faces on the ones who were listening convinced me that I would like to. I leaned farther in, and then one of them caught sight of me. Immediately the talking ceased; in the blink of an eye the cave became like all the others.

I returned several times but never again witnessed anything out of the ordinary. Now, as I took the last few steps to the verge of the cave, I was determined to find out more.

I thought I heard whispers, but they ceased as I came into view. All of the Domers appeared hard at work, lifting, carrying, positioning the huge slabs. No one spoke, and the ones who passed me bent their heads. I took several moments to compose myself, then stepped past the rough-hewn opening into the cave.

As all of them are, it was scantly illumined, less so even than the tunnels. The Domers need (and prefer) less light than we, and though I have not inspected the retinal surface of their optic globe, I am certain that it is because they possess a vastly greater number of rods. The engineers who designed them would not have failed to foresee the value of such enhanced night vision for work in the subterranean regions of shadow.

The cave was not one of the largest, but neither was it small. The ceiling was several meters above my head, high enough so that the Domers could stand upright. The floor was more or less level, and on it were scattered a vast number of stony benches. Cut into these at different levels were counterlike surfaces, upon which sat the thick slates of stone. Some were bare, while others were covered with cones of dark fungi. Around the periphery of the cave crouched Domers working with hammer and chisel-like tools to dislodge stone from the walls. The one I had come to see was among them, and I walked up to him.

"You," I said, pointing. "What's your name?"

He did not reply immediately. "Umbo," he finally said. "Kylis Umbo."

"Male or female?"

"I am a man."

"I'd like to speak to you."

He bowed his head. "We are yours to command."

"Why don't you work like the others?"

"We work. It is our duty."

"You don't. You talk. I've seen you."

"I work, Master."

"Doctor. Ebert. I've seen you, Umbo. You stopped when you thought no one was watching. Stopped and then talked. What did you say?"

"That we must work. We must fill the mouths."

"I don't believe you."

He shrugged his massive shoulders. The others around him had stopped working.

"I'm right, aren't I?" I said to them, but they cowered, as though I were about to level some wrath. "Aren't I?"

The cave filled with silence. Except for Umbo's, all eyes stared at the floor.

"What do you want from us?" he asked.

"I want to talk. I'm your doctor. You must."

"We must work, Doctor. That is what we must do."

"I order you."

He bent his head. "And the others?"

"Let them do what they want."

"What they want?" It was the first time I had seen a Domer smile. "They want to obey, Doctor. To work and do their duty. It is what we all want."

I grew angry, for I felt that he was toying with me. I ordered him to follow me to the tunnel, where I had him crouch.

"I do not take kindly to deceit, Umbo. I have power here. I could make your life miserable."

"We are born to obey. To be miserable, if that is your wish."

"I am not staff," I said, controlling myself. "I am a doctor. I am interested in understanding you. You will not be punished for speaking."

He looked at me, and for a moment I thought he would comply. His eyes, one blue, the other gray, seemed to be searching mine, and then his obsequiousness returned.

"At the end of punishment," he said, "is rest. At the end of work, Festival. We are slaves, Doctor. What have slaves to say?"

I halted an urge to strike him, wondering if, perhaps, he had not grasped the innocent and scientific nature of my interest.

"Do you understand, Umbo, that I am a doctor? Do you know what that means?"

He fingered some pebbles on the ground.

"I merely want to talk. No more than that."

He looked blankly up. "I'm just a Domer. Please, I'd like to go back to work."

I seethed and could contain myself no longer. Grabbing him by the scruff of the neck, I made to pull him forward. He did not budge. With a flick of his hand he knocked mine away.

He stood, and a line of fear ran through me. I withstood the urge to run, and in a remarkable feat of self-control turned and walked away. When I was several paces up the tunnel, my head on a plane above his, I turned and faced him.

"We'll meet again, Umbo. Sooner or later we'll have our chat."

He watched me, then lumbered slowly back into the cave. In spite of what had happened, I found myself marveling at him. He was so fat, so huge and corpulent. His awesome buttocks rolled like clouds as he walked. To him had been given the ability to survive the numbing chill, the strength to toil a day and a night without rest. He was a colossus, and for a moment I felt small.

My suit began to burden me, and the thought of stripping it from my body passed through my mind. It frightened me, and I turned to leave before doing something foolish. As I made my way to the surface, I pondered what I might do to make the man Umbo talk.

17. Guysin Hoke's Gift

When he greeted me, Guysin Hoke was covered with the pinkish gel that the girl Pook had described. It blanketed his arms and neck, and there was an oval patch on each cheek. He seemed unperturbed by my intrusion and offered me some gel of my own. I declined, at which point he excused himself.

"It will only take a moment to unpeel," he said amicably, then turned and disappeared into the bathroom. In a few minutes he emerged in the flesh, wearing a loose tunic. The areas of skin where the gel had been were pink: it looked like a sunburn, and I asked if it were uncomfortable. He shook his head.

"It's actually quite pleasant. Something like a second skin . . . You haven't tried it yet?"

"No. Nor will I."

"It's harmless. In fact, it's said to have value as a rejuvenant." I had noted before that his face was well preserved for a man his age, and was once again struck by the smoothness of his skin.

"I have no need to be younger than I am," I replied. "Nor to appear so."

"A sentiment I wish I could share. I am aging and surrounded by the ageless."

"The Domers?"

He nodded.

"I would hardly call them that. Already they are beginning

to crumble, at a rate faster than I would have imagined. Even to a physician it is a bit frightening to watch."

"You have not lived through even one cycle, Jules. This is my eighth. Stay, and you will see them return, strapping and energetic." He went to a cabinet and took out a canister. "Will you join me in a cup of brew?"

"Have you nothing else?"

He shook his head. "No other intoxicant. You've tried it?"

I nodded.

"Mine is of higher quality than most. More like a brandy."

"A snifter then. But no more than that." I settled on the couch and took up the conversation.

"You envy them, then?"

"I envy their agelessness." He brought me the drink and took a chair. "Their innocence. They need hardly to think . . ." He smiled and patted his head. "Thinking, and worrying, is what lost me my hair."

"Your genes lost it. There are practitioners on Earth who would gladly re-pilify."

He chuckled. "I am aware of the fashion. My vanity, however, lies less upon my head"—he tapped his skull—"than it does within."

"Indeed. And of what does it consist?"

"Of this, Jules." He swept out his arms in a grand gesture. "Of Eridis, and our great venture here."

"It does not taint your vanity that the Domers must die?"

"On the contrary. It reminds me of the miracle that life follows death."

"Or that they suffer so?"

He raised an eyebrow. "Is this you, my friend, who is asking?"

"I speak for myself," I replied pointedly.

"Of course." He tipped his head and drank. "You're a doctor. Aren't you accustomed to suffering?"

"Not on such a scale . . ."

"I see. You pity them, then."

"I could not practice my art without a measure of sympathy for the human condition."

"They are not human, Jules. But suppose that they were. How would you make their lives different?"

"I would give them more rest. A whole day of work is too much, even for them. And more mush."

"We give them what mush they need. More would be a misuse of resources. And rest? A day of work is optimal: it has been amply demonstrated."

"Perhaps they would live longer . . ."

"What value is there in a longer life? They will live again soon enough. If they worked less, we would have less of the drug. Less Mutacillin, Jules."

I sipped the brew. It was not brandy, but neither was it vile. Nor was it weak. "I've thought of that. It's a worrisome paradox."

"Only if you choose to make it one. Do you honestly regard the Domers as equal to the patients you treat on Earth?"

I swirled my glass and stared at the liquid within it. The question was one I had asked myself.

"They're not," he said. "They're clones, designed for a specific purpose."

"They have minds."

"Only the minds that we give them. They have no choice in what they do . . . they wouldn't want one."

"How do you know that?"

He laughed. "Look at them. Would you subject yourself to a life like that if you thought something else was possible?"

"They don't think because they've never been taught. They've never been told about anything else."

"Tell them then. It won't make a difference."

"Even if they learn the truth about Festival?"

"Tell them that, too. You'll find out what kind of minds they have. They won't listen, Jules. Or they'll listen, but they won't believe. Have you ever tried a teacher?"

I shook my head.

"Try one some time. It won't be the same, but you'll get an idea. Try it, then see if words can change your mind."

I frowned. "It's difficult, Guysin. It goes against the grain to allow such suffering."

"It serves a purpose. Think of how much there would be without Mutacillin."

"I'm aware of that. Even as it is, the drug is in short supply."

"Perhaps we should ask the Domers to work harder." He grinned.

"If Jessica is successful," I said slowly, "they won't have to work at all."

"Yes." He placed his cup on a table and regarded me. "And how is Jessica doing?"

His tone was friendly, and my head was touched with the liquor. "Well," I replied. "She says her work is progressing well."

"I'm pleased to hear it. She would be the first."

"Yes. She mentioned there have been other attempts."

"Two. The first one who tried was an idiot. The second was better, and seemed to be making good progress before the accident."

"Accident?"

"He fell down one of the mine shafts and broke his neck. We managed to save his life, though death might have been better than what he was left with. No one's tried since then. Not until Jessica."

"I see."

He stood up. "Can I offer you another drink?"

"Yes, please." I handed him the glass, which he returned full. "Wouldn't you be happier if she failed?" I blurted.

His reaction was a study in earnestness. He furrowed his forehead, then cocked his head to the side. He began to speak, stopped himself, then started to pace the small room. He reminded me of a man trying to find a gentle way to break some grievous news. After a while he sat again and leaned forward in his chair.

"No," he said. "I wouldn't. But the paradox is hers, too. Success would mean the end of everything here, including the Domers. I'm not sure that's what she wants."

"She feels a certain affection for them."

"I know. It must be unsettling to realize she could be responsible for their demise."

"And you?"

He glanced at me. "What do you mean?"

"Aren't you . . ." I searched for the proper word. ". . . fond of them too? Wouldn't their demise affect you as well?"

He reached for his cup. "I'm empty," he said. "Can I offer you a refill?"

"I'm fine, thanks."

He made no hurry pouring his drink, and I waited. Eventually he returned to his seat.

"I am attached to them," he said carefully. "In the way that an inventor is to his invention. I had a part, you know, in their design."

"Indeed."

He nodded. "Loyalty may be too strong a word, but it conveys a sense of how I feel."

"To the Domers. Or Eridis?"

"One presupposes the other. I'm attached to both." He sighed. "This has been my home for nearly forty years, Jules. It's not so easy to change."

"But you would? If she found the answer, you'd leave?"

He looked at me. "Have I told you the story of their faces?"

"Whose?"

"Theirs. The Domers."

I shook my head.

"They didn't always have them, you know."

"Indeed."

"Someday I'll have to tell you . . ." For an instant his eyes held mine, and I noted again that they were of different color. I had seen others like that recently, but the memory eluded me.

"When you get a chance," he said, "take a look." He ran a finger down the bridge of his nose. "Look at their noses." He touched his cheek. "Their cheeks. Their eyes." He smiled. "Look at their faces, Jules. See what you think."

It seemed that he was trying to make some point, but it escaped me. Perhaps I was a bit intoxicated; perhaps he meant to be obscure.

"Medically," I told him, "I am more interested in their bodies."

"Of course." He stood up. "Now you must excuse me," he said with the utmost of courtesy. "I have work that can't be put off."

I nodded, offered a similar platitude, then rose and left. Not until I entered my own apartment did I remember the question that had gone unanswered. I shook my head at the ease with which he had evaded me and wondered if there did, indeed, exist such a story as he claimed. I resolved to press him further at the next opportunity, then climbed the ladder to the floating bed. There was something else I wanted to recall, but I fell asleep before I could. The dreams I had, none of which I remember, were not my own.

18. The Fifth Pleasure

Whatever reservations I had had before about studying the Domers were dispelled by our conversation. Guysin had invited me not merely to talk to them but to speak frankly of their plight. It was a challenge, and I was determined to accept. I would study them, and I would understand.

The rigors of the profession dictated that I be as scientific as possible. After a search of the clinic's data bank I chose Greenstreet's protocol within which to frame the investigation. Twenty subjects were selected for interviews: eighteen of them gave responses similar enough to be indistinguishable. Among these was Limia Bulu, and I have taken the liberty of using him to illustrate the others. The remaining two were Kylis Umbo and Sandra-hoop.

Of the three, Bulu posed the least difficulty, and I began with him. I chose to visit him, as before, in the domeroom, and entered, then crossed the empty space in front of Service. Having become more familiar with the room, I did not pause on my way to his cubicle. When I arrived, he was on the bench, eyes closed, a teacher on his scalp. With his hand nearest me he was rubbing his knee. Rather than waiting for him to finish his lesson—at times a Domer will sit with a teacher for hours—I walked forward and poked him in the thigh. His lids struggled open and he looked down at me.

"Bulu," I said. "I am Ebert. Your doctor. Remove the teacher."

He stared at me.

"Remove it."

Slowly he lifted his arms and unpeeled the membrane from his scalp. With one hand he held it and with the other massaged his shoulder.

"Do you remember me?"

He nodded.

"I would speak with you."

He blinked, then nodded again.

"Are you comfortable, or would you rather lie on the mat?"

"Lie," he said.

I stepped back, gesturing, and with an effort he left the bench and lay on the mat. I had brought a small stool, and as he turned his head to look at me, I sat upon it.

"You may feed if you'd like," I said without thinking. "Though if it distracts your attention, I must ask you to stop."

"It is not time," he said flatly.

"When did you feed last?"

"I don't remember. I am hungry now."

"When will you again?"

"The teacher will say."

"Do you wish you could eat now?"

"Eat?"

"Feed."

"I wish to obey. The teacher will say." He rubbed his knee.

"Is your knee bothering you?"

He stopped rubbing. "It's sore."

"And your shoulders?"

"Yes."

"Are there others like you?"

He creased his forehead.

"Others who hurt," I explained.

"I suppose."

"Do you talk with them? Do you talk to other Domers?"

"Sometimes."

"What do they say?"

"They hurt. They say that."

"What do you think about that?"

"Think?"

"The fact that everyone is in pain. None of you wonders about that?"

"At the end of pain is Festival. Festival is the reward. Duty is the reward."

"Festival is a lie, Bulu. Festival is your death."

"Death?"

"The end of your life. The beginning of another cycle of suffering."

"Do not fear Festival." He closed his eyes. "Festival is the miracle . . ."

"It is your death, your slaughter."

"It is the glory. As obedience and industry are the pleasures of this life, Festival is the pleasure of the next."

"Open your eyes, Bulu. You are made to suffer. Your bodies are flawed. Fatally flawed."

"They are our bodies."

"Look around. No staff is like you."

"No staff can work as we do. None can lift, or endure as we can."

He sat up, rubbing his knees with his hands. "It is our duty and our joy to produce. What is a little pain, a little hunger, compared to that? When we have filled the mouths, we will celebrate Festival. Some will enter Carefree, others Celeste. We will celebrate and be joyful."

"I see," I said. "Does everyone believe as you?"

"The teachers have told us. It cannot be otherwise." He looked to his bench, to the membrane hanging on the peg. His face became anxious.

"I have not finished today's lesson. May I return?"

"You would obey me before the teacher?"

"You are staff. It is the earliest lesson."

"You would obey anything? Anything I command?"

"Please. May I return?"

I regarded him, noting the conflict. "Yes," I finally said. "Thank you for your time."

With some difficulty he got to his feet and returned to the bench. He lifted the teacher from its peg and fit it upon his scalp, pulling the pods down over his ears. He closed his eyes and in a moment was in a trance that seemed deeper than sleep. I toyed with the notion of interrupting him again, for I was interested in how he would react if I were to demand to borrow the teacher. I decided against it, recalling that I had already seen his response to my other attempts at provocation. I stood, and with the stool under my arm left the domeroom.

In my apartment I recorded the results of our interaction and made a few preliminary notes. I had already conducted similar interviews with a number of other Domers, though not the two from whom I expected something different. That was the next step in the study, and since I had not yet determined how exactly to approach Kylis Umbo, I decided to proceed with Sandra-hoop.

I had not discussed the investigation with Guysin, for though he had encouraged me, I feared that he would interfere if he discovered that Sandra-hoop was one of the subjects. I chose a time when I knew him to be occupied elsewhere, donned my white lab coat, and took the long walk down the corridor to the domeroom. I entered and, as I was crossing the area in front, saw a familiar face.

"Meril," I called, my voice louder than I expected. She was exiting from the head of an aisle to the right and looked up. She smiled, raised a hand in greeting, then strolled toward me in a manner I found vaguely seductive.

"Doctor," she said, extending a hand.

"Please. Jules."

We shook and then she placed the hand on a hip, letting the other dangle freely. "To what do we owe this pleasure?"

"Business, I'm afraid."

"Making a house call?"

I smiled. "Something like that."

Some seconds passed; she shifted her feet. "Confidential?"

I nodded.

"I understand. Privacy's important . . ."

"An enlightened attitude. At least in regards to the Domers."

She shrugged and played with a lock of her hair. "It's a
special thing . . . between a patient and a doctor."

"You speak as someone who's had personal experience."

"Yeah." She stuffed her hands in her hip pockets. "When I
was a kid." She stared at the floor.

"Confidential?" I asked.

Her eyes shied from mine, and she smiled. "Private, Jules.
Maybe if you get to know me better . . ."

"I hope I do."

We looked at each other rather awkwardly and then she
offered a hand. "Until we meet again," she said.

"Until then."

She turned gracefully and walked away, heading out of the
domeroom. Her strides were long and athletic. I watched until
she had almost reached the door, then disengaged my mind
from her, setting it to the task at hand.

In the observation room is a large map, upon which is drawn
each cubicle and beside it the number and name of the occu-
pant. From this I had found Sandra-hoop's location; on a separate occasion, while she was sleeping, I had passed by in order
to commit her face to memory. The cubicle was near the rear
of the domeroom, and as I approached I noted that most of the
others in the vicinity were vacant. I presumed that such an
arrangement had been contrived by Guysin. Though he must
certainly have relied for his privacy on the Domers' capacity to
block out extraneous stimuli, he probably never felt entirely
secure. The more Domers near Sandra-hoop who worked the
opposite shift the safer he must have felt.

She was lying on her mat when I arrived, eyes closed, the
feeding tube in place and full. One hand was resting near it on
her belly; the other, between her legs. Her chest gently rose and
fell.

Quite unintentionally, I reached into a pocket of my lab coat
and took out a roll, which I commenced to chew. The sound
must have awakened her, for she opened her eyes and turned

her head in my direction. She did not seem alarmed, though after blinking a few times and rubbing her eyes, she frowned.

"Who are you?"

"I am the doctor." I took the roll from my mouth. "Doctor Ebert. I am here to talk with you."

"I am feeding."

"I will not disturb that. I only wish to talk."

"I am feeding," she repeated, then turned away.

"Sandra-hoop . . ."

She pursed her lips, then sucked them back beneath her gums. "What is it?"

"I would speak with you."

"I am hungry. Tired. Can't you come back?"

"No."

She frowned. "Why have you come?"

"I have some questions."

"There are others. Why come to me?"

"I am the doctor, Sandra-hoop. The reasons are my own. I will not disturb your feeding."

"You already have."

I looked at the tube, which remained full. "You are still being fed."

"That is not what I meant."

"What, then?"

She stared at me but said nothing.

"Answer me. What bothers you?"

"The smell of your food. Watching you place it in your mouth. I do not enjoy the manner in which you feed."

I raised my eyebrows. "How interesting. It upsets you to see me eat." I held up the roll. "You are not even a little curious to see how it tastes?"

One hand flew to her nose, the other to her mouth. Her face went pale, and her body began to tremble. "Take it away," she pleaded.

I did not realize the extent of the Domer aversion to oral feeding until I witnessed her reaction: whether it was a conditioned response or a direct effect of the roll's odor-bearing molecules on her central nervous system I was not at the time certain. It was striking enough that I later made a point of reviewing the files on their systems of taste and olfaction. Sandra-hoop's reaction was no fluke.

The Domer organs of taste and smell have been modified so that most of the odors that seem natural and appealing to us are repulsive to them. Principally, these are the scents we associate with foodstuffs and edibles. Though at first glance this aversion may seem yet another instance of genetically determined torment, it is, in fact, an assurance of their survival. Were they to place an item of food—be it a tube full of mush or some contraband from staff—directly into their mouths, their lives would be placed in great jeopardy. Their mouths are for speech and breath; they are not organs of ingestion. Were food forced into them and swallowed, it would flow into their lungs. There is no other channel. They would suffocate.

I did not recall this anatomic information at the time, but I had certainly not come to torment her. When Sandra-hoop's face grew livid, I removed the roll and quickly wiped my lips of the several crumbs that had stuck to them. Her chin quivered the way ours sometimes do before we involuntarily disgorge our stomachs, and though I knew her incapable of effecting a similar vomitus, I nonetheless found myself stepping back. It was some moments before she calmed.

"I'm sorry," I said.

She looked at me with a pained expression.

"I didn't mean for that to happen."

"I've heard that before," she muttered.

"What have you heard?"

"What do you want from me? I need to feed and rest. Won't you leave me alone?"

I shook my head. "I'm sorry."

"Why?"

"I need to talk to you."

"Why?"

"I want to understand you."

"Why?"

I started to explain, then stopped myself. "You ask a lot of questions for a Domer."

"I try to understand."

"Why? That is not your task."

"Yes," she said cryptically.

"Are you not content to obey?"

"There are other pleasures . . ."

"Name them."

"You do not know?"

"Name them, Sandra-hoop."

She closed her eyes and recited. "In service, duty to Mannus, obedience to staff. The three of material life. The fourth," she said flatly, "is the wonder that is too miraculous to know."

"There are no more?"

She regarded me. "Just four, Doctor."

"I have heard it said there is a fifth."

"The teachers tell of four."

"Is it possible that there are other teachers?"

"Perhaps." Her eyes, winter gray and winter blue, flickered over me. "Perhaps I have forgotten. I am sorry."

"Are you content, Sandra-hoop?"

"What does that mean?"

"Happy. Satisfied."

"Doctor, please. I am just a Domer. I am happy to serve you. That is my pleasure."

"And the pain, in your hips, your knees?"

"It is not pleasant. To obey is at times to suffer."

"You are falling apart, Sandra-hoop. Your bodies are flawed. They are dying."

"Our bodies are beautiful, Doctor. Vast and strong. If we cease to be, it will be the end of a thing of great beauty."

"You *will* cease to be."

"Will we? You know the future?"

"I know Festival . . ."

"Do you? Then there is no more to say." She turned her head away. "Will you leave me now? I must rest. I must prepare . . ."

The tone of her request was neither servile nor insolent; it touched in some way my feelings of decency and good conduct. I found myself backing away, honoring her solicitation as I would have that of anyone in need of solitude and rest.

And yet I felt that, far from being completed, our conversation had just begun. Her responses to my questions seemed on a plane entirely different from Limia Bulu's, and I wondered what the origin of that difference could be. Perhaps it was the result of her frequent encounters with Guysin, and yet some of her comments hinted at knowledge he would have been careful to conceal. My curiosity was piqued, and I decided on a course of surveillance.

I thought I might watch her, surreptitiously if possible, at work in the mines, for that milieu seemed a potential source of valuable information. Additionally, I had still not determined a viable approach to take with Kylis Umbo and needed time to think upon it further. The mines, where I felt strangely in my element, were a perfect setting, conducive to both observation and thought.

As often as I could, then, I returned to that world, crawling with eagerness beneath the surface. In addition to the insulating suit, I wore a facial mask that some staff used for added warmth, hoping thereby to conceal my identity.

I was not able to go daily—the increasing demands of the practice kept me too busy—and had to content myself with visits several times a week. The tunnels are so extensive that it took a number of such journeys before I located Sandra-hoop; she was working in cave sixty, not far from Kylis Umbo.

Over a period of several weeks, during which I rounded anonymously, I observed nothing extraordinary. Sandra-hoop worked along with the others, toiling as they. From time to time she stopped to speak to another, though what was said I could never hear. All of the Domers on occasion grumbled, some moaning, others cursing one of a half-dozen epithets I could not decipher. If Sandra-hoop appeared to do so with greater frequency, perhaps it was because, given her unique status, she felt she deserved better. In truth, I could not blame any of them their plaints, for even as their great bodies began to succumb to the ravages of privation and disease, the demands of their work remained constant. They toiled to fill the mouths, to sate the vast Eridian gut that would not be gorged until their bodies were expended. It was ponderous to me that something so precious could come of work so pernicious, a drug that conferred life of a task that destroyed it.

After weeks of desultory observation, during which I made little progress in my investigation, a remarkable event occurred. I alone was privy to it, and it affected me in ways I have yet to fathom. I was descending the shaft toward cave sixty; ahead of me I saw Sandra-hoop leave its entrance. She was carrying a fungi-filled slab, and after depositing it in a mouth, she peered up and down the tunnel. Her glance seemed furtive, and I stepped quickly behind an outcropping of stone. Apparently she did not see me, for instead of waiting at the other mouth as was proper, or returning to the cave, she took off along the passageway that connects the sixties network of caves to the fifties. None of the other Domers seemed to pay attention to her, nor to me when I followed some distance behind.

I reached the fifties shaft, and peering around the corner saw Sandra-hoop in descent. She passed a number of caves, then disappeared around a bend. I knew the shaft: it dead-ended somewhat lower down in a small cave that had yet to be developed. I paused to consider what she might be doing there. While I was thinking, two Domers ascended and disappeared into cave fifty-four. A moment later Kylis Umbo appeared at its mouth, and after a cursory glance (my vantage was concealed) disappeared in the direction that Sandra-hoop had gone. I was at once fascinated and bewildered and, after several impatient minutes, followed him.

The shaft was steep; being relatively new, it had no conveyance for staff. The Domers had walked upright, steadying themselves by the pressure of their outstretched palms against the tunnel walls, but I was forced to back down, grabbing onto the foot- and hand-holds that had been cut in the stone floor. At the bottom it leveled out, but this was directly in front of the cave. I desired, of course, to remain hidden, and had to stop somewhat above, in the shaft itself. I found a narrow ledge that arched over the mouth of the cave, and managed somehow to gain a position upon it. The purchase was precarious but the vantage was choice: by bending my head slightly I had an unobstructed view below. There were only two in the cave, Sandra-hoop and Kylis Umbo, and they seemed unaware of any but themselves.

They were sitting side by side, their backs against a wall. Sandra-hoop's hand was on his leg; his was on her arm. He was saying something to her, his face drawn and serious, and she nodded, then whispered something in return. He smiled rather grimly and rubbed her arm. She stroked his leg. They sat for a while without speaking and then she turned her head and whispered something in his ear. He smiled again, but differently, and the two of them pushed themselves away from the wall until they lay flat. Sandra-hoop rolled up on a hip, sending shivers of fat up and down her body. He pressed himself against her, and her flesh rippled again. With her free hand she grabbed his massive buttock and shook it. His body seemed to quake and he laughed, then leaned back and pulled her upon him. He grunted and his face grew florid, but they made no move to separate. Instead, they began to writhe against one another, up and down and side to side, as though they were masses of protoplasm seeking to join. Their breathing became stertorous, and mine, louder than I wished. In a moment they had rolled over, and now it was Kylis Umbo who was on top, his back speckled with pebbles and bits of dirt. He heaved about like a wave on the ocean, then slithered down her body until his face lay upon her colossal belly. She kneaded his shoulders while he licked the edge of her stoma. He puckered his mouth and thrust his fat tongue into the opening itself. She groaned.

My breath shortened and my heart pounded against the rocky shelf on which I crouched. I felt unable to lie still and shifted my feet in order to find another purchase. The rock was slippery. My boots slid upon it like ice. Without warning my legs fell from under me, and my body tumbled down the shaft. I whimpered, then groaned as I crashed to the ground.

19. Iatrogenics

I was not damaged, though at first I wished that I were. I closed my eyes, praying to be someplace else. When I opened them, I had not moved. The two Domers stared at me in frozen fright.

I stood, brushed myself off, and folded my arms to steady their shaking. I struck an attitude of authority.

"This behavior is proscribed," I said with what force I could muster. "Illegal."

They huddled together, heads bent. How they had left their other posture I did not know. I had not seen them move.

"Well?"

They were perturbed, I am certain, though I trembled more. "Answer me!"

"What is your question, Master?"

"What are you doing here?"

"We await your command."

"I command you to answer. What were you doing?"

"Working, Master."

"Do not lie, Umbo. I saw you. I was watching."

"I know this one's voice," Sandra-hoop said softly.

"He is staff," replied Kylis Umbo. "He seeks to punish us."

"Take off your mask," said Sandra-hoop. "Let us see your face."

I had forgotten I had it on. Reluctantly I removed it.

"He is the doctor, Kylis Umbo. The one who spoke to me in the domeroom."

"We have met," he muttered.

"He said he wants to understand us."

"Let him become a Domer then."

"Perhaps he is different . . ."

"They are all the same."

"Some are different."

"Who, Sandra-hoop? Guysin? Because he tells you *you* are?"

"Hush!"

"I know about him," I told her. "I know what he does."

They were silent.

"Why is it wrong for us, then?" she asked. "If it's all right for you, why is it wrong for us?"

"Has he not told you?"

"He says it's against the rules."

"Yes."

"But you are the ones who taught us. You showed us the fifth pleasure."

"Your bodies were meant to work," I reminded her. "That is why you were made."

"Our bodies are beautiful," said Kylis Umbo. "Fat and strong. It is we who make the wealth, we who give you your precious drug. If any deserve pleasure, it is we who do."

I shivered, hugging my arms about my chest. "It is cold here."

Kylis Umbo smiled. "You are too thin. Perhaps you should eat more . . ."

"I am bigger than others. Among humans I am counted quite large."

"To us you are small, Doctor. Puny. The pleasure you have to offer is not so grand as you like to believe."

"Indeed. And what is the source of this expertise?"

He smiled and placed a hand on Sandra-hoop's leg. "Believe me, it is a lesser thing." She covered his hand with hers and their eyes met. More than before I felt an intruder.

"I am getting cold. I have been in the mines too long already." I replaced the mask, and as I did their expressions changed. They stiffened, and the tenuous link we had made seemed to recede.

"Please," I said, feeling strangely the supplicant. "I want to talk with you more. I must leave now . . ."

They watched me without speaking.

"Will you?"

"For what purpose?"

"Knowledge . . . understanding . . ."

"We will consider."

"I do not threaten."

"You cannot," said Kylis Umbo. "After life is death . . ."

"And after death"—Sandra-hoop cast her eyes at him—"life." I turned from them, for the cold had begun to insinuate itself into my mind. I imagined that I saw them with other than my own eyes, with something more than pity. Compassion perhaps. Empathy.

Suddenly I was staring at myself huddled in a cave. I was warm and fat. A man, then a woman. I felt translucent and full of light. I shivered with pleasure, and then the vision turned. A skeleton rattled bones of ice. I remembered the cold. The death. Hypothermia flashed in my mind. In a panic I scrambled up the slope and as fast as I could rushed from the mines.

I did not see either of them again for some time and kept the fact of our visit to myself. I feared that if I shared it, some hostile reaction might incur, and this I cared to avoid for each of our sakes. In my mind I returned to the conversation often, hoping to elucidate some hidden meaning, but such was not forthcoming. In the meantime I had other work to keep me occupied.

As the cycle drew on, the balance of clients in the clinic shifted markedly. For every staff I saw, I treated ten or more Domers. Initially I welcomed the change, for it afforded me a chance to examine their unique and unusual bodies. After a while, however, it grew tiresome, for their illnesses were all the same. Perhaps if I had been more zealous, more probing, I might have discovered ways in which they differed, but in our busy clinic the opportunities were rare.

Fortunately, I had Martha Higgins to keep my spirits up. Ours had become an established friendship, and her presence provided relief from tasks that had become dull and unending. During a lull one day in the stream of patients we sat chatting in the surgical suite. I had coaxed a dozen sweet muffins from Randy, and we shared these while sitting at the operating table, upon which Martha had spread a sheet. I did not know her to be a modest eater, yet found myself consuming two of the pastries for every one that she did. I asked if she had difficulty chewing.

"Because of this?" She touched the flaccid half of her face. I nodded.

"It doesn't affect my eating. Just the facial muscles are paralyzed, not the chewing ones."

"You're unusual," I told her. "Most cases of Bell's palsy recover."

She chewed for a while. "That's not what I have."

"No?"

"No." She clasped her hands and stared. "I tried to kill a man."

"Martha . . ."

"It's true. The only reason I'm here is that I wasn't successful. If I'd killed him, I'd be dead."

Her face was still. Her left eye blinked.

"I hit him with a metal brace. On the head. He fell and bled into his brain. When he woke up, half his body was paralyzed."

She rubbed her right cheek.

"He was a doctor, Jules. A specialist. At least he can't practice now. At least I did that much."

My appetite had faded. With her fingers Martha crumbled a muffin.

"They sentenced me here. To do service to humanity, meaning the government, meaning Mannus. Four cycles I'm supposed to stay. And they cut the nerve to half my face . . ." She touched behind an ear. "Here. To remind me . . ."

She sighed. It caught in her chest. "As if I needed to be reminded."

"Why? What did he do?"

"He meddled with my child."

"He raped her?"

"Him. Worse."

"I don't understand."

"He had a center. To study children. My son was having problems, and I brought him. He was twelve; I left him a week the first time. Dr. Ennis said the problems were with his sexual identity; he wanted to study him more. Ron didn't seem to mind, and I brought him back for another week. We talked a few times on the phone, and he seemed okay. But when I came to get him, he was transformed . . ."

Her eyes filled with tears. "Do you know what gonadal selectics is?"

I sucked in my breath.

"Ennis did that to him. Without my permission, or anyone's. He said it was what he needed, what his profile showed." She wiped her eyes. "He made him into a freak, Jules. I should have killed him. I tried to. I did. I tried . . ."

"Why did they punish you? Why not him?"

"They said he'd been punished enough."

"But why you? Certainly you were justified."

"We can't have people running amuck, can we?" Her voice was mocking and cold. "After all, we live in enlightened times."

"How horrible, Martha." I reached across and squeezed her hand.

"It is. I try to forget, try to make it distant. Sometimes I can. The years make it a little easier . . ."

"The child, where is he?"

"He does better than I do. He says it's not so bad being different. Sometimes he even feels special."

"It's often like that, isn't it? Easier for the children than the parents."

"He says I'm old-fashioned. That sex is different than it used to be."

"Perhaps. But gonadal selectics is hardly ever practiced now. Or it shouldn't be. It has fallen into disfavor, and I for one am glad."

"I should never have brought him there."

"You can't blame yourself."

"I can. I should have known . . ."

"It doesn't help to punish yourself."

She sighed, rubbing her face. "Every time I look in the mirror I remember."

"How barbaric we are. And here it continues."

"Did you expect something different? We made the Domers. How could they be anything but sick?"

"I was trained to be a doctor. Not a mortician." I played with half a muffin. "I always imagined that knowing the future would be a boon. But when it's the same as the past . . ."

"It's worse than not knowing."

"It is. I need a change."

She nodded. "How about a staff patient? There's one who wants to see you."

"Anything other than Domer after dying Domer."

"He says he has some urinary problem."

"Fine. Anything."

She glanced at me, then brushed her hands and stepped off the stool. "I'll go see if he's ready. Will you clean up?"

I nodded and, after she left, finished the remaining muffins. Her sordid tale, which had initially robbed me of my appetite, in the end had made me gluttonous. I swept the crumbs into my palm and tossed them into my mouth, then slid from the stool and folded the sheet. I dropped it in a linen bag and went through the double doors. Martha met me in the hall.

"He's in there," she said, pointing to her right. "I'll be in the back."

"Fine."

I washed my hands in the other room, then crossed the hall and opened the door. Meril was sitting inside.

"Doctor," she said, standing.

"You. I . . ."

She held out her hand.

"Sit down," I said nervously.

"I have a problem." She gave me a timid smile. "I feel like I have to piss all the time."

"I see."

"Only a few drops come out. I just feel like I always have to go."

"I see."

"Doctor?" She glanced at me. "Are you all right?"

I looked at her. "A few drops, you said? Is it painful?"

"No."

"Have you ever had an infection?"

She shook her head, her pretty hair springing from side to side.

"I see. I'll need to examine you. You'll have to take off the suit."

She nodded, and I opened a drawer in the examining table and pulled out a gown. I handed it to her.

"I'll wait outside the door. Let me know when you're ready."

I left and tried to think of nothing while I waited. It was impossible. I didn't want to examine her. And I did.

"Come in," she called.

She was sitting on the examining table, hugging the gown around her waist. It had the effect of accentuating her bosom.

"Lie down, please."

She did so, holding onto the edges of the gown. I leaned over and gently lifted her hands. "I have to examine you, Meril."

"I know," she said sheepishly. "I'm a little embarrassed."

"Yes. I'll try to be brief."

I spread the gown apart. My hands trembled slightly. Rising from the pubic hair was her penis. Beneath it, her vagina. I examined the organs, and her prostate. Then I had her dress.

Before I left the clinic that day I made a point of speaking to Martha. I had not seen her since Meril's visit. She was bent over the auto-analyzer.

"It was the prostate," I told her. "Congested. Nothing serious."

She looked up. "Thanks, Jules."

"That's what I'm here for." I put a hand on her shoulder. "A sweet child."

"Yeah," she said. "Yeah."

20. The Burden of Two

There have been times, Jerrold, many times, when I have felt myself inhabited by you. Your values, your aesthetic, your ambitions. As though I were the husk, and you, the kernel. I am grateful to have you, but sometimes wish I carried less of the sharp swords, the invulnerability, and more of the gentleness. It might be a commingling rather than a domination. It might be something akin to what I have found with Jessica.

I am stronger now, broader, wiser. Colors are more vivid. Deception impossible. Pain is not unknown; at times it is harsh. But I am less frail.

Jessica and I had been invited to dine with Guysin, and I stopped by her quarters so that we might go together. I had thought that she was expecting me, but when I entered I found her sitting on the side of her bed staring at the wall. Her hair was disheveled, her face blank. She was wearing a soiled suit.

"Hello," she said, glancing in my direction, then back to the wall.

"Jessica, we have a date . . . Are you all right?"

"It's easier to look here. Even though there's still interference."

"What?"

"I can project on it. Do you see?"

"Jessica . . ."

She turned and smiled. "No, of course not. The work is mine. I can tell you."

"I'm not in the mood for games, Jessica."

"My work is no game," she said, suddenly indignant. The swift change frightened me.

"I want you to come to the clinic," I said tautly. "I want to examine you."

She ran her fingers through her hair. "You're a doctor. Can you help?"

"Tomorrow, Jessica. I want you to come tomorrow."

She nodded. "I don't feel right, Jules."

"I see that."

"I'm off balance. Tense . . ."

"I've been neglecting you."

"No." She took my hand. "It's not that. Both of us have been busy."

"Is it your work?"

"I don't know. Maybe. I'm so close to getting those damn fungi to germinate. A few more weeks . . ."

"Do you ever think about what will happen when you do?"

"Yes. It bothers me. A lot."

"Enough to make you stare at blank walls?"

"Don't joke, Jules. Sometimes it feels like there's a battle going on. When I fight, that's how it feels. When I don't, when I'm tired, or weak, then it's different. Like something else is in control. Is that stress, Jules?"

"I don't know. I need to examine you."

"I'm sorry, Jules. That I'm acting so strange."

"I haven't felt quite right myself. There's an odd quality to this place that seems to breed strangeness."

"Maybe that's it." She smiled wanly. "I love you, Jules."

"Then get dressed," I said. "I'm starting to get hungry."

"How about if we have another picnic? Just you and me."

"We're supposed to meet Guysin in ten minutes."

"Are we?" She frowned. "I'd forgotten. I'd rather not go."

"We won't stay long . . ."

"I don't like him. We'll probably get into a fight."

"The man is reasonable. I imagine he wants to make peace."

"I doubt it," she muttered, then looked at me. "You promise we won't stay long?"

"I promise."

"All right." She sighed. "Give me a few minutes to clean up."

She got to her feet and unzipped her suit, climbing out and letting it fall to the ground. I followed her to the bathroom, where she stood at the sink, washing her hands and face. She dried, then stepped to the side, in front of a long mirror. From the doorway I watched as she gazed at herself. She was thin, though still lovely. She made a face, and I stepped forward and embraced her from behind.

"We are beautiful," I said.

"No. Too thin."

"No. Melded."

"You're squeezing too hard."

"It is you who are holding me."

"Jules . . ."

The moment vanished. I saw my face behind hers. It seemed odd to find it there. I relaxed my hold.

"Be more gentle," she said. "I don't like it when you hurt."

"I'm sorry." I leaned forward and kissed her neck. "I can't resist you."

She wriggled out of my grip and picked up a brush. Tilting her head back, she began to brush her hair. "Let's not stay long, Jules. All right?"

"As short as possible without being rude."

"Good. If you want to help, you can bring the clean suit from the closet."

I brought it and handed it to her. "I'll wait outside."

In a few minutes she came out, and we walked the short distance from her door to Guysin's. Each of us had dined with him before, but this was the first time we had been invited together. The door opened just as we arrived, and Randy's face appeared. With a flourish of his arms he made a small bow.

"Welcome to dinner."

"Hi," said Jessica. They kissed on the cheek and then he turned to me.

"Doctor." We shook hands.

"Your host awaits your presence."

"You are the caterer for this affair?"

"For all affairs." He lifted a hand to forestall a reply. "The menu is fixed, Doctor. I regret there are no choices."

"I have become accustomed to your cuisine, my friend. Except for the stew I find it quite adequate."

He looked at Jessica. "Is that a compliment?"

"I think it is."

He bowed again. "Rejoice then, for there is no stew. If you'll excuse me, my other patrons clamor for attention." He cupped an ear and with a feigned look of concentration leaned in the direction of the dining hall. "I must be off."

He left and we walked inside. Guysin was standing in the living room and looked up as we entered.

"Ah. Welcome."

We exchanged greetings and spent the next half hour in desultory intercourse. By that time each of us had finished a cup of brew. Guysin poured refills, then motioned us to the table. I was ravenous, and my participation in the conversation ebbed while I consumed what was before me.

The vichyssoise was excellent, and I felt cheated by a mere cupful. The algae was simple and to my taste, but the brisket was tough. Its sauce, however, was persuasive, and I guessed that Randy, knowing of the poor quality of the meat, had sought to conceal it. It was a valiant effort, and I promised myself to compliment him.

Neither Jessica nor Guysin ate as much as I, while they seemed to be drinking considerably more. As long as they stayed civil, I was not inclined to interfere. On the contrary, I felt that a brace of disinhibition might help to loosen the constraints of their relationship.

When the meal was almost finished, Guysin raised his cup. "A toast," he offered. "To my friends."

He took a long swallow, and after a moment Jessica did the same. I laid my fork on the table, a small piece of beef impaled on its tines, and lifted my cup to join them.

"And to our host," I added. "For this fine repast."

The three of us drank (Jessica belatedly), and I returned to my plate.

"To the Domers," I heard her say.

"To them," he answered, eyeing her over the cup. "And to pleasure."

"Mutual pleasure," she replied.

"Of course."

"Between equals."

"As you wish." He drank, and she matched him.

I felt the air between them thicken, and I raised my own cup. "To good health." They did not seem to hear.

"To good health," I repeated.

Guysin nodded and took a drink. Jessica watched him.

"Will you not toast to good health, Jessica?"

She began to reply, then looked at me. I held my cup aloft, and finally she touched it with her own.

"Health." She took a sip.

A silence ensued, which Guysin broke.

"May I speak frankly, Jessica?"

"If you can."

He smiled. "Let us put our swords aside for a moment, shall we?"

"Say what you have to say."

"I'm worried about you, Jessica. You're not happy here; you're at odds with the community."

"With you."

"You are wrong to see me as your adversary, but leave that for now. I am talking about the colony."

She played with her cup, swirling what was left of the liquor. A few drops spilled on the table.

"What happens if you succeed, Jessica? What happens then?"

"I will succeed," she said bluntly. "I almost have. It's just a matter of time."

"Then what? What happens to us? To Eridis? To your precious Domers? What happens to them?"

"I can't see the future, Guysin."

"I can. Do you want to hear? When Mutacillin can be made anywhere, this place becomes a liability. Too far and too expensive. Mannus closes down the operation, and we go home. Except that this is home for me. This is where I belong."

"I'm sorry."

"And what about the Domers? You despise me because I treat them like slaves. Better slaves than nothing. What do you suppose Mannus will do with them?"

"They have no right to do anything," she retorted. "They're not chattel. They're people. You don't seem to realize that."

"It doesn't matter what I realize. I don't own the planet. Mannus does. And they own the Domers."

"No," she said. "No one owns them. You could teach them that, Guysin. Give them new lessons. Tell them how the world really is."

"That would not save them, Jessica. Even if they could talk brilliantly of themselves, of life and death and slavery, they would not be spared. It would not be in Mannus's interest."

"Then make it in their interest. The Domers could mine the rock here, or we could find some other place where they could. They're strong, they can work much longer and harder than we can. Find a place where the gravity's less, and they'll live longer, too."

"It would be much easier to extinguish them. There's no reason to do anything else."

"They are a people, Guysin. They have the right to survive. Find a reason."

"Stop your work, Jessica. Leave things as they are."

She shook her head. "I can't."

"You must."

"Don't threaten me, Guysin. Don't ever threaten me."

"I am not the threat, Jessica. You are. If they die, if this ends, you are to blame."

Jessica put her palms on the table and leaned forward. Her face, like his, was red. Her voice was deadly.

"You are the architect of this place, Guysin Hoke. In every way you mean it to cater to you. What becomes of it lies on your head. On yours, not mine."

His face strained to keep calm. "You would change it. I would have it remain the same."

"There is no such thing," I interjected, but neither of them paid attention.

"Yes," Jessica said angrily. "And I know why."

Guysin stared at her, his eyes glimmering.

"Speak frankly, Guysin. Isn't that what you wanted?"

"What difference does the reason make? Those with different motives can still unite."

"I couldn't, Guysin. Not with you."

"You judge yourself different?" His face twisted with scorn. "Better?" He laughed. "You are too proud, Jessica. You are as human as I am."

"I would never try to dominate someone. Never work to mold them like putty."

He looked at me, then back to her.

"Jules knows," Jessica said.

"Of course. And about you? Does he know about you?"

I swallowed the last of the beef. "Yes. We have no secrets."

"And what is your judgment?" he asked. "Do you stand with her?"

Having been excluded for some time from the conversation, I leapt at the opportunity to speak. "Each of us has his addictions," I began, "which, except under extraordinary circumstances, we cannot alter. Nor in the main should we try, for they are a source of vitality and invention. Indeed, obsession has been responsible for great moments in art and humanity, not to mention medicine and other endeavors of science—"

"Get to the point," Jessica snapped.

"Yes. Please."

"Of course. It is this: there is a point beyond which an addict must not go. Regardless of intent, he must not foist himself upon another. If he harms himself, he has my pity, and I will offer my help. If he harms another, then he must be chastised."

Jessica nodded. Guysin smiled. "You have vindicated me," he said.

"Hardly!" she snarled. "You force yourself on her. You force her to have sex!"

"She likes it, Jessica. Just like Kylis Umbo. She asks me to come back."

"Kylis Umbo?" I muttered. "He is the one?" But I received no reply, for Jessica was locked with Guysin.

"Now? She asks you now?"

"Less now. But that's natural. She's more tired, she needs more rest."

"But you still force her." She slapped the table with her palms. "I know it! You still do!"

"Calm down," I said.

"I will not!" Her voice rose as she jumped from the chair. "He abuses her! All of us! He forces us to be slaves!"

"Jessica . . ."

"Don't touch me! It's too fast. Too many. It's him! Him!" She stumbled into the table, sending plates and utensils to the floor. Liquor spilled into my lap, and I kicked my chair back.

"Jessica . . . what's happening? Calm down." I went for her and she backed away, into a wall.

"No!" she cried. "Please! No!"

I grabbed her hands. "Jessica!"

Her stomach convulsed, and she vomited at my feet. Twice. Three times. I did not let go.

"No!" she cried. "No! Help me!" Her eyes flickered, then rolled back in their sockets. I pulled her toward me as she went limp.

"Call Martha," I said, lifting her in my arms. "Tell her to meet me at the clinic."

"She drank too much. She's not used to it."

"Call her. Now." I kicked a chair out of the way and went toward the door.

"Is she all right?"

"She's drunk. Call Martha." I left.

Martha met me with a gurney and emergency cart at the entrance to the clinic. I was panting and my arms were sore. I laid Jessica face up.

"It's not an emergency," I said. "She's breathing."

"Guysin said she drank too much."

"She did, but not that much. There's something else."

We wheeled her inside, down the corridor, through the waiting room and the hall beyond. At that hour the clinic was empty.

"I want her in the surgical suite, Martha."

"Right."

We slapped the foot of the gurney through the swinging doors and stopped it near the operating table. By that time Jessica had begun to show signs of consciousness; she was rolling her head from side to side and moaning.

"Jessica." I bent in front of her face. "Jessica."

Her lids opened but the eyes beneath wandered aimlessly. For a moment they seemed to focus; she began to mutter. I put my ear to her lips.

"What's she saying?" Martha came up with a plastic intravenous bag.

"It's unintelligible . . . Let's get some blood before we give her that."

She took a syringe with a large-gauge needle from her pocket, and I held Jessica's arm while she punctured the antecubital vein. Jessica did not flinch. Martha took the blood and apportioned it into a half-dozen tubes she held in the other hand. Then she inserted a small cannula into the other arm, hung the bag, and began to infuse the solution.

"I'll start running this stuff," Martha said. "You want everything, right?"

"Yes. Toxic screen too."

"She a user?"

"Just do it, okay? I don't know what she is." I studied her face. "I'm not even sure who . . ."

While Martha worked at the counter, I examined Jessica. Her mental status continued to fluctuate, but otherwise there was nothing remarkable. Her vital signs were stable; her heart, lungs, and belly normal. As the results came in, Martha called them to me.

"CBC okay. You want the breakdown?"

"No. Go ahead."

"Lytes: 138, 4.0, 24, 102. Glucose 125 . . ."

"She just ate."

"Right. LFTs, calcium, phosphate, creatinine . . . all normal. Some of this stuff is going to take a while, Jules."

"You in a hurry?"

"Don't be like that. I just thought you might want to sit down, instead of pacing all over the place."

"If I want to sit, I'll sit."

"It makes me nervous."

"Just do the tests, all right?"

She turned on her stool and faced me. "Don't take it out on me, Jules. You're upset. I understand. There's no reason to take it out on me."

I looked at her, then away. "I'm sorry . . ." I paced. "It's my fault, Martha."

"Don't be silly."

"It is. I should have seen it coming . . . I did, only I didn't do anything."

"This has happened before?"

"Not like this. Moments. I always thought it was something else . . . strain, preoccupation . . ."

"It could be, Jules. It happens."

"No. She's sick. I think she has Barea disease."

She frowned. "What makes you say that?"

"The way she's been acting. This isn't her, Martha. It's not."

"But why Barea disease? It could be anything."

"She was exposed. Probably more than once." I shook my head. "I shouldn't have waited so long. I should have thought of it earlier."

"Aren't you jumping the gun a little? We haven't gotten half the results back."

"It is. I'm sure."

"Even if you're right, it's not your fault. You can't blame yourself, Jules. That's your own advice."

"It's easier to give it," I said grimly. "Will you check to see if anything more is ready?"

Nothing was, and I reexamined Jessica. She seemed better, calmer. In a while she had begun to respond to my voice with gestures, then simple replies.

"No toxins," Martha called. "Alcohol 0.1 percent. Not very high."

"Who's that?" Jessica asked softly.

"Martha. We're in the clinic."

"Is something the matter? What happened?"

"You fainted. Do you remember?"

"Not really. I remember the dinner. Did I throw up?"

"On me," I said.

"I'm sorry." She managed a smile. "I guess I can't hold my liquor."

"I'd rather you did on me than anyone else."

"You're sweet."

"How do you feel?"

"My head hurts. It's spinning."

"Anything else?"

"Like what?"

"Voices? Hallucinations?"

She closed her eyes, then opened them. "Uh-uh. My stomach's sore."

"I don't doubt it."

"What's wrong, Jules? What happened?"

"I don't know. I want to do a test. I need your help."

"I feel so tired." She yawned. "Can't you do it later?"

"No. I want to do it now."

She looked at me. "You're worried, aren't you?"

I nodded.

"All right." She licked her lips. "Can I have something to drink first?"

I brought a cup of water, and Martha came to watch her while I fetched the binopticon. When I returned, the back of the gurney had been elevated and Jessica was propped up.

"She said she wanted to sit," Martha told me.

"Good. It's easier this way."

"What do I have to do, Jules?"

"There's a light inside. Two lights, one for each eye. All you have to do is look at them."

"Can I blink?"

"Yes. Just keep your forehead against the bar. Don't move away."

"Okay."

"You need me for anything?" Martha asked. She yawned. "I could use some sleep."

"Go ahead. What time is it anyway?"

"It's late. Or early. Not very long before the clinic opens."

"You want to close it today?"

She shrugged. "I'll be all right. How about you?"

"I'm not tired yet. Let's see how I feel."

"Everything's on automatic," she told me, then turned to Jessica. "No more fainting, all right? Not until I get back anyway."

"I promise. I'm in good hands."

Martha patted one of mine. "The best." She yawned again. "Call me if you need anything. Otherwise I'll see you at six."

She left, and I hoisted the instrument onto my shoulder. With one hand I braced it and with the other positioned it on Jessica's eyeballs. When she was comfortable, I switched on the beams of light. For several seconds they tracked in random circles, then, when they had warmed, aligned themselves with her optic nerves. I flicked a switch, and impulse generation began.

Some thirty minutes later I turned it off. I had scanned her occipital lobes three separate times; the punctate gaps on the screen had remained the same. They were concentrated in the cortical region, but not confined to it. Nowhere that I sent the probe were they entirely absent. There were lesions throughout her visual system; by inference, throughout her brain.

I took the instrument from her orbits and held it in a hand. I played with one of its levers, avoiding Jessica's face.

"Well?" she said.

"I'm not sure."

"You found something, didn't you?"

I nodded.

"What?"

"I wish we were on Earth."

"Tell me, Jules."

"You've got lesions all over your brain," I muttered. "Everywhere, Jessica."

She sucked in her breath. "What are they?"

"I'm not sure. I need help."

"Don't lie to me, Jules."

I sighed, then looked her in the face. "I think it's Barea disease."

She started to speak but the words caught in her throat. She tried again, and her voice trembled.

"You think, or you know?"

"I'm not that good with this thing. I could be wrong . . ."

"But you don't think you are, do you?"

I shook my head.

"Could you do a biopsy?"

"Of your brain?"

She nodded.

"No," I said flatly. "Never."

"But we need a diagnosis."

"We have one."

"You're not positive. I want to know for sure."

"The tissue doesn't regenerate. You know that."

"It doesn't have to be a lot. A few cells would be enough."

"I won't cut into your brain, Jessica. Not for three cells, not for one."

"I'm not afraid, Jules."

"It's not a question of fear."

"I trust you. Touch my mind. Take it." Smiling, she reached for my hand.

"Jessica . . ."

She gazed at me, her face the mask of an innocent child. Slowly, the truth, the folly of the situation dawned on me. That she had argued, begged even, for me to slice into her brain, to tamper with the very essence of her consciousness, meant that I could no longer trust her. Her mind had become addled. The burden of decision had fallen to me.

"Jessica. Listen to me. It is late; neither of us is thinking clearly. We need to rest. Can you rest?"

She held my hand. "With you beside me."

"In the morning we'll decide what to do. We'll think about it, and then we'll decide."

"Yes." She closed her eyes.

I stood there, aware suddenly that I was exhausted. I bent down, careful not to let go of her hand, and lay the binopticon on the floor. I gripped the edge of the gurney and wheeled it to the center of the room. I cranked up the head of the operating table, then kicked off my shoes. Still holding Jessica's hand, I climbed onto the table. The surface was hard, but it was a bed. I closed my eyes.

It took a long time to fall asleep. I could not get what I had seen through the binopticon out of my mind. Nor the frightening thought of entering Jessica's brain.

21. A Cage Is Better

Morning came too soon. I was in the trough of a troubling dream, translucent sacs falling upon me from the sky. They lay scattered about the twisted land I wandered, forcing me down unmarked paths. One sac fell dangerously close, landing on the ground with an audible slap. I woke, and the sound gradually faded.

"Jules."

I felt a hand on my shoulder and then a face came into view. It was Martha.

"You slept here."

I rubbed my eyes and wiped my mouth. "I would hesitate to call it that." Stiffly, I swung my legs over the side of the table. "Bad dreams. Too many."

She nodded sympathetically. "How's Jessica?"

I looked over; her chest rose and fell easily. The bag of fluid was almost empty.

"She's not good, Martha. Not good at all." I told her what I had found.

"Are you sure it's Barea disease?

"Surer than I would like to be."

"What are her chances? If it is, I mean."

"When I left Earth, they were reporting twenty to thirty percent mortality . . ."

"Maybe it's changed since then."

"It's probably worse. We were seeing just the tip of the iceberg."

"You don't know that, Jules. Maybe they've found something new. Maybe even a cure."

"The agent hadn't even been identified when I left."

"You've been gone a long time."

"I wish I were back."

"Why not send a transmission? Consult with someone there."

The thought had not occurred to me.

"There must be doctors on Earth who know more about this than you do. Who are better with the binopticon. Maybe you'll find out it's not as bad as you think."

"I don't want to lose her, Martha."

"You're not going to." She took my hand. "Why don't you get some rest?"

"I might have it too," I mumbled.

"What?"

"Nothing."

Martha cleared her throat. "I think Jessica should be quarantined, Jules. Until we find out for sure what she has."

"I hate to do that."

"She could be contagious."

I sighed, then nodded. "She can stay in my place; it's larger than hers."

"I'll get someone to watch her."

"Is that necessary?"

"Do you trust her the way she is?"

"Make it outside the door then. If she's going to be in a cage, at least she can have some privacy."

I pushed myself from the table and stretched. I felt weary beyond lack of sleep. "I'm going to clean up. Keep an eye on her, will you?"

She nodded and I dragged myself from the clinic. Sleep had bestowed neither vigor nor hope, and I was in a disagreeable frame of mind. My stomach growled as if in affirmation of my despair.

I returned to my quarters, where I bathed and changed into fresh clothing. The larder was empty, and I was forced to attend the refectory and its company of staff.

The place seemed brighter, perhaps because my eyes were so bleary. I kept my gaze to the floor. As I approached the counter, I commanded myself to be civil.

"A large portion of everything," I said to Oona.

"You look beat."

I nodded. "I've been up most of the night."

"Business or pleasure?" She grinned.

"Please, no jests."

"Is something the matter?"

"I'm hungry, that's what's the matter. And tired. Will you serve me so that I can eat?"

"Don't take it out on me." She slapped a hill of potatoes on the plate.

"I'm hungry."

"Yeah, and I'm feeding you."

She dropped some eggs on the potatoes and handed me the plate.

"Thanks," I said, but she had turned her back to me. I shrugged and slid my tray to the end of the counter, where I loaded it with biscuits, wedges of cheese, jellies, a hamlike substance and other breakfast items. I filled two cups with coffee, then carried the meal to an empty table at the periphery of the room.

I had hoped to dine in solitude; though troubled, I deemed my own company better than another's. Such was not to be. No sooner had the edge been taken from my hunger than he whom I had most hoped to avoid appeared at the table.

"Jules," he said. "May I join you?"

Two slices of the porcine substance were in my mouth and I took my time chewing them. When they had become all but liquid I swallowed, chasing them with a brace of coffee.

"I would invite you to do so," I said, squinting up, "except that I am in a hurry. I am here only because I must eat. I am in no mood to chat."

"I understand." His face looked drawn and his eyes were rimmed with red. His scalp, which was always smooth and polished, bristled with a narrow halo of dark hairs.

"How is Jessica?"

"Better."

"She is not used to so much liquor."

"No." I turned to the biscuits.

"Jules," he ventured, "I would not have this matter with Jessica come between our friendship."

"She is all at the moment that matters to me." I continued to eat.

"She is not a happy woman, Jules. She should not have come."

"Leave it! I know what she is and what she isn't." I dropped my fork to the table and stood. "You don't look so happy yourself, Guysin. Maybe you need a rest. Maybe all of us do." I strode off, leaving him staring. My tray, with the coffee steaming above it, was still half-full.

I went to make the transmission, then remembered that I could not do so without the binopticon. I fetched it from the clinic and on the way back composed in my mind the message. I had it ready when I entered the communications room, but I found Rollin slumped against the console. He stirred as I came close.

"Rollin?"

He sat up and rubbed his eyes. Across his forehead was a thick band of gel.

"Are you all right?"

He yawned and stretched. "Sleepy. I think I left it on too long."

He reached up and peeled it off. Beneath, his skin was red; there were several small blisters. "It's sore."

"You should not be allowed to use it here. What if a transmission comes?"

"Hardly ever does. It gets recorded anyway."

"What if it's an emergency?"

"Hasn't been one since I've been here."

I scowled. "I have a matter of some urgency to transmit. Are you competent to do so?"

"A Domer would be competent, Doc. Whad'ya got?"

I explained it to him. Despite appearances, he performed with the fluidity of a person experienced at his job. He hooked the binopticon directly to the console so that when he sent the information it did not replay on the screen, for which I was grateful. He coded my list of questions into a language that was as foreign to me as my patois probably was to him, sent it, and sat back.

"That's it."

"When shall I expect a response?"

"Whenever they get around to answering."

"There's no delay?"

"Not much. As long as everything's working."

"And is it?"

He shrugged. "Has been so far."

"Let us pray it continues. Please contact me when the response arrives. Be it day or night."

"Will do."

"Thank you."

I took the instrument and left, returning dyspeptically to the clinic. I was relieved to find no one in the waiting room and went back to the surgical suite. Jessica was awake; the tube was out of her arm. She was sitting up, her legs dangling from the edge of the gurney.

"Jules," she said. Martha looked up from across the room and came over.

"How do you feel?"

"Better. Hungry."

"No hangover?"

"Did I drink that much?"

"Not really."

"The rest of the results are normal," Martha told me.

I nodded.

"Then I'm okay?"

I looked at Martha. She shrugged.

"You don't remember?"

"What?"

"Last night? You don't remember last night?"

"What? Guysin? That we fought? I knew we would. I told you I didn't want to go."

"But after that. After the argument. What do you remember?"

"Getting drunk? I passed out, didn't I? I guess I can't hold my liquor . . ."

"And after that?"

She shrugged. "Waking up here. The tube in my arm. Martha over there. You must have thought I was pretty sick to bring me here."

"You are sick, Jessica. We talked about it last night."

"What, Jules?"

I studied her. She pulled on her lip.

"Don't look at me like that. I feel okay now. Just hungry." She began to climb from the gurney.

"Wait a minute." Both of us moved at once. "Where do you think you're going?"

"I need some clean clothes. It's time to go to work."

"No work today, Jessica. Rest."

"That's silly," she tittered. "What would Dr. Ebert say?"

"Dr. Ebert says rest," I said.

She looked at me sternly. "How would you know?"

"Jessica . . ."

She broke into laughter. "You're so serious. If you want me to rest, I'll rest. I can put off work for a day."

"No work until we know for sure what you have. It might be contagious."

"That's silly. I won't give anybody anything." Before I could stop her, she had reached over and grabbed my breast. "Or anything they don't want." She grinned.

"This is not a joke, Jessica." I took her hand from my chest. "You are ill. It might be contagious. I've sent a transmission to Earth, and we should get a reply soon. Until then, we've arranged for you to stay in my apartment."

"Stay there? What do you mean?"

"Until we know more, you need to be quarantined."

"That's ridiculous. I'm as healthy as you are."

"Evidence indicates otherwise."

"It's just a precaution," Martha said gently.

"What about my work? I need to be in the lab . . ."

"What you need now is rest."

"Whose idea was this? Guysin's?"

"He has nothing to do with it. The decision is strictly a medical one. A precaution."

"But my work, Jules. I'm so close—"

"It will keep. Your health is more important."

She looked at me and her eyes turned glassy. "Keep it," she said. "Will you? It's deep. A cage at least is better than none at all."

She brought my hand to her lips. "I'm tired." She kissed it. "I'll wait for you on the cloud."

She lay back and closed her eyes. I felt ready to weep.

"I'm afraid, Martha."

"She's exhausted. Give her time to rest. Something to eat. She'll perk up."

I held Jessica's hand in mine, then laid it in her lap. "Will you take her? I need some time to myself."

"Of course."

She secured the side rails and wheeled her from the room. The double doors slapped past one another, stilled. I felt painfully alone. The air in the room was stale and filled with Jessica's odor. Tears trickled down my cheeks. I bent over the surgical table, my head in my hands.

Don't cry, a voice said. And again. Don't cry. Work.

I blinked and cocked my head. I wiped my face.

Go ahead. Get to work.

I sighed, too tired to argue. I straightened my clothes, then followed the gurney's path to begin my day of service.

22. An Interesting Man

It was busy in the clinic; the line of Domers waiting to be treated seemed endless. No stall remained vacant for more than a few seconds; as soon as one patient left, another took his place. I thought of closing the doors but decided against it. Had I not been occupied with work I would have been preoccupied with worry, and after taking a brief break for lunch I returned to my toil.

The first stall I entered housed a Domer who complained of hazy vision. To the naked eye there was nothing of note, and I made the circumstantial (and routine) diagnosis of bilateral immature cataracts. She asked what I could do to help her.

"Nothing, I'm afraid."

"Will it get worse?"

"It will not improve. It may stabilize."

"What do you mean?"

"The fatter you are, the faster it will worsen. You are thinner now—"

"They feed us less."

"Yes. It's better for your vision. Your eyes won't get hazy as fast."

"I don't like to be hungry."

"I'm sorry."

"I'm afraid of stumbling in the mines. I can't see like before."

"Yes. I know. Is there anything else I can do? Do your knees hurt? Your hips?"

"Of course. Everything hurts."

"I can give you something for the pain. Would you like an injection?"

"Will it help my eyes?"

I shook my head. She chewed her lips with her gums.

"All right."

I left the booth and returned with a long-needled syringe.

"This will sting."

I drove it into her thigh and depressed the plunger. She winced but made no cry, and I withdrew the needle.

"You'll feel better soon. Come back if you need another." I held aside the curtain while she struggled to her feet. Her eyes were brimmed with tears as she came out of the stall. She hobbled off, and I dropped the syringe and needle into a tray full of others. I took a breath, exhaled, then turned to the next booth.

The Domer was sitting on the pallet, legs bent, his forehead resting on his knees. As I entered he looked up.

"You!" I exclaimed. "What are you doing here?"

"I need help."

"Do you?" I raised an eyebrow. "Why come to me?"

"You're a doctor. It's your job."

"Indeed. Pain is a powerful persuasive, isn't it, Umbo? What hurts? Your knees? Your hips?" The corners of my mouth curled involuntarily up. He grabbed my arm.

"I did not come for an injection, Jules."

"My name is Dr. Ebert. Let go of my arm." He dropped it.

"I came to talk."

"Did you? Why now?"

"I have questions—"

"Indeed. Why come to me? Why not someone else?"

"I was advised to."

"I am no longer so interested in you, Umbo. There are other more pressing matters on my mind."

"Jessica told me, Jules. She told me to come."

Her name from his lips was like a blow to my chest. It was only the night before that I had learned it was he with whom Jessica had breached my trust, and his physical presence now made me tremble.

"You presume to tell me of her?"

"She loves you," he said gently.

"That is not your affair."

"She told me you could help."

"Did she? And what else did she say?"

He looked at me guilelessly and shook his head.

"Innocence does not become you, Umbo. I am acquainted with her needs. I am aware of what happened before I arrived."

"She told you?"

"Of course."

He nodded. "I learned from her. About pleasure. And cycle. How we live and die and live and die." His voice was grim. "And about the world beyond."

"Is that what you tell the others? What you preach to them in the mines?"

"Until I am hoarse. A few listen; mostly because I'm a novelty. A distraction from the montony . . ."

"Yes. I've talked to them myself. They don't understand what I say. Or they can't."

"It's the teachers. They take our memories and replace them with their own."

"Yet you are somehow immune to their effect. How do you explain that?"

"I can't. Sandra-hoop is too. If only we could teach the others . . ."

"To what purpose?"

"We should not be treated as we are." He looked me in the eye. "We are not chattel, Jules."

I held his gaze, then shook my head sadly. "You are, Kylis Umbo. That is why you were created."

"Our minds are human. Our bodies are strong. There must be a way to keep them from falling apart so fast."

"Do you know what genes are?" I asked.

"Of course," he snapped. "I am not a fool."

"Indeed. Then you know that they make you what you are. To prevent your deterioration would require an alteration of your genetic matrix."

"What kind of alteration?"

"Making you smaller, for example. Less corpulent."

"No . . ." His voice trailed off. He rubbed his knee. "That would change who we are. Couldn't you give us stronger bones? A larger pancreas?"

"What do you know of the pancreas?"

"It controls the blood sugar. We are diabetics, aren't we? Isn't that why we get cataracts?"

"How do you know these things? You are a Domer."

He shrugged. "Couldn't you? Couldn't you change our pancreas just as easily as our size?"

"I don't know. I'm not an engineer. I imagine if it were possible it would have been done."

"Maybe they were in too much of a hurry. Maybe it wasn't profitable."

"I wouldn't know."

"Is it in our genes to be docile, too? To be submissive?"

"No," I said flatly.

"Are you sure? How do you know?"

"I am a physician," I said.

"But couldn't it be coded like anything else? Just because it isn't blue or gray doesn't mean behavior can't be defined. Isn't that right?"

"Why is it so important? For you it's a moot point."

"No," he said. "There are futures, and there are futures. We need to understand."

"Understanding is predicated on memory."

"Yes. And change requires conflict."

"Indeed."

He looked at me and a gleam came into his eyes. "Fat and slim, Jules."

"What?"

"Life and death."

I frowned, and suddenly a voice entered my mind. "Snow and dirt," I heard myself say. The words echoed, and my body transformed itself. I wanted to touch Kylis Umbo. I moved my hand.

"Jules?"

I halted.

"Jules?" The curtain opened and Martha looked in. "Are you all right?"

I stared, then nodded.

"You seemed gone a long time. Do you need help?"

"Help?"

"Jules? Are you okay?"

An image faded. A sensation. "I'm all right."

The one side of her forehead wrinkled. "Are you sure?"

"Yes. We were talking. For a moment I had a funny thought." I pressed my temples between my palms. "This is an interesting man, Martha. Kylis Umbo, meet Martha Higgins. Martha Higgins, Kylis Umbo."

He nodded but said nothing. Martha looked at me as though I were daft.

"You're exhausted, Jules. I'm going to close the clinic. Go back to your apartment and get some rest." She left.

"She doesn't seem to agree with you."

I shrugged. "She doesn't know you. She might feel differently if she did."

"Kind thoughts won't change our lives, Jules. Hers, or yours."

"I have to go now," I told him. "Is there something I can do for you before I leave?"

His face seemed to struggle briefly with itself, and then it softened into a smile. "Yes," he said and lay back on the pallet. He placed his arms limply upon the floor and closed his eyes. Slowly he spread his legs.

"What are doing?"

The posture was frighteningly familiar, and the voice . . . the voice was hers.

"Jules," he whispered, and my breath stopped. "Jules."

"No." I choked, backing away, terrified that he would say more. "No!"

Turning, reeling, I fled from the stall.

23. The Fall

Just as all of us have our phobias, hidden though they may be, there is for each of us a disease that we dread above all others. It is the challenge of medicine to uncover it, for the fear of its occurrence lies at the base of a hundred other complaints. I discovered mine in the days following that meeting with Kylis Umbo, and it filled me with dread.

I feared psychosis, Jerrold; at times I felt I had already succumbed. An unfamiliar presence seemed to hover about my every thought, infiltrating even the organs of my senses. What seemed large was also small; cool was warm, and soft, hard. I felt eyes within my eyes, and another tongue upon my own.

Bizarre impulses struck like currents of electricity, exciting me one moment, terrifying me the next. Sexual fantasies were prominent, masturbatory eccentricities, homosexuality and other forms of intimacy hitherto inimical to me. What I drove from my mind by force returned in some other guise. A scene in the shower, the face of a strange mother, the flowing of blood. I felt frozen in time, in worry and fright.

That this was no disease, that it was in fact the opposite I know now. But then, nothing was apparent.

I was fortunate to have my job. It provided a sense of order, a structure, at least, around which to assemble the days. It gave me that, but little more. The Domers were sickening at an alarming rate, and I attended to them with a rising sense of futility.

As a physician, those were the worst days of my career. I was preoccupied, which made the work burdensome, and helpless, which made it depressing. The ministrations—of medication and advice—that had once been a source of reward to me now became the instruments of duplicity and lie. While I tried to convince myself that I was not to blame, inside I believed otherwise. I felt at once the abuser and the abused.

I sought out Rollin several times a day. When I was not there, or at the clinic, I was with Jessica. She was less troubled than I—in truth, she was not troubled at all—and this disturbed me more than had she been raving.

On the fourth day of her quarantine we shared a breakfast that I had assembled in the kitchenette. It was modest fare, for my appetite of late had lessened. Hers, as always, was scant. I finished a bowl of porridge, wiping the sides with a wedge of apple, and embraced her.

"I'll be back at lunchtime," I told her, then departed.

Outside the door, sitting on a stool, was the girl Pook. Her attention was riveted to a small screen balanced on her knees, and she barely acknowledged me as I passed.

"You are the attendant today?"

"Um-hm."

Her presence did not overwhelm me with confidence.

"Are you still using gel?"

She mumbled a reply.

"Speak up, young lady."

"No, I said."

"Good. I'd like a word with you."

"Sssh! Damon's just about to kill himself."

"Pook . . ."

"Sssh!"

I reached down and flipped the power switch.

"Hey!" She looked up angrily. "What's the idea?"

"Just a question, and then I'll be gone."

"What?"

"Are there interludes between the climaxes? Moments, perhaps, a bit less compelling?"

"Huh?"

"I was wondering, Pook, if from time to time you might be able to tear yourself from the drama and see how Jessica is doing. That is the reason you are here."

The words seemed to penetrate. "You want me to go inside?" she asked.

"That would be nice, if she wants it."

"Isn't she contagious or something?"

"She's here for precaution. You won't get anything by just talking."

"Okay," she said. She played with the switch on the set. "Anything else?"

"I'll be in the clinic if you need me. I'll be back for lunch."

She nodded, and I turned to go, then stopped.

"Do you want him to die?" I asked.

"Huh? Who?"

"The one you said is going to kill himself."

She shrugged. "It doesn't really matter. He'll be back."

"Indeed."

"Yeah. He's died before. A bunch of times. They'll just give him a new heart, or brain, or whatever he needs. He'll be back."

"That simple, is it?"

"He's the star, Doctor. He can't really die."

"I suppose not. I wonder how he enjoys his immortality . . ."

"Huh?"

"Nothing. Enjoy your show. And don't forget Jessica."

I crossed the pavilion, feeling as I suppose a parent does when leaving his child with a sitter. One never knows for sure, and yet there is no choice but to trust. As I entered the corridor, a strange indolence took me. The present, so rife with hardship and worry, seemed to slow and spread out like a lake. The sharp arrows that for days had been rushing at me from all directions lost their momentum, came to a halt, drifted off into space. Haste seemed to end; I felt on the verge of a great premonition.

The feeling passed.

I neared the clinic, and from the other direction came a

Domer. He was limping severely, and I slowed my pace to allow him entry first. At the door he pressed the upper plate, then dragged himself inside. I followed.

The morning was dismal: I must have performed more than a hundred injections. By the time Martha closed the clinic for lunch, the muscles surrounding my thumb were weak and my hand trembled from fatigue. We walked down the corridor, parting at the passage that led to the communications room. Martha continued on, and I went to see Rollin. He looked up when I entered, then reached to the counter and held up a folder.

"Hot off the press, Doc."

"Their reply?"

He nodded, and I grabbed it from his hand, riffling through the pages. I found a chair and sat down.

"You going to read it here?"

"Do you have some objection?"

"I was on my way to lunch."

"You do not have to stay on my account."

He smiled. "I was hoping you'd say that."

"There is the possibility I may want to respond."

"I'll be back in an hour or so."

"Good." I turned to the folder.

"So long. Good luck."

I muttered some reply and began to read.

It would be redundant to describe each and every particular of the report I received; by now the information is common knowledge. In brief, it stated the following:

The patient you describe and the results you have transmitted raise a number of possible diagnoses. [It went into several of these, systematically excluding each.] . . . The most likely, then, is the Herpetic Anamnesiac Syndrome, or HAS. This nomenclature has superseded Barea disease and other less precise designations. Its pathogenesis has been described adequately only in the past year or two.

The disease is caused by a virus, one remarkably similar to the herpes viruses of the past. The virion consists of an internal core of double-stranded DNA, a stable icosahedral capsid, and a surrounding membranous envelope. Its shape, weight, and immunologic characteristics mark it a member of the herpes group, but it is distinct from the zoster or simplex particles that in the past afflicted mankind. It is a new agent, at least new to man, and has garnered the name herpesvirus hominis schizis, or HVHS. It is responsible for the HAS.

Infection with HVHS is primarily a venereal disease. The virus readily crosses mucosal surfaces, with an infection rate upwards of ninety percent. The initial lesion is most often a clump of tiny vesicles, which rupture in a matter of days. Sometime between a week and a year later the virus completes its cycle, and the vesicles recur. This is the stage of contagiousness, and for reasons as yet unknown, it spans a period of months before to months after the reappearance of these lesions.

The primary infection often passes unnoticed, though usually the vesicles are sore until they rupture. An inconstant number of patients experience an evanescent rash in the following weeks. It is self-limited and requires no treatment.

Weeks, months, in some cases more than a year elapse without further signs of disease. The virus resides, as its predecessors were known to do, in the neural roots and ganglia. During this period it is engaged in active replication, and when a certain critical mass of particles has been produced, it begins to ascend the dorsal columns of the spinal cord. Eventually it reaches the rudimentary portions of the brain, and from there disseminates throughout that structure. The virus concentrates in the cortical regions but spares no part. At this point, or soon thereafter, the anamnesiac syndrome begins.

The syndrome is, in actuality, a misnomer, for what occurs is not truly anamnesia. It appeared so to the early investigators, who believed that the personality changes were disinhibited behavior, the acting out, as it were, of forgotten or repressed personality traits. We understand now that this is not the case, but HAS remains entrenched in both lay and medical literature.

Once inside the neural cell HVHS acts as any virus, invading the nucleus. But instead of commandeering the nuclear DNA to reproduce more virus, it simply insinuates itself among the strands. No new virions are produced at first (later in the cycle they are, and travel in a retrograde fashion to the point of initial exposure), but slowly the neural cells are altered. Extremely subtle changes in anatomy and, later, electrical potential take place. Soon, the major clinical manifestations of the disease emerge.

What initially was thought to be a kind of schizophrenia, with delusional behavior and disturbances of affect, has been identified as something else entirely. The mind of the patient remains intact, and into it, as though by graft, is introduced the mind of another. Another's thoughts, experiences, memories: these are somehow transmitted by the virus. How it does so is the subject of debate: the plethora of proposed mechanisms is evidence of our continued ignorance.

The manifestations of the HAS are protean, varying from mild and infrequent bouts of emotional lability to severe, psychotic-like reactions. Many seem hardly aware that they are infected, while others, for reasons that are obscure, are not only aware of the presence of another mind but able to tolerate it with equanimity. The majority of these never come to the attention of a physician. Those who do, estimated at twenty to thirty percent of the total infected, have the poorest prognosis. Decline is predictable, though in some is protracted. Mortality is extremely high, often by self-inflicted means. Fortunately, our efforts at control of the virus and, lately, at eradication have been more successful than our understanding of its mechanisms of action.

Initially, Mutacillin was tried, before we knew the illness to be of viral origin. It, of course, had no effect. Recently, however, a drug has been developed (Binaricide, by MSD) that detaches the viral genomes from the native DNA and destroys them. It is extraordinarily effective, with a response rate upwards of ninety percent. Loss of the dual personality occurs in three to four months. Those who do not undergo a cure experience at

least a reduction in the mental interference. Side effects of the
drug are mild, and it is currently the treatment of choice.

A more important breakthrough has been in the field of
public health policy and enforcement. The NHD has issued
recommendations, the most notable of which is the mandatory
dosing of all groups suspected of harboring the virus. Both the
judicial and legislative branches of the government have come
out in support of these guidelines, and recently they have gone
further. It is now law that all patients with known disease, as
well as those in high risk groups, receive Binaricide. These
individuals will soon be required to carry proof of treatment.
Enforcement will be strict and penalties, severe. Further, the
NHD is currently discussing a proposal whereby the entire
population, as a prophylactic measure, will be required to receive treatment. With this on the horizon we hope to have the
disease eradicated in a matter of years. . . .

[The report elucidated its findings and predictions with various graphs and tables of clinical and epidemiological data, then
continued:]

In conclusion, we believe your patient to be infected with
this new and toxic strain of virus. If her clinical condition and
course bear this out, you should obtain Binaricide immediately. This, we remind you, is required by law. Additionally,
it might at the same time be prudent to treat the entire
Eridian colony. . . .

The report continued for another paragraph with references
and bibliography, then ended. I re-read the section on treatment and the high rate of cure. For the first time in days I felt
something other than hopelessness.

I wanted to request the drug immediately, and cursed Rollin
his lengthy lunch break. I paced the room, finally becoming too
impatient to wait. Bursting with excitement, I rushed out to tell
Jessica the news.

Pook was seated where I had left her, slumped over the
screen on her knees. As I approached she seemed to startle.

"Hi," she said sleepily, sitting up and rubbing her eyes.

"Have you been napping, young lady?"

She yawned. "I went inside and we talked for a while, and then she got a call. After that she said she wanted to take a nap so I came back here."

"Who was it that called?"

"I don't know." She yawned again. "I guess I fell asleep, too."

"You were supposed to be vigilant," I chided.

"It's boring sitting here."

"I suppose it is." I managed a smile. "Hopefully we won't have to do it much longer. There's a cure, Pook."

"That's nice," she said. "Can I go now?"

"Of course. Thank you for your help."

She nodded, then put the screen under her arm and ambled off. I pressed the buzzer and when there was no response palmed the door and went inside.

"Jessica?" I called. There was no reply. I looked in the living room, then climbed a few rungs of the ladder to check the bed.

"Jessica?" I said louder. I searched the kitchen and bathroom. She was not there and I shouted once more, then rushed from the apartment. With frightening and absolute clarity I knew where she had gone. I prayed that she had been intercepted by staff; at the least, that she had thought enough to wear a suit.

Midway down the corridor I stopped to catch my breath, and then again somewhat further. Pools of sweat had formed beneath my breasts; my chest heaved. At the entrance to the mines I halted again, panting and dizzy. I had no suit, but there was no time. I planned to enter without one.

I took a step, then stopped when I saw a Domer coming up the tunnel. It was Kylis Umbo, and in his arms he carried a body. My throat tightened.

"We found her at the bottom of the sixties shaft," he said grimly.

She was limp, and her skin was dusky. I touched her and she was cold.

"Put her down," I choked.

"Here?"

"Yes. Put her down."

He laid her on the floor of the corridor, and I bent over her. Her head was twisted unnaturally to one side; she was wearing a thin bedroom garment. Without hope I felt for a pulse. I watched for a breath. I lifted the lids of her eyes and saw the deep and fixed black of her pupils.

"She's dead." My life seemed to clot in my chest.

"Help her, Jules. You're a doctor. Bring her back."

"She's dead!" I cried. "Look at her. Look!"

I knelt beside her and wept.

Sometime later, sobbing still, I looked up. A small group of staff had gathered about. All were from the mines, save one.

"You!" I cried. "Are you happy now? Are you satisfied?"

"Why do you say that?" His face was troubled. "We had our differences, but we were friends."

"You called her, Guysin. You told her to come, knowing she was sick. You killed her!"

"Don't be ridiculous."

"Why are you here then? You were in the mines!"

"I visit them frequently. I was told that she fell."

"Fell? Or was pushed?"

"You're distraught, my friend." He shook his head sadly. "We all are. Perhaps this is a time for you to be alone."

He turned and began to walk away.

"I won't forget this!" I screamed after him. "I won't! I won't!"

Some of the others offered condolences, but I scarcely noticed. When the last had gone, I buried my face in my hands and wept.

Minutes later, or hours, I stopped. My grief was not spent but my body's strength was drained. With an effort I managed to get to my feet, and discovered that I was not alone. Kylis Umbo was behind me, standing quietly. I heaved a sigh and turned to him.

"Was it truly Guysin Hoke?" he asked.

"Truly? I do not know. He had a reason. And grief longs for a target . . . Help me now, my friend. There is a task I must do."

"What task?"

"Carry her to the clinic for me."

He lifted her easily, and I led him to the clinic's door. I went for the gurney, and he placed her upon it.

"I must leave you now," I told him. "You cannot fit where I am going."

"I should return to the mines."

"Why not wait? Rest in one of the booths." After a moment's thought he agreed.

"After all," I said, "We have much to discuss." The words surprised me. He nodded.

"Will you be long?"

"I suspect so. I have need of a skill that for years has lain dormant. And love, too, might make me linger."

I turned away, wheeling the gurney down the curved hall, through the waiting room and examining area, past the swinging doors into the surgical suite. I turned on the room's lights, and when I had acclimated to their brightness, pushed the body beside the operating table. I walked to the opposite side and leaned over. With one hand on the thigh and the other on the shoulder, I pulled it onto the table.

I brought over a large instrument stand, making certain there were a sufficient number of trays and jars of fixative. I then gowned myself and snapped on a pair of plastic gloves. I turned on the operating lights above the table, adjusted them, then reached into the pack of instruments for forceps and scalpel. With them in my hands and the body of the woman I loved before my eyes, I began the dissection.

24. The Act of Seeing with One's Own Eyes

I do not intend to recount the specifics of my approach; you probably have a notion of what it entailed. Much of the examination was improvised, a fact that I hope will temper such criticism as those of you with more expertise might want to exact.

The first cuts of the knife, to the thorax and abdominal wall, were the most difficult. They were the most painful. It was a corpse, to be sure, but it had not ceased entirely to resemble she whom I had loved. To puncture its flesh, that part which we regard, however wrongly, as the envelope of our being, was to commit a defilement. The care with which I slid the blade along the skin consoled me little. I felt lightheaded, and grabbed onto her nearest thigh to steady myself. The moment passed, and I returned to the dissection.

Once beneath the flesh it became easier. Some of the organs were still warm; not all felt as dead as the body itself. I touched them, marveling at their beauty, removing those I thought to examine further. Liver, kidneys, pancreas: they seemed to glow in my hands, and I imagined briefly incorporating them somehow into my own body. Each organ I touched seemed familiar, and the familiarity grew as the body became more exposed to my senses. The smell was rich and strangely full of life. The textures were soft and pliant. I stifled an urge to thrust my face into the abdominal cavity.

None of the organs seemed seriously diseased or injured. The heart was small and appeared healthy. Near it one of the great vessels had a small rent in its wall, caused probably by the force of the fall. I severed the heart's attachments and removed it for further study. Holding it in my hands I began to weep, for my empathy seemed to have grown such that I felt it were my own I was cradling in my palms. It was a painful moment, but tender, too. With trepidation I moved to the head.

I had planned to incise the thick skin of the scalp as quickly as possible, and to cut through the bones of the skull to the brain. I had hoped to avoid the face, where memories seem to linger longest. I found, however, that I could not, and I paused to gaze at the mask of death.

The lids were down, cloaking eyes I did not wish to see. The nose was as before, more prominent even, as the plain of the face beneath it drew away in rigor. The lips were drawn, thin and taut as they had never been in life. I outlined them with a finger, and the mounds of the cheeks. They felt artificial, rigid, as though they had been sprayed with a coat of some fixative. I removed a glove and touched the skin again. It was the same, only colder.

Of the various faces in my mind this was none. It was not a face at all, hardly a mask. It was the dead part of a fire, the ashes, and as that realization grew in me, and the inkling of where the flame still burned, I smiled. It was not an expression of joy, but neither was it one of despair. It was a moment of insight, akin, perhaps, to when man first sparked a fire, or thought upon himself the universe and discovered infinity.

I replaced the glove and felt for the occipital notch, where I began the long circumferential incision of the scalp. The head was twisted far to one side, but it did not impede my progress. I grasped it in the crook of an arm, using the incision I had made with the blade as a guide for the saw. The skull was thick, and it took an effort to detach it. Finally I succeeded, and held the bony dome in my hand. Glistening beneath the bright lights lay the brain.

If the flesh evokes feelings of intimacy, and the face, fondness and familiarity, then the brain educes mystery and reverence. I gazed at it, wondering what still existed there. I pondered how thought, dream, imagination, which seem so different, so utterly opposite to the gray matter from which they derive, can be so bound to it that they vanish when it dies. Might they not still exist, but in some other, inexpressible form? How do molecules, animate only in the spin of their atoms and the forces that bind them, contrive to produce matter that thinks? At what point does consciousness begin? How many cells must be linked together? If a million, why not a thousand? Why not a hundred? Ten? One? If one cell has consciousness, why not a part of one? Why not an atom? An electron? Does energy itself, in some way we will never comprehend, think? Does it have motive? Volition?

Even as these thoughts occurred to me, my fingers were fondling this last and most precious organ. In medical terms it held no life, but touching it, I felt charged with vitality. I severed the stem and lifted the brain from its cavity. I felt a great wash of empathy and knew, even were the tissue to fall apart in my hands, I could do it no harm.

I placed it gently on the table beside me and bent one last time to the body. Beneath the foramen magnum I found the cause of death. The first cervical vertebra, the atlas, had fractured in the fall, severing the spinal cord at its highest point. Death, I suspected, had been instantaneous.

There was nothing more of the body that interested me, and I turned from it to the table beside me. Except for the brain, the organs sat in trays and jars of fixative. I had done this as a matter of course, in case the need arose to study them in more detail. I knew this would not be necessary, but my habits, even during that trying and stressful time, were meticulous. I placed the brain in a dry tray, then carried it across the room.

At the microtome I began the final task. With the broad dissecting blade I made a series of coronal cuts, examining each section for evidence of pathology. To the naked eye there was none. I took a single section and placed it on the microtome; in a matter of minutes I had a dozen microscopically thin slices of tissue. I stained a few as best I could and, when they had dried, took one to the microscope.

It took no time to discover the pathology: the brain swarmed with particles. Dark dots they were, surrounded by a thin halo of transparency. The tiny, invisible virus I knew to be at their core. I thought of the visit I had had with the coroner and the slides he had shown. I remembered the holograph.

I leaned away from the microscope and rubbed my eyes, then bent again to the long tubes. The particles were everywhere, but the cells were undamaged, as though the one lay in symbiosis with the other. I gazed at the lovely web of her tissue, and then by some trick of the eye it transformed itself. The cell bodies, the axons and dendrites became a terrain, a land of gentle hills and streams and forests; the haloed particles were its inhabitants. I imagined that I was among them, a symbiont with the land. I to it, it to me. A world was there, or a blueprint for one.

Jessica, I whispered, I have no desire for fear. I am a physician, I must guide. Physikos. I must see what nature would have. Phyein. I must help to bring it forth.

I removed my gloves and gown, and turned from the room. The gutted body had surrendered its mysteries, and I wanted nothing further to do with it. My mind held something potent, and I went to find Kylis Umbo. In the hall outside the waiting room I met Martha.

"Jules," she said, embracing me. "I came as soon as I heard."

"There's nothing left to do."

Tears streaked her left cheek. "It's awful."

"She died instantly, I think. At least she didn't suffer."

"They leave that for us."

"Yes." I heaved a sigh. "I did an autopsy . . ."

Her eyes widened.

"I had to, Martha."

"I would have done it, Jules. We could have waited."

"No. I wanted to. I needed to."

She stared at me, trying to comprehend. "She died from the fall?"

"Yes. It broke her neck. Severed the cord."

She nodded solemnly. "I closed the clinic, Jules. Indefinitely."

"Yes. The body . . ." The word choked me unexpectedly. "I left it, Martha."

"I'll take care of it." She took my hand. "Is there anything special you want me to do? With the body, or anything?"

I shook my head. "It's no longer Jessica to me. Do what you want."

"Why don't you take a break, Jules? You could use a rest."

"Yes."

"When you're ready for company, let me know."

"Yes. Thank you." We embraced again, then I left her and went to the Domers' treatment area.

"Kylis Umbo," I called softly. In a moment he emerged from behind a curtain.

"Jules," he began, but before he could continue, I took hold of him. My arms made barely a half-circle around his waist, yet it was enough. I thrust my face into the folds of his belly and kissed the soft flesh.

"Kylis Umbo," I said, drawing back for air. "Shall we talk?"

"All of us," he replied with a grin.

I told him of the virus and HAS, and then of my vision. He listened thoughtfully, and when I had finished, pulled on his lip the way Jessica sometimes did.

"I have the germ of an idea," he said slowly. "I need to think it through."

"Yes. I need time, too. Despite this new mind a part of it must grieve."

"I am not dead, Jules."

"No. But I still have an office to uphold. Now, perhaps more than ever, we must consider the ramifications of what we do."

He nodded. "I will talk to Sandra-hoop . . ."

"Yes." I began to weep. "You see? My emotions overcome me."

"You cry for yourself."

"I need to rest, Kylis Umbo. I must go."

He hoisted me up and hugged me to his chest. If the weight of my body taxed him, it did not show. In a moment he let me down and lumbered across the room to the door. Palming the plate, he left the clinic.

25. What Nature Would Have

Even as before we argued.

> It's not like that.
> How, then?
> Caterpillar—cocoon—butterfly—cocoon—
> What next?
> I don't know. The next step.
> This is a disease.
> No. A symphony.
> It kills . . .
> Links.
> Thirty percent dead. You yourself . . .
> Am here. Alive.
> In me. Only in me.
> No. It is you who are alive in me . . .

Not long thereafter I met again with Kylis Umbo. He had spoken with Sandra-hoop and carried with him her proxy. After a lengthy discussion we came to an accord, though not without misgivings on my part. It seemed that what we planned might merely substitute one mind for another.

"If you knew the teacher," he told me, "you would not say so. It is no mind, or none that deserves to guide us."

"Still, it frightens me. I am not without corruption. Perhaps we will end up replacing one kind of slavery with another."

"No, Jules. There will be no replacements. Only additions. We will have three minds, four. And later . . . who knows how many later?"

I recognized who was speaking; she was right. We agreed to take one step at a time. Before we began the first, however, an event of some moment transpired.

After Jessica's demise I had found myself spending long stretches of time in the observation room above the domeroom. That locale, of all on Eridis, seemed most able to soothe my mind and clarify my thoughts. I was there one evening near suppertime when I saw the small figure of a man cross the floor below. It was Guysin, and as I watched further, it became apparent that he had come to tryst with Sandra-hoop.

He reached the head of her aisle and, after glancing about, hurried to her cubicle. She seemed to be waiting for him. They touched, and in a short while she lay down. At first Guysin seemed tentative, but soon his mood changed. He climbed upon her belly, grabbing folds of her flesh with his hands and thrusting his face between them. He seemed in the throes of some fever, and for a while Sandra-hoop let him play. Then she guided him down into the crevasse between her legs.

Several minutes passed. From time to time I glimpsed the tip of his buttocks above her upsloping thighs. Sandra-hoop began to heave; her body trembled. The pace of her movements quickened, and then a spasm shot through her. Her legs, which were spread apart, suddenly clapped together. There may have been a muffled cry: from the room I could not be certain. The moment passed.

She lay back, panting, and spread her legs. Between them lay Guysin Hoke's crumpled body. She stood and lifted him in her arms, then carried him down the aisle and across the empty domeroom floor. Below my window they disappeared from sight.

Later, I heard that Guysin had been found at the bottom of the sixties shaft. His suitless body was frozen by the time it was discovered. Apparently he had fallen.

His departure affected me variously. Though I never counted him friend, neither was he foe. That he may have been responsible for Jessica's death remained a canker; it was tempered, however, by realizing the extent of her disease. The virus occupied her ubiquitously; even had I the drug, I do not in my heart believe she would have survived. The fall, in truth, may have been caused by the germ, not the man.

It saddened me, in all honesty, to have him die. I felt, too, a sting of conscience. But stronger than all was compassion: It was obsession that ultimately killed Guysin Hoke, and passion. To neither of these have I ever been a stranger. In a different time, perhaps a different world, he might have been me.

The period following his misfortune was not an opportune one to initiate our scheme, but there was little choice. Festival was rapidly approaching, and we had need of haste. I was determined to proceed, and at the same time was full of fear. Had it not been for Jessica I might have faltered.

She reminded me that the first step was not a task but a pleasure, that the Domers were opulent and beautiful.

You are the fruit of a new seed, she told me. The seed of a new fruit. Be brave.

My flesh quivered; my penis stirred.

She laughed, I blushed, and we began.

For weeks we rutted about the domeroom, Kylis Umbo, Sandra-hoop and I, attempting to infect as many of their folk as we could. I had hoped that the Domers, once told of our purpose, would be amenable, even enthusiastic, but such was not the case. To my most fervent exhortations they reacted with a maddening lassitude. Most were in such a state of discomfort that they did not want to be bothered, and in many cases we were obliged to force ourselves upon them. Bewildered though they were, they accepted the act with a certain equanimity, at least they did so with me. They still regarded me as their doctor, and I was not timid in using the power inherent in that role. After failing on several occasions to persuade with words, I simply prescribed the sexual act as treatment for their ills. I was careful to be garbed always in my white coat, for in this guise (dingy and spotted though the coat became) none had the temerity to refuse me.

Sandra-hoop and Kylis Umbo had more difficulty than I, for they were regarded with the suspicion that is common toward deviates. The unenlightened Domers were resistant, and for this reason the two of them preferred to work as a team. When it became necessary, one sat upon the chest of the uninitiated while the other did what was necessary to assure adequate contact. In general, they did not have to resort to such a rapacious method, for most of the Domers were too weak to mount an effective defense.

We had no way of knowing which of us was contagious, or to what degree, and it was this uncertainty that forced us into the ambitious program upon which we embarked. Within a month's time we managed to expose virtually the entire Domer population. Most of the burden fell to me, for Kylis Umbo and Sandra-hoop had to continue to work in the mines. Nor were they in the best of health.

I, on the other hand, felt healthier than ever. Augmented by Jessica's presence, my energies seemed to blossom. In an awesome display of sexual vigor I mounted Domer after Domer, urging my erectile member into contact with as much flesh as possible. It was a challenge from which I could not willfully release myself, and each day of venery ended only when I became too exhausted to continue.

The month flew by rapidly, and by some stroke of fortune none of us was ever caught in our acts. Had the two Domers been apprehended I am not sure what would have happened. Probably nothing, for cycle was near to ending and punishment would have been more trouble than it was worth. As regards myself, I was careful to carry my bag of medicinals whenever I entered the domeroom; had I been questioned, I would have fabricated some esoteric treatment to explain my actions. Or perhaps I would have said nothing, relying on the authority of my position to silence inquiry.

One morning I was recuperating from a particularly strenuous session, when Jeen appeared at the door to my apartment. Her buzzing awakened me from a deep and dreamless slumber, and I stumbled down the ladder, grabbing a robe on the way to the door. On seeing me, her face registered surprise, and she quickly turned away. I frowned, self-consciously hugging the edges of the robe tighter about my sides. It was then I realized that I had inadvertently taken Jessica's and that it fit me no better than a tatter, concealing nothing.

"Excuse me," I said, more confused than apologetic, and retreated from the doorway. I returned some moments later with my own garment tied securely about my waist.

"I didn't expect to find you sleeping," she said.

"Grief . . ." I muttered. "Sleep is a respite."

"May I come in?"

I stepped back and motioned her toward the living room.

"I sent Mannus your reports. They accepted the deaths as accidents." She gave me a look. "They appointed me interim Manager."

"Congratulations."

"They're not in order," she snorted. "I'd rather not have the job."

"Guysin Hoke's a hard man to replace."

"Sure he is." She leaned against a wall. "This place could be run by anyone, Jules."

"Then what does it matter whether or not you're Manager?"

"Something funny's going on. Two deaths within a week. And the Domers seem different. Restless . . ."

"Maybe Guysin's death upset them."

"Maybe. I told Mannus I wanted to move up Festival."

"Oh?" My voice was sharper than I would have liked.

"Does that bother you?"

I manufactured a yawn and shook my head.

"We're having it in four weeks. Get this cycle over with and start fresh."

"I see."

"It'll be easier for you. You won't have to doctor them much more."

"I suppose not."

"You don't sound very happy."

"Festival means returning to Earth. Looking for another job."

She glanced at me. "I would have thought the sooner for you the better."

I shrugged. "I've grown accustomed to this place."

"How you've changed," she said. "When we first met, you despised it here. Now you don't want to leave."

"Is there anything else you wanted to tell me, Jeen? If not, I'd like to be alone."

She eyed me. "Jessica's dead, Jules. You can't bring her back."

I nodded gravely, relieved to have turned her attention to my sorrow.

"Grieve for her," she said, "but don't let it consume you. Don't let her memory replace your own."

I forced myself to be calm, escorting her out before allowing my anxiety to surface. She had spoken as if she knew, or at least suspected, what was in my mind. Perhaps, I thought, she was one of us. Perhaps a foe.

I wasted little time after that, resting only when it became impossible to continue. Every possible hour I spent in the domeroom, if not mounting an unexposed Domer, then speaking to one I already had. I was searching for a word, a gesture that recalled to me either myself or Jessica. Some sign to show that the virus was taking hold, that the transformation was beginning.

Slowly it began to happen. The emergence of a new race of Domers. We identified them at first in the mines, where Kylis Umbo and Sandra-hoop preached without end. More listened to them, and more began to understand. A following developed, albeit a tentative one. The penetrance of our minds had yet to grow strong.

We did not have the luxury of patience. If Festival began before our plan was set in motion, we could be robbed of the freedom that seemed now within our grasp. If all the Domers died in the bath and the virus itself did not survive, then I alone would be left. One man to infect an entire colony. I might not be able. I might be caught. At the time I did not even know if I would survive.

A week before Festival was planned, we called an assembly in the domeroom. It seemed premature, but we had no choice. It was the dinner hour, and staff was eating. Sandra-hoop, Kylis Umbo, and perhaps two dozen Domers had already gathered in the area in front of Service when I arrived.

Conversation halted, and all eyes turned in my direction. Several Domers came up and fondled me, as though I were some rare and magical fabric. For some moments I allowed it, and then I brushed their hands away.

"Please continue," I said. "I did not mean to interrupt."

The Domer who had been speaking resumed. His voice was angry. "What if these new thoughts are just another kind of teacher? Something to confuse us?"

"What teacher would tell us of another world?" replied a Domer next to him. "A whole different way of life . . ."

"I don't believe there is. I think it's a trick."

"It doesn't make sense," said another. "It makes me mad . . ."

"Me too. We're being used. We're nothing to them."

"I'm ashamed at what we put up with," one of them confessed. "Ashamed of ourselves . . ."

"Don't be," I said.

"No? Why not?"

"You're beautiful."

"We're ugly. Our bodies are weak. Fat, sick—"

"No," said Sandra-hoop. "We're strong. Beautiful. The others fear us."

"I do too," said one. "I fear what we might do."

"I fear Mannus. But I hate them more." There was a murmur of assent.

"Kill them," someone hissed. "Kill, kill, kill . . ." A few others took up the chant.

"It won't help," I said.

"Kill them! They kill us. Over and over . . ."

"They kill us forever. With pleasure."

"I just can't believe it," said one. "Festival is . . . it's Festival. It's our reward."

"It's our shame," said Kylis Umbo. "It's their victory."

"They're stronger than us. They're brutal . . ."

"We're stronger!" one of them crowed. "They think we're robots, weak and beneath notice. We're not robots. We have minds—"

"And we make their precious drug!"

"It makes me want to cry," said another. "To think how we suffer. To know their plan . . ."

"To know there are other places besides this. Other worlds. That we live and die without ever seeing a sun, or a sky."

"I like it here," one said proudly. "I like the cold. And the mines. If only we didn't get so sick . . ."

"I always thought that we deserved to be sick. Just like staff deserves to be staff."

"Yeah. And Mannus deserves the drug."

"Freedom is better than slavery," Kylis Umbo said. "I've been saying it for years."

"But the teacher," replied another, a puzzled expression on her face. "The teacher is freedom. Duty and obedience . . ."

"Our pleasures?" A few of them laughed. "And perpetual death our reward?"

"It's perpetual life, too."

"Mindless life. Perpetual servitude."

"It can be changed," I said. "All of you know that it's possible."

"Changed to what?" one asked.

"A better life," I replied.

"More food," chimed another.

"Less work," several said at once. The crowd murmured.

"Contact with the outside world," added Sandra-hoop. "Maybe even a new place to live."

"The fifth pleasure." There were many nods.

"Mannus can research new genetic designs," I told them. "Ones that would obviate your suffering. Lighter bones, for example. Stronger joints that resist the arthritis."

"We will demand control over our lives," said Sandra-hoop. "Only Domers will be allowed in the mines. The others can visit us in the domeroom, but only at arranged times. Otherwise, only by invitation."

"It is not enough," one of them argued. "A little freedom is worse than none at all. We should demand complete autonomy . . ."

"Yes," agreed another. "Independence."

Kylis Umbo shook his head. "It cannot be. We rely on staff for too much. Our food, the disposal of our waste, the processing of the fungus. Later we will be our own masters, but in the beginning we must be willing to accept less."

"If we ask too much," said one in a worried voice, "Mannus might decide to give nothing. They might decide to abandon us completely."

"Asking anything will be asking too much," I pointed out. "But they will have no choice."

"Our lives mean nothing to them. We are worth less than the rock of this planet."

"That will change," I said, "when we plant the bombs. When we blow up one of the caves."

"They may just wait until we blow ourselves up."

"No," I replied. "They won't wait. Each explosion will make them take us a little more seriously. A troublesome situation will become an urgent one. And then a crisis."

"I'm afraid of dying . . ." one said softly.

"We won't," said Sandra-hoop. "We'll live on, just like before. Only this time we'll be reborn with our minds intact."

"We're not sure of that," someone said. "What if the virus doesn't survive Festival?"

"That's why we have to wait," Kylis Umbo explained. "No matter how tired we get, how hungry or sick, we can't give up. We have have to wait until we know if the virus survives."

"And who will volunteer?" one asked. "Knowing what we know, who will volunteer to walk through the door to their death?"

There was a silence, as the brave people there groped with

that difficult question. Some certainly had a better sense of what was being asked than others, but all, I think, understood the nature of sacrifice. That I gathered by watching their faces, and waiting, as the silence grew on.

"I will go to Festival," said Sandra-hoop. There was a collective sigh. "I will make the teacher's words ring true. The greatest pleasure it will be. The unspeakable joy."

"And I," said another. "The chance of a future is better than the pain of this body."

Another spoke up, and then another. By the end there were ten who had volunteered to pass the doors.

"But what if the virus doesn't survive?" repeated the one who had asked before. "What happens then?"

"One step at a time," I cautioned. "No one knows the future."

"No." Sandra-hoop smiled. "But it's to our advantage that staff and Mannus think they do."

I nodded, and most of the others joined me. For a while longer we talked, sharing concerns and discussing the particulars of our plan. Finally, we dispersed. In each our separate ways we waited.

On the day before Festival the band of Domers stayed in the mines. As well acquainted as they were with the passages, they were able to avoid the staff who shepherded the others back to the domeroom. In the haste to begin Festival early they were not missed. There were so many other Domers to account for, after all, and the one staff member who cared enough to count each one was gone.

In each cave was planted a bomb, the same ones used to enlarge the tunnels. The fuses were joined so that a single detonator controlled a half-dozen caves. Over each detonator presided a pair of Domers, one a messenger, the other a bomber. Kylis Umbo presented the list of demands to Jeen, who laughed in his face. An hour later caves thirty to thirty-five were blown out of existence.

Jeen took a more serious attitude. She ordered that Festival begin immediately for the others and sent an urgent missive to Mannus on Earth, requesting instructions. Their response, received in record time, was terse. "Get them out of the mines."

Jeen armed a small militia of staff and attempted a swift attack. One Domer fell before half of the sixties shaft disappeared beneath a thunder of falling rock. Staff retreated and tried a countermove. Caves fifty to fifty-five were detonated and gone in a matter of seconds.

"They're crazy," Jeen said, fretting what to do next.

"Like foxes," replied Martha. She and I, at Jeen's behest, were meeting with her.

"I don't understand it. Nothing even close to this has ever happened."

"They're downtrodden," I said. "Treated worse than slaves. What did you expect?"

"Every other cycle they've gone to Festival without any problem. Gleefully."

"Maybe it was just a matter of time," said Martha.

"I wish they'd waited another cycle. Then I wouldn't be here."

"Why not give them what they want?"

"What? More food? I can't. Less work? Mannus decides how much Mutacillin to mine."

"Then let Mannus decide what to do next. You don't owe them anything."

"I'm just glad we started Festival early. At least we don't have any other crazy Domers to deal with."

"Why not give them what they ask, Jeen?" said Martha. "You're leaving. It's no skin off your back."

"I don't like to be manipulated." She scowled. "Besides, I haven't been authorized."

"Mannus said to get them out of the mines," I reminded her. "Agreeing to what they're asking should do it."

"They don't want to come out. They say they're going to stay there until the new crop of Domers is grown."

"But they won't destroy any more caves. That's what Mannus cares about."

Jeen ran her fingers through her hair and swore. "I hate this. I wish Guysin hadn't died. I keep thinking that somehow all this is his fault."

"He gave them faces," I muttered. "You can give them freedom."

And she did. As much as anyone. She convinced Mannus that the Domers meant business, that they would blow up the whole colony if they had to. Mannus gave in, and then they fired Jeen. They fired all of us, for that matter. Which was moot. Except for Martha the entire staff was headed back to Earth anyway.

We left several months later, after the new staff had arrived and been oriented. Parting with Martha was painful. I felt in my heart more than a passing sadness, and her brave, choked farewell was almost too much to bear. She cupped my hands in her own, her face more alive for being half dead, and whispered, "You have my blessing." Those were her final, resonant words, and I realized then that she knew. Knew, and accepted. More, she wished me well. Such was the parting gift of a great lady, and it touched me deeply. I shall never forget.

Not long before our departure, it had become clear that the virus had survived the bath. Baby Domers in their vats were showing precocious motor and intellectual development. Some already had speech, voicing thoughts and memories of unsettling familiarity. It was strange and wondrous; I brought the news myself to the rebel band.

Victory was plain to see in their eyes, but their jubilance was muted. Their already exhausted bodies had suffered through weeks of cold and deprivation. Once they gave up their siege, many had to be physically assisted from the tunnels. I was one of the first to offer help, for I knew it would be my last opportunity to see them before they would be recycled.

I found Kylis Umbo and helped him to his feet. He was drawn, thinner than I ever would have imagined.

"We won." He smiled weakly.

"Yes."

"And you return to Earth . . ."

I nodded. "There are Domers there, of a kind. To me this is but the first step."

"You are a giant, my love."

"And you." We embraced. "If only Jessica and Sandra-hoop were here to join us."

"They are here." He touched his head. "Soon they will be everywhere."

I smiled, and we touched a last time, separating quickly at the sound of staff. After they passed, I placed a hand on his bowed spine. His hips were nearly fused, and he moved with the tortured shuffle of a man in great pain. With my assistance he struggled up the steep shaft, stopping several times before finally reaching the surface. He took a minute to catch his breath, then turned and faced me.

"Service, duty, obedience," he said. "Those were the three pleasures of material life. The fourth was Festival, so great that it could not be told." He smiled. "The fifth we know. And now we have the sixth."

He turned and hobbled toward Service. Then he stopped. "Freedom, Jules. Freedom."

It was the last I saw of him, of any of them. But I did not forget. As much as the words were his, they were my own.

Part Three

EARTH

26. A Haven for Some

I returned to Earth amid no shouts of greeting, no cries or hailments. Jessica welcomed me with a feathery touch of the limbic system, narcotizing me during the flight from the desert base to Barea. A wave of euphoria bathed me as I first glimpsed the city. It sprawled below like a great hunger; I felt umbilicated to every piece of its life.

We approached from the south, at my request cruising at a high altitude. Sowall stretched out as vast, vaster than ever. The Twins had become the Triplets, their shiny orange coats contrasting with the gray roofs that had begun to creep up the sides. Pimplehill appeared to the west, its top charred and full of debris. It seemed as though some catastrophe had erupted there and laid it waste. There were neither buildings nor people, only ruins. It pained me to look, and I shut my eyes. When I opened them, we had nearly reached the wall.

It had changed since I had been gone. The southwest part of it had evaginated, gobbling up a large section of northern Sowall. The wall was no longer circular, resembling instead the uneven edge of an amoeba, or a malignant corpuscle. We flew over it, and a stab of pain pierced me. My eyes filled with tears and I shuddered. The feeling passed.

We had entered the ring. The pain had been Jessica's, the terror memory of the Guards. We landed, and I wiped the tears away. It took some time for my breathing to calm.

The craft engaged one of the visitor ports of the Pimella Arms, where I had arranged a temporary residence. I was shown to the unit by the manager, who to my surprise recognized me immediately. She inquired how my trip had been (she did not know where I had gone) and said that she was pleased to have me back. I vaguely remembered the woman and was certain that she had never cared much for me before.

"You're coming back to live at the Arms, are you?" she said brightly.

"On a monthly basis for the present."

She nodded. "It's still a good place to live."

"Indeed. I hadn't supposed there would be a vacancy."

"Never used to be," she muttered. We arrived at the suite, and from her bag she took a palm plate and fitted it into the empty space next to the door. "We save all the plates. In case people come back."

"Why are there vacancies now?"

She glanced at me. "How long have you been away?"

"A few years."

"Oh." She turned back to the plate. "A lot of people left Ringhaven when the HAS epidemic hit. They're starting to trickle back, but they're still afraid."

"What do they fear?"

"Going crazy. Dying." She looked at me accusingly. "You're the doctor."

"I've been away . . ."

"They say they've almost got it under control. In Ringhaven anyway. Outside . . ." She shrugged. "You know how it is out there."

"Indeed," I replied. "I know it well."

"The Guards come on every hour now. To make sure the outsiders stay out."

"I see."

"And they've stopped doing implantations. Until the HAS thing is wiped out. That's another reason why we have vacancies. No new tenants to replace the ones who left."

"And yet Ringhaven continues to grow . . ."

"I wouldn't know. The Arms is my home." She finished inserting the plate and turned to me. "Try it."

I placed my hand on the metal square and the door slid open. She picked up her bag.

"I hope you decide to stay. If you need anything, give me a call." She smiled and left. I entered the apartment.

It was much like my old one, save for the absence of my customized furnishings. There were four rooms and two windows, both of which looked out upon a tall corrugated building to the east. I deposited my few belongings on a table and called the company to whom I had entrusted my refrigerator and the items within it. They promised to deliver all within a week, a delay I found insufferable. To my credit I did not engage them in argument. It would have been futile, and I did not wish to waste time. I had an urgent desire to be in the streets, and as soon as I hung up left the apartment.

The elevator took me down and I walked briskly from the lobby. My thoughts held neither purpose nor destination; simply to have my feet on Barea's ground seemed enough.

The streets were cool and somewhat dim, trapped as they were in the shadows of the buildings that loomed above. Some were of glass, and inside I could see people bustling. Idly I wondered how many had been born there, lived, and would die there without ever setting foot beyond. I felt a sudden urge to confront one, to discover what that life was, and hurried across the street to a building's entrance.

I peered through glass into the lobby; it was full of electronic machines and brightly painted robots. Some wore wigs, and one of them began to come toward me. As it drew nearer, I backed away, and when it beckoned to me, I turned and left.

It was day, but the streets of Whitehill were empty. Before, outsiders had come to Ringhaven to shop, gawk, drift, but now there were none. At first this puzzled me, and then I recalled what the woman at the Arms had said. The Guards were now activated hourly; obviously, no outsider would dare venture far from the wall. I was curious to know if any at all entered Ringhaven and wandered toward the wall to find out.

Upon arriving, I found a crowd of people gathered about. All or nearly all hovered close to the plastic barrier. Some held bags with items to hawk or trade; others seemed there merely to socialize. All had timepieces strapped to their wrists or hung about their necks, and these they eyed nervously every few minutes. Why they were even inside I did not understand, unless it was a matter of habit. Or perhaps the lure of danger.

For several hours I stood on the corner of a street across from the wall, watching the ebb and flow of the crowd. Ten minutes before the Guards came on, the people began to disperse. Five minutes later nearly all were outside the wall, and in two minutes more the area was empty. During the final sixty seconds single individuals came sprinting toward one of the wall's openings. Some were pale with fright; others laughed in high-pitched voices and beat their chests. These were mostly youths, come, I supposed, to test their courage.

On one such occasion a young man slipped in his race to the wall, twisting an ankle. He struggled to his feet, but collapsed to the ground when his ankle proved unable to support him. From beyond the low barrier people yelled at him to move, and he began frantically to hop toward them.

Ten meters from the wall he stopped to catch his breath. I stepped nervously from my corner. He resumed his efforts to get to safety, and then the Guards activated. With a shudder he fell to the ground and began to scream. I ran toward him. His face was contorted, his fingers clawing at his skull. I lifted him in my arms and rushed beyond the wall.

The crowd opened, and I placed him on the ground. He had been exposed for less than a minute, but it took easily ten before he calmed. People muttered while we waited, but I registered none of the words. I was full of horrifying memory.

Gradually it weakened its grip on me, and I looked at the boy. He was no more than sixteen, his dark skin covered by loose pants and a bright shirt. His hair was matted and tied with red bands. I lifted his shirt to be certain of his heart, and on his chest, in white, was a tattoo. It was a geometric shape, and while he recovered, I counted the sides. There were twenty.

When he was able to speak and sit, I left him and walked back through the wall. Others had begun to re-enter, but the people there no longer held my interest. I was tense and disturbed. A knife seemed to be twisting in my heart.

After that incident my life took on a new character. The simple thought, the cursory glance became an unacceptable ruse. The most trifling circumstance demanded my complete attention. A gust of wind, a crack in a building, in a face begged for study and commitment.

I developed strange compulsions, craving intimacy with dirt and metal as well as flesh. One moment I felt elated; the next, full of wrath. I was vulnerable, invincible, nonplussed. The minds of other living creatures—birds, insects—mesmerized me.

At the time I believed these disturbances the result of re-culturation. The symptoms, if you will, of anomie after a prolonged absence. I regarded Jessica's presence within me as additive, not causative. I was wrong, but then such can be the blindness of the eye turned inward. Now I have not two pairs but dozens to help me see.

In the early weeks after my return I kept mostly to myself. Jessica was active within me, providing what companionship I felt necessary. Our thoughts constantly mingled, for I had not yet learned the art of control. Often I was she, with her strength and tenacity. I held the memories of her squalid life as a child and felt, too, her anger and frustration. For the first time I saw myself as she did: with respect, wariness, exasperation, humor, love. I felt more attached to life, and more vulnerable. It seemed there was more at stake.

We spoke (in my mind) endlessly of the Domers and the lessons of their triumph. We walked about the city, looking, smelling, listening to its abundance. We pondered life. Gradually, our plan took shape.

I took the first step by visiting a physician to whom I had referred a number of patients in the years prior to Eridis. As a specialist in infectious disease he would be privy to the most current information on HAS.

While I had been gone, he had moved his office to one of the towering new buildings in Goldmont. It was located on the two hundred and thirty-first floor and afforded a panoramic view of the city. Its luxury bespoke his continuing prosperity.

I was gazing into his tank of exotic and mutant fish when he came through the door to the waiting room and greeted me.

"Jules," he exclaimed, grabbing my hand and clapping me on the back. "It's been a long time."

"Hello, Bandy."

"Come in, come in." He guided me through the door and into his office. I sat in an armless chair, while he took the one behind his desk.

"So, you just got back from Eridis."

I nodded.

"Wasn't there some kind of trouble there? A coup or some such thing?"

"The workers asserted a claim to better conditions," I said. "Is that what you mean?"

"Could be that." He leaned back. "I remember getting a notice about Mutacillin. Mannus warned that there might be less of it for a while."

"Has there been?"

"We've never gotten as much as we need. And now it costs more, but then everything does." He shook his head as though aggrieved by his lot in life, then leaned forward. "So what can I do for you, Jules?"

"I'm thinking of opening a practice in Whitehill. I was hoping you could help pass the word."

"I don't see why not," he said after a moment's thought. "I'm overbooked as it is, what with this HAS thing and all."

"I would appreciate it."

"Fact is, we could use some good docs in Ringhaven. Seems like half of them have left in the past couple of years."

"Indeed."

"Bunch of sissies, if you ask me. Worried that they'll get HAS, even if they won't admit it." He seemed disgusted. "We've got a damn good medicine to treat it, but they're still afraid."

"You're not?"

"Sure I am." He leaned back in his chair and chuckled. "Fact is, I already had it once. Strangest thing, it was. I started hearing my wife's voice all the time. Day and night, when I was with her and when I wasn't. First I thought I was going crazy, and then I realized what it was."

"Did you give yourself Binaricide?"

"Of course. My wife, too. And the lady she got it from."

"And it worked?"

"Do I seem different to you?" He stood up and put a hand on his hip. "Like some woman?" He thrust the hip toward me, laughing. "Or some crazy?" He laughed again and sat down. "Sure it worked."

I struggled to control myself. "I see," I said, managing to keep my voice even. "This actually pertains to one other request . . ."

"Shoot."

"I was hoping to get some current information on the HAS epidemic. I assume that it still exists."

He nodded. "We're close to licking it in Ringhaven. The NHD started sending teams outside the wall a few months ago. It's harder out there, of course, the way people are and all . . ."

"The drug's still effective?"

"Damn effective. Ninety-five percent cure rate. The ones who aren't cured seem to be the ones who die anyway."

"Yes. The report I received mentioned that."

"There's a bill being considered that requires every person in the country, whether or not they have HAS, to get treated. Makes it a felony not to be. If they'd get off their duffs and pass it, we'd be in business."

"Will they?"

"Sooner or later they have to. It's our best bet: dose everybody and eliminate the reservoir. And hope that the virus doesn't decide to mutate before we do."

"And the mortality?" I asked. "Is it still twenty to thirty percent?"

He shook his head. "Never was. Closer to one, maybe even less. The NHD circulates those higher figures just to make sure everybody takes HAS seriously."

"Who wouldn't?"

"Beats me. I sure didn't want someone else inside my head." He laughed. "Especially not my wife."

Jessica's scent exploded in my olfactory bulbs. My mind reeled, and then I burst into laughter. Bandy regarded me strangely, then smiled.

"Preposterous, isn't it? Do you know there is a cult that encourages people not to get treatment? They claim that the disease is not a disease at all, but some kind of spiritual breakthrough."

"Interesting . . ."

"It's crap. They should see it from behind my desk."

"What is this group?"

"Felons," he said contemptuously. "Crazies. Most of them are behind bars by now. Dosed out with Binaricide. If you ask me, their minds should be sucked and replaced with something useful."

I began to get nervous, fearing I would commit an outburst. I pleaded with Jessica to control herself, to allow me my professional mien.

"Why was a law made?" I asked.

"Are you serious?"

"I was gone when it was passed," I said quickly. "Everything I've heard since talks mainly about the high mortality. And now you say it's a fabrication."

"You have been gone, haven't you?" He scrutinized me, and then to my relief assumed a professorial air.

"The mortality was bothersome, Jules." He leaned back and clasped his hands behind his head. "But it wasn't what aroused us to make the law. We—and I include all the major lay organizations along with the medical community and government—recognized early on the danger of the disease. Think about it. What would happen if people's minds started to coexist on a large scale? Poor with rich, women with men, children even with adults? How would it be if, as a doctor, you were infected with the thoughts of your patients? What would happen to your perspective . . ."

I remembered the awe as I entered Jessica's brain, the joy of having her with me then, and since. I swallowed a rebuke.

"How long would it be until the social fabric was in tatters? Until total chaos replaced order? Think about it, Jules. A society without privacy. Without boundaries. It would be havoc. I'm not sure we'd survive . . ."

"Certainly not as we are."

"Not as anything. It's a virus, Jules. A disease. If we don't kill it, it will kill us."

I wonder how long we have, Jessica whispered sarcastically. Shut up, I told her.

"I see your point," I said.

"I laugh about the thing with my wife," he went on, "but underneath I take it seriously. I take this whole damn thing seriously."

"I can see that you do," I replied, standing up. "I can understand why."

He nodded thoughtfully, then leaned forward and left his chair. He followed me to the waiting room door, which was open. The chairs had filled while we were together, and a roomful of faces looked up.

"I appreciate your time," I told him. "I know you're busy."

He clapped me heartily on the back. "It's good to see you again. Let's get together sometime." He began to retreat down the hall. "Let me know when you're set up."

I nodded as he disappeared; the people in the room returned their expectant eyes to magazines and laps. On my way out I passed the fish tank, just in time to witness an ancient aquarian scene. A small fish was in the process of being swallowed by a larger one. I paused to watch, as its body, then tail disappeared into the other's mouth. The added weight seemed momentarily to disorient the larger fish, and it drifted toward the bottom of the tank. Waiting there, hidden in the colored shell of a large snail, was a creature of whom only the tentacles were visible.

They were purple, and as the sinking fish drew near they came alive, writhing like worms. One of them touched its ventral fin, and in a moment the fish's life was forfeit. Its body jerked spasmodically, then fell into the purple arms. They wrapped around it and slowly drew it into the shell. Minutes later the shell burst, and from it emerged a creature that astonished me. It had the body of a crustacean, but its face was humanoid. Flat, with two eyes and a crenated mouth. Above its forehead sprouted long tresses of purple hair.

I stumbled from the office, inexplicably moved by what I had seen in the tank. The drama seemed to hold for me some lesson, yet I could not decipher it. In the elevator the air began to vibrate, then slap at my face and head. I sank timelessly to the ground, and the doors slid open. I thought of lips, and a mouth. The glands beneath my tongue began to water. I wanted suddenly to swallow, to ingest, and I rushed from the elevator. Smells of vinyl, metal, living bodies surrounded me, and I pushed through them to the street. With the instincts of an animal on the prowl, I went in search of food.

27. Naturopathy

Can you understand, brother, why I did not choose the treatment that by law I should have sought? If you have ever lost a loved one, you will not judge me harshly for wanting to hold onto Jessica. That was my first justification, and if it was venal, then I must reply that I have never aspired to sainthood. But I had, in addition, a second reason.

I thought to follow on my own planet the hope we had conceived on Eridis: to unite our disparate spirits and reverse the diaspora that kept one man's heel forever on another's throat. That Jessica had cleaved to me (and I to her) was the paradigm, and I could not allow it to be riven from us.

I set up a practice in Whitehill, for my intent was to cater to the affluent and privileged of Ringhaven. Despite my long absence my name was still remembered by many of my colleagues, who referred to me those clients whom they either could not or did not wish to see. I was not particular, wanting only to build the practice as quickly as possible, and received whomever passed through the door. In the first few months the flow was little more than a trickle, and I held hours only in the morning. In the afternoon I took walks, at first only in Ringhaven but later outside the wall. For the most part I wandered randomly; in retrospect, I realize that I was strengthening my resolve. I was in Barea for nearly a year before I returned to the party.

Somehow I wandered there from the south, so that I came

upon the swarming, noisy avenue almost by accident. I climbed through a loosely constructed barricade of plastic products, pushing aside jars and bottles in order to reach the throng. I managed to stuff the rolls of sheet plastic I carried for protection into my pockets before I was engulfed by the mass.

If possible, it was even more crowded than it had been before. Curiously, though, the mood was less frenzied. People shouted and jostled one another, but this was the exception rather than the rule. The festivity, though no less than I remembered, was of a different quality. Subdued. Portentous.

I moved somehow without walking, the flow carrying me westward, past intersections where stood barricades similar to the one I had crossed. People joined or departed the crowd at these points. Those who came added their pieces of plastic to the other items; those who left picked up an object or two to protect themselves. I realized that the barricades were designed primarily as deterrents (they could not possibly halt a hungry hound), to divert the attention of the Fagos dogs from the crowd inside. At the next opportunity I took the bulky rolls of plastic from my pockets and threw them onto a pile.

I reached the park, which seemed to have grown in size from what I remembered. People spilled from its edge like rising water, into the streets and alleys beyond. On my first visit, marked as it had been by distress, I had failed to notice much of the surrounding milieu. This time I was more attentive and took note of a large structure rising conspicuously on the far side of the park. I counted five identical levels, each with a walkway fronted by a railing. Drawing nearer, I saw that each level was composed of a series of doorways paired with windows. The structure's color was gray, and much of it seemed to be crumbling.

I thought it at first a tenement, but the number of people who hung upon the railings and passed in and out of the doorways convinced me otherwise. It seemed to be a giant bazaar of some sort; idly, I wondered what goods and services might be exchanged there. Just when I had made up my mind to see for myself, my attention was diverted by a young woman who was pushed, it seemed, into my arms.

Her hair was braided into stiff plaits, which brushed against my cheek; her face, when I saw it, was gifted with animation. I assumed she wore a mask, though even at close range I could discern no seam. She gave me a lovely smile, making no attempt to disengage herself from me. I was determined to suffer no intimidation, and I returned her smile with one of my own.

"Good day," I said.

She rubbed herself against me, nodding slightly and smiling, as though there were no need for any other discourse.

"My name is Jules."

She touched my temple with a finger, then touched her own. I wondered if she were mute.

"Can you speak?" I flapped my lips together and pointed to my mouth.

She giggled and nodded, then drew her face so close that our noses were touching. Her eyes were nearly black; I felt them pour into my own. And then the reverse.

I swallowed dryly, and the woman stepped back. She took my hand in hers and led me through the crowd.

She guided me with the subtlest of touches, as though from her fingers sprouted wires to each part of my skeleton. Their tips lay upon my palm and through them I felt the beat of her heart.

To no surprise she led me to the tiered building at the edge of the park. We climbed stairs to the second level, then edged down the long walkway to one of the doors. Many of the folk who lounged upon the railing greeted the woman as we passed. She responded in kind, usually with a simple gesture or smile. I remained for the most part silent, content to bask in the strong scent of the lady's wake.

She led me through a door and we entered a small, dark room. It quickly grew darker, as my companion closed the shutters of the only window. She lit a lamp in one corner, lowering the wick so that it did not smoke. Then she sat against a wall.

I looked at her and then at the room. The walls, floor, and ceiling were covered with rugs, of hues both dark and light. The ambience was of great luxury, though on close inspection most of the rugs were balding or torn. The faint smell of animal pervaded the room.

I returned my gaze to the woman, who was sitting casually with her legs crossed in front of her. She was clothed simply, and her feet were bare. Around her neck she wore a delicate chain, and from it hung a jewel.

I felt a tremor of indecision, then took a deep breath and went to sit beside her. Except for her eyes, which followed me, she made no motion.

"I would like to hear you speak," I said.

"Fornication," she replied, turning her face to me.

I chuckled, strangely put at ease.

"Pleasuredome. Blastula."

I touched her wrist, stroking the pale veins on the back of her hand. She placed her fingertips on my jaw.

"Fusion. Swallow. Goiter."

"I see," I said, touching her knuckles with my lips. "Prurience. Lust."

She looked at me as though she had heard nothing, and I became fleetingly apprehensive. The light in the corner pained me.

"Jewels," she said.

I heard thunder.

"Facets. Entry."

She snaked upon me, and in a moment we were coupling maniacally. I rose time and again from exhaustion, which seemed to please the lady. She anticipated me at every turn, and when I could finally rise no more, she knew that, too. She swathed me in a loose remnant, then sat naked beside me while I fell asleep. I did so swiftly, staring at the many-sided jewel that hung between her breasts.

When I awoke she was not there. I had expected this and was unperturbed, having faith that the questions I had would find answers when and if it became necessary. Gathering my clothes, I left the room.

Night had fallen, but the scene outside was unchanged. People were everywhere, and the sounds of music rose through the air. The candescent brightness of Ringhaven glowed to the east, casting the park in a lavender light. I decided to return home, for I was far from engorged with sleep, and hungry besides.

Making my way through the park was not as effortless as it had seemed before; I was accosted twice more before I achieved the avenue. Its flow was strongly against me, and I left it at the first intersection. On my way through the barricade I grabbed a broken hull of plastic, holding it before me as a shield until I reached the ringwall. There I discarded it, for the dogs inside are tamer and obedient. Unencumbered, I finished my journey home.

By the time I reached my apartment I was too tired to eat properly and contented myself with a loaf of bread and wheel of cheese. They were sufficient to take the bite from my hunger, and without further delay I collapsed on the bed. The remainder of the night I passed like a stone.

The next day, and for many (weeks, months) thereafter, I followed the same routine. Working in the morning, wandering in the afternoon. As many days as not I ended up at the party, though not all of those culminated as it had the first time. Many did, however, for the men and women were about, and I myself was not so timid. In the beginning it was Jessica who urged me on, but as we melded I could no longer distinguish between us. And others began to grow.

As far as my practice was concerned, it too grew, until my office was as full as Bandice Monk's had been when I had visited him. Initially I followed convention, diagnosing and treating according to the accepted strictures of traditional medicine. My clients came to depend on me, and over the course of time many came to trust my judgment in lieu of their own. In the past I would never have encouraged such blind faith, but my plan necessitated it. It was vital that my patients maintain complete confidence in me, and I used whatever leverage my position allowed to bolster my authority.

Once I had achieved their trust, I began gradually to turn them to my purpose. In each session I found some way to interject a word or two about sex. In many cases this took the form of a proverb, perhaps some maxim culled from medical lore. If there were a current movie or video that dealt candidly with such matters, I took the opportunity to recommend it. When possible I tried to be didactic, counseling them on the healthful aspects of a strong libido and urging them to seek its discharge as often as their lives would permit. I posted signs in the waiting room with messages of encouragement and printed leaflets to the same effect. To some of my patients, whose lives were already marked by license and orgy, such advice was unnecessary, but to the majority it was otherwise. Startled at first, wary, they gradually came to accept my counsel as medically sound. It was not, after all, so heretical, and indeed, I found that those who were most vociferous in denying the therapeutic value of sex were the same who, once converted, praised it most fervently. This was the second step of my plan, and when all or nearly all of my patients were convinced, I moved to the third.

It was the most exciting part, and the most challenging. In place of the general exhortation to fornicate I suggested an action more specific. I suggested that my patients fornicate with me.

It was a step both easier and harder than I had imagined. Easier, because the taboo, which I had believed so unshakable, dissolved for me so readily. Rather than feeling as though I were committing some heinous crime, I felt a liberation, the release of a great and clotted power. A handful of my patients were eager to join, seeking, I suppose, some parity with the figure they held in such esteem. Many, however, were reluctant, and these were the ones who made the step difficult.

They played on my shame and fear of reprisal. They tried to portray me as a miscreant, a diabolist seeking to corrupt and defile. I did, in truth, feel a certain guilt, but their resistance only made me more resolute. I countered outrage with conviction, disapproval with persuasion. I believed then (as I do now) that I held within me the possibility of a new future. I felt incumbent to share it.

With those to whom seduction was as commonplace as the

exchange of currency I was blunt, and often we copulated within minutes of my suggestion. With others I had to use more cunning, hinting over the course of several visits with artful phrases and subtly provocative examinations. I used whatever mental powers I could devise toward my end, but never did I force myself physically upon a client. Nor was I ever cruel. Except with those who desired something different I was always gentle, at times even affectionate during our acts.

The manipulation that I practiced, had it not been justified by the end I served, would have been insufferable. It would have corrupted beyond repair the relationship between physician and patient. As it was, I found it difficult to advise my patients on the smaller matters for which they consulted me. I knew that sooner or later I would be unable to continue in any form my practice; in the interim I did what I could. In truth, once we had coupled I did not much care if a patient chose to seek another practitioner. As long as the exodus was not of such proportion to jeopardize the last step of my plan.

The last step. The most dangerous one. I began to advise against the treatment of HAS.

Once I had begun my campaign of dissemination, it was only a matter of time before patients began to appear with the syndrome. They complained of a great variety of symptoms: dizziness, disorientation, hypersensitivity to a wide range of phenomena. All who came were worried, even though some actually felt better than before. Most had heard of HAS and asked specifically for treatment.

"It's not necessary," I told them. "The figures circulated regarding death are grossly exaggerated."

"Why take the chance?" most replied.

"There is a risk," I said. "There is to anything. But there are possible benefits if you allow the germ to take hold. Great benefits."

"What?"

"Seeing things truly. Power in oneself. Unity."

"I don't like having another person in my head," many told me.

"It takes time to understand. Words do not suffice."

"It could kill me. Already I think I'm crazy."

"Wait. Give it time. It can become something more."

Most were not convinced. "Please, Doctor. I want treatment."

In the beginning I gave it to all who asked, who persisted. Fortunately, not everyone did. Some believed me; others were intimidated. The reason to me did not matter. What did was that the future had been germinated in Ringhaven.

Sometime later, as I had fully expected, I received a visit from the authorities. To my surprise the face was one I knew.

"Dr. Toppas," I said, welcoming him into my office. "It has been many years."

He eschewed my hand and sat. He seemed to have aged immensely. His eyes were tired and the side of his mouth out of which he spoke had slackened to reveal the line of his gum. He gazed about the room without interest, absently pulling on the lobe of an ear.

"Are you still our coroner?" I asked.

"Haven't been for years."

"An administrator now?"

"Officer of the Board. Licensure division."

"My congratulations." He brushed me aside with a wave of a hand.

"I've had reports that you haven't been treating your HAS patients."

"From whom?"

"From them, Doctor."

"I see." I folded my hands in an attitude of calm. "These patients . . . have they other complaints?"

"Like what?"

"I can't imagine. Many who visit a physician are inclined for one reason or another to exaggerate. Some even find it necessary to lie."

"It's against the law not to treat the disease," he said bluntly.

"I have never withheld treatment from those who wish it."

"The law says nothing about wishes, Doctor. Everyone gets treated. No exceptions."

"It's irresponsible not to advise them of the benefits and risks. It's a violation of medical ethics—"

"I'm not talking about ethics. I'm talking about the law."

"Do you disagree?"

A hint of interest crossed his face, then disappeared. "What I agree or disagree with has got nothing to do with it. If you don't give Binaricide to a patient who has HAS, even to someone you only think has it, you're breaking the law."

"What if he doesn't want it?"

"Then he's breaking the law."

"I see."

"Good," he said without enthusiasm. "That's why I came." He rubbed his eyes and got to his feet. "By the way, how was your trip?"

"Trip?"

"Didn't you go somewhere?"

"You mean Eridis?"

He frowned. "Was that it? Did you have a good time?"

I looked to see if he were serious.

"I could use a vacation myself," he muttered. "A long one."

"Indeed. Eridis is a remarkable place."

"Barea's not what it was. I need to get away." He seemed already some other place, and it was not an appealing one.

"Is there anything else?" I gestured to my desk. "As you can see, I am quite busy."

He shook his head and wandered toward the door.

"I appreciate your visit," I said cordially. "I shall bear in mind what we discussed."

He nodded and muttered some farewell, then left. I returned to my office, wondering briefly at the change he had undergone. He seemed enervated, listless, devoid of purpose. Perhaps it was his new job, to which he seemed almost indifferent. Perhaps something else. I never found out, for the next and last time I saw him he did not see me. Nor did the circumstance on that occasion warrant a friendly chat.

At my desk I considered his warning. He had made no threat but had been nonetheless explicit. If I continued what I was doing, I would not be summoned before the Board of Medical

Examiners; I would be tried in a court of law. I would certainly be stripped of my license; I would probably be incarcerated as well. If they found out that I carried the germ, I would be dosed with Binaricide. The thought chilled me. Even were I to become reinfected, how would I ever find Jessica again?

They can kill a visionary, she told me, but not a vision.

> I raged   Thunder
> in the earth, the sky.
> Peals of
> Shivers of
>   laughter
>   lightning . . .
> It's simple this way.

I rose, not Jules at all. Not dizzy. And fucked a roomful of patients, missing lunch in the process.

28. Certainly Not as We Are

I am nearing the end of my narrative, for reasons purposeful as well as exigent. Words become more cumbersome; they seem to convey little of the meaning I would choose. I say one aloud and it hangs in the air for hours. Or it dissipates even before it leaves my lips. I fear that soon I will be reduced to monosyllables, or grunts, to avoid miscommunication.

I am a fugitive too, Jerrold, and may at any moment be apprehended. In the dim light of this cellar I hasten to finish the tale I began so long ago.

There is a hum to everything, bodies, sunlight, air. In the beginning it was worrisome, but now I have grown accustomed to it. It swarms about me wherever I go. I feel protected.

Everything is in motion; nothing is still. When one part of me is sleeping a thousand others are awake. I sample a tree and see a tree, a face, a forest. I taste fruits from branches that are withered and feel sap stick to my fingers. I am a fugitive girl hiding in a bush, a spear notching the bark. Upon exposed roots I pant, I am a tongue, a tunnel. The air around me is too bright, too sweet, too dark. I walk (or hobble or leap) and a gray building is blue, it is pink, it is too tall and not tall enough. I am a fat man. A cachectic.

Weeks ago it became clear that as much as I have passed the bright germ I have received it. The capacity of my mind, of all of ours, astounds me; daily am I filled with more diversity. Earlier I believed that this was the nature—the value—of the virus: to laminate endlessly and thus to mend our divisions. I was not wrong, but I was far too mundane in my vision. I am a new being, and we are on the brink of a new age.

Dr. Toppas's visit had an effect quite the opposite of what he intended. I increased my activity, both within my practice and outside it. As my mind vibrated with the lives of others, my powers of empathy grew immensely. I became able to understand patients immediately, even before they opened their mouths to speak. I knew their pains and their pleasures, their needs and their fears. With such intimate knowledge I became utterly compelling. Few were able to resist me, but the price I paid was steep. I ached with grief and passion, with my patients' primitive and twisted emotions. On many occasions I had to steel myself so that I did not laugh out loud, or weep.

My forays outside of Ringhaven were my respite, and I wandered the streets of Sowall and Westvale at every opportunity. I always spent time in the park, for there life seemed most to approximate my state of mind. One evening I met a youth, a boy not yet in his manhood. The face was familiar, and I recognized he whom I had rescued from the Guards. He seemed not to remember me, or at least gave no sign. In the manner of adolescence his speech was spare, and it was I who broached, then carried the conversation. When I asked of the tattoo on his chest, he narrowed his eyes.

"What tattoo?" he said.

"The one under your shirt," I replied casually.

His eyes darted to mine and then he spun around. I grabbed him by the arm. "I saved you once from the Guards. You probably don't remember."

He tried to shake his arm loose; I let it go.

"I'm not police," I said. "I think I'm one of you. I'd like to talk."

He gave me a blank look, then turned and began walking through the crowd. Without hesitation I followed.

He took me to the tiered building, the fourth level. He did not lead me as the woman had, but neither did he attempt to escape. We entered a small room, and his bravado wavered. I felt his bashfulness as he went to light a candle.

The room was barer than the others I had visited, its walls cracked and crumbling. A single rug covered the floor, a collection of pelts sewn together. With every sense I recognized them as the hides of Fagos hounds. I sat with my back to the wall and watched the boy.

His chocolate skin was so beautiful that it made me ache. The candle made shadows on his face. Black, blacker. He was nervous, frightened, excited. I shivered with his conflicts.

Next to the candle he lit a stick, which trailed a line of smoke to the ceiling. It was faintly sweet, but after a minute its smell was lost in a thousand others. The boy came and knelt beside me.

"Who are you?" I asked. He put a finger to my lips.

"Lay down," he said.

There were two pillows in the room, and I inserted one between my shoulders and the floor. "It's as close to flat as I am able," I explained, reclining. I began to feel drowsy, and a faraway voice cried out a warning. The boy had removed his shirt, was bending over me, his chest inches from my face. The voice cried out again, but to me it was unimportant. The tattoo became the sky, and then it fell into my eyes. I dreamt a world where every object, every person was made of twenty sides.

When I woke the boy was gone. In his place was a scent I recognized at once. But the face was none I had ever seen.

Jules.

The word echoed out of nowhere and I turned my head to see who had spoken. Save for the old woman the room was empty.

I'm pleased to see you. Pleased that you remember.

"Ann? Where are you?" I sat up.

Here. (A seam of light blinded me.) Everywhere. (I opened my eyes.)

"Talk," I said to the woman. "Use words."

She smiled, bunching the slack skin of her cheeks. "Long time no see."

"How . . . I mean, what . . . I . . ."

"Have many questions."

I nodded. "For example . . ."

"WhyamIhereamIillwhowastheboywhywhoareyouwhats
goingonthesmellarousesIdontunderstandanxietyperplexion
excitementperplexionwhatsgoingonwhatiswhatiswhatis . . ."

"You speak well for an old lady."

She burst out laughing, and I saw that, in addition to being
nearly bald, she had no teeth. "I can speak better if you let me."

She began reciting the bones of the body, their articulations
and muscular attachments, faster even than she had spoken
before.

"Is that from you?" I asked. "Or me?"

She shrugged. "Just words. We're better without them."

"Please." I held up my hands to ward her off.

"A silly gesture."

Suddenly my thumb was in my mouth and I was sucking it.
With my other hand I began to play with myself. "Stop it!"

"I'm not a witch."

"Please. I'm sorry."

"You're frightened. Worried. Puzzled."

"I can do that, too. You're amused. Affectionate. Happy to
see me."

"I am."

"Then be nice."

Her eyes twinkled. "Hermine told me you have many questions."

"The boy?"

"He said you snored in your sleep."

"I was drugged."

"He wasn't sure what to do. So he came and got me."

"Why didn't he fall asleep too?"

"He knows how to protect himself. I can teach you if you'd
like."

"Later." I stared at her. She smiled.

"You don't believe it's me, do you?"

I shook my head. She grunted and pushed herself to her feet.
"I *am* Ann Donovan," she said. "As much, anyway, as you are
Jules Ebert."

Her back was hunched, her fingers burled and arthritic.

There was a tremor in one hand, and her walk was a shuffle.

"It hasn't been that long, Ann. You were lovely. Beautiful. What happened?"

"You think me unattractive?"

I mumbled a reply, and she laughed. "Turn around."

I hesitated, then did as she asked.

"This will take a few minutes," she said. "If you'll be quiet, it'll be easier. I still have to concentrate."

I occupied myself by conjuring visions of the Ann Donovan I remembered, especially that sensuous creature I had last seen gyrating but a stone's throw from where I now sat.

"You can turn around."

I did so, and sucked in my breath. Before me stood she whom I envisioned, turning a lazy circle, caressing with her fingers the soft fur that covered her body. "Not bad," she said, pleased with herself. "It's been a while since I looked like this."

"It's a trick," I stammered. "You were in disguise." I looked around the room for discarded garments or a mask.

She smiled and came toward me. "Isn't this who you wanted?"

"Don't toy with me. I'm drugged, aren't I?"

She shook her head, then retreated and stood against the opposite wall. "I'm sorry. Sometimes I get carried away."

"Talk to me, Ann. Please. Explain what is happening."

I felt subtly entered. Various of my organs seemed to react, and then a tiny digit appeared at the base of my thumb. It grew until it became a thumb itself.

"See," she said. "It's easy."

I stared at it and flexed the joint. "You did that?"

"You did. I just helped."

I was stunned. Speechless.

"I have many minds aiding me," she explained.

I nodded dumbly.

"Ontogeny recapitulates phylogeny, Jules. We are built genetically on the units of our ancestors and carry the information to become any living thing. Polyp, tapeworm, vertebrate. Anything. The virus unlocks this store. It transmits the genetic, the chemical information that makes a person what she is. It allows another to be that person. Or any part. Soon you'll be as strong as I."

"It must be hormones," I said foolishly. "And neural regulation. And blood flow, and secretions . . . You can alter your own metabolism . . ."

She sent an image of a maze with infinite choices. "I can alter anything, Jules."

"I don't understand," I stuttered. I was frightened. "Make it go away."

The thumb disappeared.

Questions. Ask questions.

"Why choose the guise of an old lady?"

"Safety. The police aren't apt to pay me much attention."

"What could they do to you? With your powers . . ."

"They could use Binaricide. Or kill me. I'm not deathless."

"How would they ever know you?"

"The same way I know you. They have people like us, Jules. Finders. People who have the virus, the abilities."

"It's against the law," I uttered inanely.

"Man-made law. We carry the germ of a new age, Jules. Our plan is the same as yours."

"There are many of you?"

"The numbers grow daily. Mostly outside the wall."

"The icosahedron," I muttered. "That is your mark . . ."

She nodded. "Some wear it. Mostly the less developed. The ones who need a symbol."

"A young lady I met some months ago. She wore a jewel. I thought it rather pretty . . ."

"I wore it once myself. Now I have no need."

Suddenly I was filled with ecstasy. And reverence. She laughed.

"No need for that. Soon we'll make love. Then if you want to worship someone, worship yourself."

I blushed and cast aside the thought of laying my head at her feet. I stood up and went to her. We embraced.

"Your days as a doctor are numbered," she told me. "You must know that."

"I feel more a healer than ever."

"Yes." She smiled. "But they will close your practice and arrest you."

"I am many places. And far away. They will have trouble finding all of me."

"We could use your help, Jules. Only a handful of us are able to operate in Ringhaven. We still haven't discovered a way to neutralize the Guards."

"Blow them up," I said.

"The idea has crossed my mind, too. But our way is better. Slower, but better. Someday the people inside will themselves tear down the wall."

"Harm to all things vile."

"Show me," she said, grabbing handfuls of my belly in her fists.

"What?"

"I'm hungry." She pushed me down.

"Ann . . ."

"Let's eat."

29. Life Is Short, the Art Long

A week ago my practice was closed. Toppas came with two officers of the law. Had he been able to find me I am sure he would have had me arrested. Fortunately, I heard the commotion in the waiting room and was able to secrete myself in one of the examining rooms. By the time they found me, I had become an old and stopped man with dark complexion and pustular sores on my face and hands. Toppas hardly looked at me before moving on.

I have not returned to my office or apartment since that day. I live in a small cellar in Westvale, which Ann found for me. I have learned to change my shape and voice, but am unable to sustain for long the transformation. Until I can, I must reside here, where it is relatively safe.

By the time you receive this, Jerrold, it will be four years hence. If it in any way places a burden upon you, then I must apologize. I do not mean it so. What you choose to do will not by then substantially alter our lives. Guard the work, or make it public. I trust your judgment as I do my own.

I have no great words of wisdom with which to end. Already I have probably said more than I needed and less than I hoped. Lately I think often upon the Oath I took so long ago. I ask myself what it is to be a good doctor. A healer. At times it seems that it must be a shadow, shifting with each hour of the day. At others, an embrace. At this moment I imagine it to be a perpetual and deepening autopsy.

Do not be harsh with me, brother. I love you and have chosen decently. The art has guided me to see what nature would have. The perilous moment is always. The future is everywhere.